DISPOSABLE

Magic

BY: PHIL MANISCALCHI III

To my daughter Corinn who encourages and inspires me every day, and my son Dominic for asking the question, "Will you tell me a story?".

I love you hobos!

CONTENTS

DISPOSABLE Magic

"There's nowhere you can be that isn't where you're meant to be..."

— John Lennon

PROLOGUE

A Stormy Night

"…. it's 9:45. Here's Wendy Raines with the latest weather forecast on Detroit's best place for rock, WDTR."

"Thanks Mike. We're looking at clear skies and a temperature of sixty-five degrees tonight. Perfect weather to get outside and watch the Perseid meteor shower. So, grab a blanket and some popcorn because it should be one heck of a show. Tomorrow's forecast calls for partly cloudy skies with a high of eighty-two and a slight chance of….,"

Randy Bennett switched off the radio and gazed out the window. "Clear skies?" he muttered to himself. He was sitting alone in the solace of his single car 'man-cave', enjoying his second cold adult beverage. Randy was only partially listening to the radio as the oil slowly drained from his 2002 Dodge pickup. Vehicle maintenance was something his father had instilled in him at an early age. "Take care of your car and she'll take care of you," Randy Sr. had told him on more than one occasion. Randy Jr. had taken this, and many other sage bits of fatherly advice, to heart.

As he sat looking out the garage window, remembering his father, Randy heard the roll of thunder. "This one's going to be bad," he thought. What was it his father had said about weather forecasters? "How many other professions allow you to be right only half the time?" or something to that effect. "Well, it seems that Ms. Raines is certainly going to be wrong tonight," he said to himself. The moon, which had been full and bright not more than a few minutes ago, had vanished; completely obscured by a cloud cover which surely meant an intense storm was moving through. And fast.

A sudden wind gust rattled the garage's large overhead door, startling Randy. "This is going to be bad." His thoughts immediately went to Maggie and Rose. The hair on his arms and neck stood up as Randy flung open the side entry door and sprinted for the house.

Up in the master bathroom, Maggie Bennett was giving her three-year old daughter, Rose, her nightly bath. This was a ritual both Bennett girls looked forward too, and Maggie felt blessed. She had a wonderful husband, a handsome, smart, funny man who cared deeply for her. They had met in college and she fell in love with him the moment their eyes met.

A Stormy Night

Maggie never believed in love at first sight until she met Randy. After a brief three-month courtship, they were engaged, and married the following year. Maggie was pregnant almost immediately after their wedding. "If not sooner," she often thought. Rose Grace was born on June 12th, exactly nine months to the day of Randy and Maggie saying their "I Dos". Rose was a beautiful, healthy, happy girl who was the light of her life. To top things off, they had recently moved into the perfect house, in a neighborhood Maggie had always imagined herself living. Yes, she felt truly blessed.

If there was anything Maggie would change, anything that could improve her already perfect life, it would be to give her husband a son. Rose Grace was the daughter Maggie always imagined having, but she knew how much Randy wanted a son. Since his father passed away, in that horrible accident last year, Maggie knew having a son meant even more to Randy. Unfortunately, the difficulty Maggie went through during Rose's birth meant that having another child could be fatal to both mother and baby.

She was feeling the pang of sadness and loss deep inside her knowing she couldn't give Randy the son he always wanted, when Maggie felt Rose squeeze her finger.

Maggie looked down at her little girl, who was making her

now famous, attention grabbing 'fish face', and burst out laughing. She splashed the warm soapy bath water at Rose and soon the Bennett girls were splashing and laughing hysterically. But the laughter was quickly interrupted when Randy burst into the house screaming.

"Maggie! Magg's, where are you? We need to get to the basement now!" he yelled.

She was startled out of the beautiful moment with Rose at the sound of her husband's voice. Randy was always calm no matter what the situation. Even when his father had passed so sudden and tragically, he never truly lost his composure; at least not that Maggie saw. Without hesitation, Maggie grabbed a large white bath towel, swaddled up Rose and ran for the stairs. They were headed down the steps when she saw Randy standing there, a panicked look on his face. The look in his eyes was pleading her to come with him. "This is bad," she thought.

The second Maggie's feet hit the landing, Randy swept his girls through the kitchen, to the basement door. "We need to get to the downstairs, now," Randy urged as he threw open the door, flipped on the light switch and hurried his girls down into the lower level. Once in the safety of the dimly lit subterranean room, Randy tried frantically to explain what was happening.

He was speaking so quickly and with so much anxiety that all Maggie could understand was: 'Wendy Raines', 'clear skies' and 'my ass'. But she didn't need Randy to explain what was happening. Maggie could hear the wind howling and the lightning crashing. This was a massive storm and they'd be lucky to come out of it unscathed. Then, the home's vinyl siding began to rattle and the lights flickered.

"Oh, please no," Maggie thought just as everything went black.

The Bennetts huddled together on their old green sofa and waited. It was all they could do. As quickly as it came, the storm was gone. They sat there, the three of them, in complete darkness, huddled together for safety and comfort. Randy could feel Maggie's heart beating hard against his chest and it steeled his resolve. He had to be strong for his family. The storm seemed to have passed but it was better to be safe than sorry, so they waited in the dark for a few moments longer.

Rose was cradled in her mother's arms and, though her laughter had faded when her mother first scooped her out of the tub, she was remarkably at ease now. To Rose, this seemed like just another one of 'daddy's silly games'. And as if on cue, daddy did what daddy does, "Where's my Rosey?" she heard him ask. The little girl ducked her head under the towel as daddy asked again, "Where's my Rosey? I'm gonna get those toes."

Rose was giggling now as daddy grabbed for the towel and started to tickle and nibble at his little girl's toes. The sound of her daughter's laughter helped put Maggie at ease. Her Randy always had a way of lightening even the darkest of days. Before she knew it, the Bennetts were in a full-fledged, no holds barred tickle fight. "Yes," Maggie thought as her adrenaline ebbed, "my life is perfect."

When the tickle battle was over, and Maggie was declared the winner, the Bennetts made their way back upstairs. Her anxiety was back as Maggie opened the basement door. As she stepped into the kitchen, to survey the damage, she felt Randy's hand on hers.

"It's only stuff Magg's," he assured. "That's what insurance is for."

The man truly was her rock.

She stepped into the kitchen but could see no damage. Although the power was still out, the clouds had cleared and the moon shown through the window as bright as any spotlight. The house, it seemed, came through unscathed.

"At least the kitchen did," she thought.

As Maggie continued to survey her home for signs of damage, she heard Randy unlatching the front door. She called to him and urged, "Please be careful." He shot her a quick smile which was meant to calm her, but Maggie could see he was worried about what he might find outside. "And hey," she yelled as he closed the door behind him, "that's what insurance is for."

When Randy Bennett Jr, flashlight in hand, stepped into the warm summer Clarkston night, his life would never be the same.

1

And Then, Poof...

I'm going outside," he yelled, as he slid the glass door
closed behind him, for the final time. The cool spring
air filled the boy lungs as he stepped onto the wood
deck. "Today is the day. It's finally here," he thought. He had
been waiting for this day for years and it was finally here! "I'm
twelve!" he exclaimed.

Dominic Philip Bennett had a feeling of pride this morning,
like he had achieved some great accomplishment. Today, he
felt like a King. He knew it was a silly thought; after all, it was
just his birthday, and other than living through another year,
he hadn't accomplished anything special. But for a reason he
couldn't put into words, he felt powerful, like he was
something more than just another twelve-year old boy from
Clarkston, Michigan. He felt like a man. No, it was more than

that, he felt like the ruler of a kingdom. Like a great leader who others would follow into battle without question. And if he really thought about it, Dominic had always felt like more than a just a kid.

He was a good-looking boy with brilliant blue eyes, wavy brown hair and was, what the middle school girls called, "dreamy". At 5'10", Dominic was the tallest kid in his school. Except for the three-inch scar running across his left cheek, his complexion was perfect. Although, he didn't pay attention to his looks, or what others thought of them. He was happy with who he was, and the opinions of others were not a top priority.

Now, standing on his back deck, surveying his land, Dominic reached into his pocket and pulled out his most prized possession: an antique watch. The time piece was made of brass and looked to be hundreds of years old. There was beautiful hand carved filigree on the back and an image of what appeared, to Dominic, to be an eye; however, it was hard to make out exactly what the image was. Years of weathering had created a thick layer of patina which obscured much of the intricate, hand carved design. On the right side of the watch were two buttons, which apparently had no purpose at all; at least not one that he could see. With the crown at the top, he could adjust a series of numeric dials on the face of the watch, from □□□ to 999. The problem was, no matter what he did, the dials didn't seem to do anything. They weren't date wheels and, other than being decorative, did not seem to have any function at all. The boy wanted to ask his dad what the dials did but he hadn't even told the man that he had found the watch yet.

He could just imagine the conversation:

"Hey dad, check this out!"

"Where did you find that, son?"

"I was cleaning out the bushes, like you asked, and it was just lying there."

"Son, that looks like an antique. Someone must have dropped it, perhaps the mailman or the FedEx guy. Sorry but you can't keep it. I'll have to try and find the owner and return it to him."

No way was he going to let that happen. This was going to be his secret alone.

He slid the watch back into his pocket and patted it, to ensure it was safe. With his treasure secured, the boy stepped into the yard. As soon as his feet touched the grass, he unsheathed the plastic sword he had tucked in his belt and imagined himself standing on a battlefield, surrounded by his enemies.

And Then, Poof...

Dominic surveyed his yard, which was now a vast open plain of tall grass and large oak trees. He could hear the cries of the enemy horde approaching and turned back towards his house; which was now a great stone castle. "Protect Castle Bennett at all costs!" he yelled and, with sword in hand, Dominic charged through the wooded yard beheading every ferocious dandelion and disemboweling each traitorous bush that dared cross his path. He sliced and diced his way through the battlefield yelling, "Leave no survivors!"

When the battle was over, and his enemies were vanquished, he stopped to survey the damage he had inflicted on his cowardice foes. What he saw snapped Dominic back to reality.

Strewn across the well-manicured lawn, were the heads of dozens of tulips and rose buds. "Mom's flower garden!" he gasped. The flora had taken great casualties during this epic battle. But Dominic knew when his mother saw what he had done, *he* would be the real casualty of this battle. Panic set in and the boy raced throughout the yard, gathering up every flower bulb and rose petal he could carry, and stuffed them under a nearby yew. The punishment he would receive for his crime would be unavoidable. "But not today," he thought. "Not today."

Disposable Magic

For as long as he could remember, Dominic had loved stories of knights and castles and often imagined himself as a great king in some far away land; fighting to defend the honor of his family, and his kingdom. Then it hit him, today wasn't just any birthday. Turning twelve meant he could finally achieve his lifelong goal: battling the Black Knight!

"Well, not the *real* Black Knight," he thought.

For his birthday every year, Dominic's parents took him to *Medieval Days*; a renaissance themed restaurant which catered to the days-of-old enthusiast. And after all, he was the biggest enthusiast he knew. The boy had read every story of every knight, and king, he could find. His favorite place in the world was *Medieval Days*. "Why would anyone want to spend their birthday eating pizza with a cartoon mouse?" he asked his mother one day. To Dominic, *Medieval Days* had the sounds and smells of .... well .... a better time. He pondered this thought for a minute, "A better time?"

He was only twelve and didn't know anything of time before this, but 'a better time' felt right. It was an age when knights were beloved and the maidens swooned at the sight of these fierce men-of-men. Oh, if only he had lived back in those day. In his mind, he would have been the ruler of the greatest kingdom ever known.

But, the Bennetts lived in rural Clarkston, Michigan. "The furthest place from the days-of-old one could get," Dominic often thought. He knew he was different, and for as long as he could remember, he felt like an outsider. Like he didn't belong. No matter how hard he tried, he never seemed to fit in with the other kids.

When he turned six, Dominic's parents had planned a *Knights of the Round Table* themed party at the Bennett home. It was the best party ever had by a kid, (by anyone for that matter!).

For the 'party-to-end-all parties', Randy and Maggie dressed in silly costumes and completely transformed their backyard into something out of medieval times. His mother had made a dozen blue and yellow flags, each with the family crest emblazoned in the center, and hung them around the yard. In the center of the yard, sat a large round table for his guests to eat and be entertained. His parents even hired a court jester to juggle and tell jokes for the boys as they ate.

For dinner, along with the usual potatoes and rolls, each boy received his very own turkey leg! And to top it off, they drank their ale from a real medieval style mug; although in this case the ale was of the ginger variety. The birthday cake was a beautiful three-layer vanilla and chocolate castle, with a tower at each corner connected by a corresponding parapet, a drawbridge and even a mote made with crushed Oreo cookies! It was truly the most epic birthday party in history.

Dominic thought back on that special day and smiled. It was by far his favorite birthday and, until today, he thought nothing could top it. "But battling the Black Knight…." He paused at the thought of being in the ring with the infamous beast of a man, a smile widening across his smile. However, the more he thought of standing face-to-face with a man more than twice his size, the more his smile faded; until a feeling of panic filled him.

"I need to prepare," he said.

Thinking better of razing any more of his mother's flora, Dominic sprinted towards Eden.

In the center of the Bennett backyard stood a small group of trees. The ground between the trees had been meticulously landscaped by Mrs. Bennett when the family first moved to Clarkston. For groundcover, Maggie had planted, what was by far Dominic's favorite name for any plant: Mondo Grass. The Mondo grass covered the large area between the three giant oak trees, which were, in Dominic's opinion, the most unique thing about their property. The trees were laid out in a perfect triangle formation. But that wasn't what made them unique.

And Then, Poof...

What was most interesting about the oaks was that they were the same size and had the exact same branch structure. And, if that weren't unique enough, the trees were spaced the exact same distance from each other.

The small grove was a beautiful spot to sit and watch the sun rise in the morning, or nap in the afternoon. Randy would often lay on the Mondo grass and marvel at the precise geometry of the natural equilateral triangle of trees. It was such a perfect setting, Maggie had named the area 'Eden'. And, it was Eden where Dominic currently found himself.

The boy had just laid his foes to waste, and all which stood between him and victory were the three huge knights currently surrounding him. Should he wait and let them make the first move, or go on the offensive and end the fight quickly? Without warning, Dominic turned and thrust his sword at the Red Knight who was flanking him from the right. Red was apparently caught off guard and could not react in time. The knight howled in agony as King Dominic's blade sliced through him like butter. The Red Knight stood silent for a moment, grabbed his chest and collapsed to the ground. "One down," the king thought.

King Dominic quickly pivoted to his left, so to keep the last two men in his sights. These knights were skilled, they were strong and they were fast. But they were no match for the King of Clarkston and Dominic could sense they knew this as well. The knight to his left, the Grey Knight, charged the king, but the king was fast too, and he quickly and gracefully avoided this feeble attack. As the knight overshot his prey, Dominic sliced his sword across Grey's back. The Grey Knight fell to the ground; dead before he landed. "Two down, one to go," Dominic thought as he turned to face his final opponent.

There he was, at last, face-to-face with his archenemy: The Black Knight. "This will be a duel which will be talked about for ages!" he shouted.

The two warriors stood assessing each other, searching for their opponent's weakness. The first move would be crucial. Now was not the time to underestimate the giant standing before him. The Mondo grass on which they stood was about a foot tall and very thick. King Dominic knew he needed to step carefully. He couldn't rely on a direct charge at the Black Knight with this footing, as was evidenced by the recently deceased body of the Black Knight's, Grey partner. No, he had to get his opponent to make the first move.

In an attempt to catch the Black Knight off guard, Dominic faked a forward thrust; it was really no more than a twitch. As expected, his adversary reacted to the move; but not the way the king anticipated. The Black Knight charged King Dominic with the speed and grace of a panther. This caught the king by surprise and he had no choice but to take a large awkward step back. As King Dominic stepped back, his right foot landed directly on something buried deep below the grass. For a moment, the boy thought he'd keep his balance; until he felt his ankle turn. Dominic crashed into the Mondo grass with a sharp 'thump' and, before he could react, the battle was over. The Black Knight had vanquished him, again.

Distraught, the boy picked himself up off the grass. His ankle was fine, but his pride had taken another massive blow. "How can I beat the real Black Knight if I can't even beat the imaginary one?" he shouted to no one. Dominic pounded his foot onto the grass, searching for the traitor who had contributed to his monumental defeat. When he stepped on the object a second time, he decided he'd better excavate it. "Wouldn't want that to happen again," he thought.

The boy dropped to his knees and carefully pulled a clump of the Mondo grass back to expose the object; he didn't need to add grassicide to the list of crimes against his mother's garden. Partially buried in the dirt, was an old blanket wrapped tightly around something solid. Using his plastic sword like a garden trowel, Dominic carefully removed the soil around the blanket; the way an archaeologist would unearth the bones of newly discovered brachiosaur. After a couple of minutes of digging, the small package was freed from its tomb.

Dominic sat in the middle of Eden, imagining what could possibly be wrapped up in a blanket and buried in the middle of his yard for who knew how long. The cloth was pale blue and made of wool. It was tattered and frayed and looked to be hundreds of years old.

"What could be in here?" he thought.

Images of various artifacts ran through the boy's mind: an old skull, a gun from the Wild West, maybe even a stash of gold coins! Then he remembered. "It's my birthday. I might as well open my first present," he said to himself as he carefully began to unwrap the blanket. Although he *knew* he was alone in Eden, he couldn't help feeling he was being watched. Whether it was the guilt of carving up his mother's flowers, or the fact he found something which was obviously meant to be hidden, he swore he could feel eyes watching him. He surveyed the area and decided he was alone. Or so he thought.

The blanket had been wound tightly around its prize for years and the boy struggled to untangle the old cloth's grip. When the last of the fabric had been unwrapped, he laid it aside on the Mondo grass next to him. In his hands, Dominic now held a very old glass bottle.

And Then, Poof...

The bottle was about six inches tall and four inches wide. Pressed deep within the vessel's neck, was an old brown cork. Using the old cloth, Dominic wiped the dirt from the bottle so he could see what was inside the ancient relic. The glass was clear and flawless; no cracks or chips. Not even a single air bubble from when it was blown into life. The bottle was, in this young boy's opinion, perfect.

He peered inside the bottle, expecting to see something valuable. "Why else would someone take such care to bury this in our yard," he thought. To Dominic's disappointment, the bottle was empty. "Or is it?" he mumbled. The boy peered deeper into the bottle and spied what appeared to be a purple wisp of smoke, and it was moving. The vapors clockwise rotation reminded the boy of the way a hurricane moved. "Whoa!" he exclaimed, as he watched the purple storm turn. Then he felt a sudden chill run through him and quickly stashed the bottle back beneath the blanket. He surveyed the yard again. Someone was watching him, but who, and why? After assessing the yard for a minute or two, he convinced himself that he was just being paranoid (although what did dad say, "Just because you're paranoid, doesn't mean they're not after you."). When his paranoia had passed, he retrieved the bottle and studied its contents.

Disposable Magic

The purple hurricane was mesmerizing. "What is that?" he said as he reached for the cork. The boy paused as a flood of thoughts ran through his mind: "What if it's a poisonous gas? What if it's a virus that starts the zombie apocalypse? Who put this here?" Then another thought struck him. He studied the hole where he had unearthed his treasure and compared its relationship to the oaks. The treasure was buried in the exact center of the stand of trees. "It was as if the trees were put here to guard this," he thought, looking again into the bottle. "This means something," he said, to no one in particular.

The boy gripped the cork tightly and proclaimed, "This is mine!" Unlike the idea of unleashing a zombie apocalypse, he knew this to be true. "This is mine," he asserted. He grabbed the cork with his right hand and pulled hard, but the cork wouldn't budge. "Of course not," he thought, "it's been buried for decades." The boy adjusted his grip and pulled harder on the cork, which remained locked firmly in place. "This is mine!" he yelled again as he regripped the cork. His grip on the bottle was so tight that for a second, he thought he might break the glass. With every muscle in his twelve-year-old body, Dominic yanked on the cork. When he felt it move, ever so slightly, he *knew* he would soon be liberating the cork from its host. The moment he realized he had beaten his cork

foe, Dominic spotted a strange old man standing at the edge
of Eden, watching him.

The oldest man the boy had ever seen was standing behind
an oak tree leering at him and holding what appeared to be a
blue crystal. "Who…" But before he could react to the
stranger's sudden appearance, the cork let loose with a 'pop'
and when it did, Dominic Bennett vanished.

2

Awakening

W hat a dream," he thought. It was pitch black in his room and the King of Clarkston was just waking from the most amazingly realistic dream. He reached for his cell phone, to check the time, but grasped only air. The feeling of cold dampness startled the boy. He leapt to his feet and quickly realized he was no longer in his room. In fact, he wasn't in any kind of room he'd ever known.

As his eyes attempted to adjust to the black space, Dominic slowly worked his way around the dark room, arms outstretched, searching for something familiar. Slowly and methodically, he investigated the lightless, cramped, damp space, searching for a window, a light switch or a door; anything which could help the boy figure out where he was.

Awakening

As he searched, what was clearly a round, room, Dominic remembered his dream. "Ok," he muttered to himself, "I just woke up in a weird round room, with no lights and no windows. How is that possible? Am I still dreaming? The last thing I remember is losing to the Black Knight. The bottle! I opened the bottle and..."

"Step aside," bellowed a voice from outside the room.

Dominic hurried across the room, towards the voice, and felt what he thought was a heavy wooden door. "I said step back or I'll have your head jailer," the man's voice asserted. The voice outside the room grew louder, but the door was thick and the boy could barely make out what was being said.

"Sir Orgen, as you are aware, this room has been off limits for nearly twelve years. No one is to enter by order of the king!" a second, less assertive, voice argued.

"Then I suggest you inform the king of my treachery. Now, I will say this only once more, step back from the door."

After a long pause came the sound of a large metallic object being hefted from the door. The handle rattled and suddenly, Dominic's cold dark room was flooded with light.

For a moment, the boy was blinded. He quickly shielded his eyes behind his hands, allowing his pupils time to adjust to the sudden flood of light. Peeking through his fingers, he spied the silhouette of a very large man standing in the doorway. As the figure approached him, it appeared to Dominic that he was wearing armor. Black armor.

"This is obviously some kind of joke," the boy thought. What else could it be? Only seconds ago, he was dreaming of fighting the Black Knight and now the giant was standing right in front of him.

Then the giant spoke, "King Dominic, are you in here my lord?" The room was dead quiet. Again, "King Dominic, my lord, is that you?"

"Hello? Who are you? My name is Dominic Bennett. I have no idea how I got here, but whoever is playing this joke on me, it isn't funny," the boy whimpered.

"Sire! It is you! Are you alright my lord?" the large man in the black armor exclaimed. The giant rushed into the room, wrapped his arms around the boy and squeezed him tightly.

"The Black Knight has come to kill me!" Dominic thought, as he struggled to pull himself free from the giant's grip. The boy began to tremble at the thought of dying in this place, alone. At that moment, he wanted more than anything to be in his mother's arms. Then, as though he could sense the boy's panic, the giant suddenly released his grip.

"My apologies your majesty. I did not mean to frighten thee," the giant said remorsefully.

"Wuh, what's going on?" Dominic asked.

"Sire, you have returned to us just as you said you would!"

"Like I said I would?" Dominic was suddenly aware of someone else in the room with them. The second man, while not quite as large as the giant who most certainly bruised one of the boy's ribs, could certainly be the giant's slightly smaller brother. He too was wearing armor, but a different color. "Is his armor red?" Dominic thought.

"What do you mean I have returned?" Dominic asked, confused by what he was hearing, and seeing.

"Sire, you are our king. You left your kingdom twelve years ago and said you would return this very day. When we heard the storm, well…here you are," the second man exclaimed.

"What, I…uh…I don't understand. I'm not a king," the boy mumbled. "Who are you guys? Where is my mom?"

The two knights gave each other a look, and for a moment they were silent. Then the man in the black armor turned to Dominic, knelt and declared, "King Dominic Philip Segarius, I am Sir Brenden Fredrick Orgen of Munkelstein and I have sworn my life to protect you. In your absence, and per your instructions, I have tended to the kingdom these many years.

27

We have been eagerly awaiting your return and here you are!
Sire, I have assembled the lords in the War Room as you had
instructed before your departure. Now that you have returned,
they will want to see you with their own eyes. And sire, there
is something I mu…"

"But, I've never been here before," Dominic interrupted.
"My name is Dominic Bennett not Dominic Sagittarius. I was
born and raised in Clarkston, Michigan with my mom Maggie,
my dad Randy and my sister Rose. This isn't funny anymore.
Where am I, and where is my family?"

"Sire, I am Sir Burton Michael Redjon, of West Canyon,"
the man in the red armor declared, kneeling before Dominic.
"I can assure you, what Sir Orgen says is true. You are the
King of Munkelstein. Your returning home today was foretold
more than a decade ago. The knights await your presence in
the War Room, sire. As Sir Orgen has stated, the situation is
dire. The Knights of Munkelstein, must be assured that you
have indeed returned as you had promised them you would.
They have been patient for twelve long years; however, I am
afraid their patience is at an end," the man calling himself Sir
Redjon explained.

Dominic felt utterly alone. His mind spun as he tried to
make sense of what was happening. Two large men in armor,

"Knights?" he thought, were kneeling before him, telling him he was the king of a kingdom he's never heard of. "Guys, honestly, this isn't funny," he replied. But as he is said the words, Dominic had the worst feeling: 'this isn't a joke.' "In fact," he thought, "it somehow seemed familiar." The two men kneeling before him, while strangers, seemed very familiar to him; particularly the giant. Was he an uncle, or a friend of the family? Had Dominic met these men before? Maybe they were friends of his dad's, hired to make his twelfth birthday one to remember? He thought about it for a moment, but he knew this wasn't the case. Deep down, Dominic knew they were not joking. The problem was, he also knew that what they were saying wasn't possible.

When Sir Orgen spoke again, it was with a little more urgency, "Sire, please come with us. The situation can no longer wait. We must brief the men of your return. They have been waiting in the War Room for you all day."

Dominic was at a loss for words. He started to take a step towards the men then had a thought. "Wait a minute. Twelve years?" he asked. "Before you opened the door, I heard one of you say that this room has been closed for twelve years by order of the king. Is that right? I've been gone twelve years and this room has been locked for twelve years by my order, I mean the king's order?"

"Yes, sire, 'tis true. Not a soul has stepped foot in this dungeon as you commanded before your departure," replied Sir Redjon.

"Ha!" Dominic laughed. "I knew this was a prank."

"Sire?" asked Sir Redjon.

"Today is my twelfth birthday. How could I be king and order anyone to close this room off if I wasn't even born yet? And stand up, you're creeping me out." He *knew* this was a prank and now he had caught them. "Checkmate!" he thought.

The two men rose in silence. "Sire, it is apparent that you have no recollection of the past or who you truly are," said Sir Orgen. "I wish I could explain everything to you now, but we simply do not have the time. All I ask, for now, my liege, is for you to look deep inside yourself. Does this place not seem familiar somehow? Do you not feel we have met before?" the giant asked.

If Dominic was being honest with himself, yes it all did feel familiar. He knew these men. He wasn't sure how, but Dominic knew he had met these men before. The thought sat uneasy in him as his head began to spin again and a queasy sensation filled him. Feeling faint, he leaned against the nearest wall, to keep from falling over. He wanted to say something, to tell them to stop this cruel joke, but, "It's not funny anymore," was all the boy could muster.

Awakening

Before he could utter another word, a young woman hurried into the room. "Sir Orgen my lord, the knights are becoming restless. Sir Thomas Jameson has demanded to speak to you at once and says if you do not return to the War Room immediately, with a sufficient explanation as to why he has been kept waiting..." The young girl hesitated, whatever the message from Sir McConnell was, she was terrified to deliver it to the giant.

"Who could blame her," the boy thought, "the man is massive."

"Go on, girl" growled Sir Orgen.

"Sir Jameson, umm, he said if you do not return to the War Room at once, the prince would be the least of your worries," the girl said reluctantly.

Dominic could sense anger rising in Sir Orgen. The giant obviously did not like to be threatened.

The young girl continued, "The others are becoming angry as well, my lord. Sir, they are asking if King Dominic..." The girl stopped midsentence as she spotted the pale young boy, in the strange outfit, leaning against the dungeon wall. Her mouth gaped as if she were staring at a ghost. "Sire?!" she exclaimed as she dropped to the floor and knelt before Dominic. "Forgive me sire, I did not see thee standing there," she pleaded.

31

As Dominic was processing this new bit of strangeness, Sir Orgen took the boy by the arm and said, "Come, sire. Please, come with me and I assure you things will become clear very soon." But the boy seemed oblivious to Sir Orgen's urging. The giant asked again, this time pleading, "Sire, we must hurry, before the men leave!"

Dominic looked up at the large man in the beautiful black armor and, for a moment, no longer felt frightened. Ten minutes ago, the boy was in his yard preparing for an epic battle, now he was standing in a cold damp prison cell surrounded by strangers telling him an even stranger fairytale. A sudden wave of familiarity washed over him. Call it déjà vu, remembrance or an awakening, Dominic *knew* he and Sir Orgen had been here before, in this very room. With each passing moment, he felt his resolve stiffen and Dominic knew, just as he knew the bottle was his, that he could trust Sir Brenden Fredrick Orgen with his life.

Sir Orgen saw the sea change in the young king's eyes and thought, "This seems familiar to him."

"Follow me, sire," the Black Knight said, as he turned and exited the room. Dominic hesitated for a moment and then slowly headed for the door. As he was stepping across the threshold, the boy turned to see the frightened girl still kneeling face down on the cold stone floor. He paused and asked, "Excuse me ma'am. What is your name?"

"Isabella, my lord," she replied without looking up.

"Isabella? Do you have a brother named Marcel?" he asked, and then immediately thought, "How could I possibly know that?"

"Yes, sire, I do. He is your stable boy," replied Isabella.

"*My* stable boy," Dominic thought. He turned to leave and stopped once more, "Oh, you can rise Isabella. We're leaving and it's cold in here. Please, tell Marcel I said hello," Dominic said, as he left the room and hurried after Sir Orgen.

3

In the War Room

In silence, the two large men escorted the boy up a tall stone spiral staircase. The stairway was narrow and the climb steep. Dominic was replaying recent events in his head, trying to make sense of what was happening. No matter how he looked at it, the only thing which made sense to him was that this must be an elaborate prank. If he was indeed the king of this castle, how could it be that he hadn't been here for twelve years? He was exactly twelve! It made no sense.

They had been climbing the stairs for a few minutes; passing only the occasional window. Each of the arched, ornate, panes was glazed with intricate, colored glass. Some windows depicted images of fierce beasts and others depicted knights on horseback. The opaqueness of the stained glass made it impossible for Dominic to survey what was outside. If he could just see his surroundings, he might get a clue as to what was really going on.

After another minute of climbing, the boy heard voices, faint at first, but with each step they grew louder. While he could not make out actual conversations, Dominic was able to pick up bits-and-pieces of dialogue: 'Sir Orgen is a fool,' and, 'King Dominic is not returning.' As he got closer to the upper landing, he heard something which sounded like, 'Sunrise.' Or was it 'Surprise'?

"Aha!" he thought, "They said 'Surprise'. This must be where the surprise is!" Excitement filled the boy. This was definitely going to top any of his previous birthdays. "My parents are geniuses," he mumbled.

"Sire?" questioned Sir Redjon.

"Huh? Uh, nothing," the boy replied. He was just about to ask the giant how much further they needed to go, when they arrived at the castle turret's landing.

Dominic stood there, at the top of the tower, exhausted from the climb. They were atop a small landing, facing a large oak door which was ten feet high and braced with strips of steel plates. Even a twelve-year-old boy could see, this was a secure area meant for authorized people only.

As he was mentally preparing himself to step in to the room,

Dominic noticed a pungent odor permeating the landing. The smell was so strong, he swore he could taste it; if tasting an odor was possible. It was an odor he recognized immediately.

Dominic Bennett had never been the kind of kid who played organized sports. That's not to say he wasn't athletic. On the contrary, his father had always been impressed with Dominic's natural abilities and had urged his son to join baseball, soccer, lacrosse and the like. The truth was, Dominic had always shied away from interacting with other boys. They were either too immature for him to relate to, or they would ridicule him for his love of all things medieval. Nothing proved this point better than his relationship with Tyler Cole.

The Cole family had moved to the neighborhood just after Rose was born. Dominic's mother was very friendly and she welcomed the Cole's with open arms. Maggie Bennett and Stefanie Cole got along immediately and soon became very close friends. Of course, this meant that, like it or not, the boys spent a lot of time together.

Tyler was into Power Rangers and Pokémon, which didn't mesh well with Dominic's, 'D' to his friends, love of knights and castles. The boys got along fine, for a while. D learned the names of all the Power Rangers, and all about Zordon. "Did you know that Zordon defeated Rita Repulsa and threw her in a dumpster on the moon?" Tyler asked D one day. However, when it came to playing knights, Tyler had no interest. "Knights is for babies. I don't play baby games," he told D one day.

Dominic remembered feeling crushed by this comment and ever since, had shielded his hobby from other kids. From that point on, he and the "Cole Kid", as Dominic referred to him, didn't get along; which suited D just fine. But this wasn't the reason Dominic didn't play organized sports. It was Dominic's inability to follow rules.

When D was seven, Randy signed his son up to play soccer. The boy had never watched the sport and didn't know any of its rules, however, when the coach put him in as a defender and instructed, "Just don't let anyone near the net, ok D?", the boy was thrilled.

"A challenge," Dominic thought. "I shall defend this net with my life, sire," he told Coach Noah.

D was as excited as he'd ever been. Unfortunately, this excitement ended only moments later when the first attacker came charging down the field towards D's net. "I shall defend it with my life," he thought again. D waited until the attacker was within striking distance and, like a cat cornering a helpless bird, he sprinted full speed at the boy and pounced on him.

The poor unsuspecting kid fell to the ground with a loud 'THUD'; which could be heard across the soccer field. But D and the boy, Scott, were the only ones to also hear the soft 'CRACK' sound which came from the general vicinity of Scott's tibia.

During the ensuing pandemonium of whistles blowing, cries of pain, parents screaming and his coach yelling, "Dominic, get off him,", all Dominic could think was, "I was just defending my territory." He tried explaining this to coach Noah, as well as his parents, but no one would listen.

On the drive home that day, a ride for which he counted no less than ten 'what-were-you-thinkings', and six 'you're-groundeds', his parents refused to let the boy explain his side of the story.

Years later, he chuckled at the thought of his entire organized sporting career lasting a mere five minutes-two seconds. "That must be some sort of record," he told his friend Adam one day. The next time he participated in organized athletic activities was in middle school.

At Clarkston Middle School, every child was required to attend gym class twice a week. Anyone who knows anything about middle school locker rooms, and middle school boys in particular, knows that neither have a pleasant aroma. Multiply the average middle school boy's oniony B.O. bouquet by a factor of thirty and you could understand what a middle school boy's locker room smells like on any given day. It was this aroma which hit Dominic's nasal passages as he stood outside the War Room.

Sir Orgen paused before opening the door. "Sire, if it pleases ye, I would like to address the men first, to let them know of your return. And, also, to explain your current, umm, condition," the Black Knight suggested.

"Yeah, yeah, whatever," Dominic said dismissively. He just wanted this hoax to be over with and, the sooner he got in the room and everyone yelled '*surprise*', the better.

Too excited to contain himself any longer, Dominic pushed past the giant and entered the War Room. "The king is in the houuuuse!" he yelled excitedly as he stepped into the large, smelly room. He expected to see his parents standing and yelling, "*Surprise!*" or his aunts and uncles or at the very least his best friend, Adam. Instead, what he saw made him reel.

D found himself in a large, round room. Approximately forty feet wide and built entirely of large granite blocks, the room was like something out of the middle ages. Standing in the center of the room, was a large round table, twelve feet in diameter, made of a single three-inch piece of solid cedar, and resting on, what appeared to be, a base of black onyx. Hanging above the table was a chandelier unlike anything Dominic had ever seen.

The fixture, which was suspended from the ceiling by a long, wrought iron chain, was made entirely of stag antlers. The warm glow emitting from the chandelier was not electric light, but the faint flicker of fifty candles, each in its own glass bowl. The bowls were interspersed along the drops and branches of the luminous behemoth fixture. As unexpected as the room's architecture was, what caught Dominic by surprise, and knocked the breath from the boy, were the chairs; or more precisely, the 'party' guests seated in the chairs.

There were eight large wood and iron chairs positioned around the table. Seated in these chairs, were five of the largest men Dominic had ever seen. Their sizes varied, but none was shorter than 6'05", or weighed less than 250 pounds, and each man was adorned in beautiful armor of varying colors. The worst part was, none of the men were his parents; or anyone even remotely familiar looking, for that matter. Dominic felt ill.

There was a long moment of absolute silence. He had often heard the term, 'you could hear a pin drop', but it wasn't until this moment that Dominic knew exactly what dead silence felt like.

The knight in the grey ornate armor, with the Bull embossed

in the chest piece, broke the silence. "Bahaha," he chortled. "Brenden, you've out done yourself. This jester is hysterical. Look at those fantastical clothes. He looks like a young girl playing dress-up…." The man stopped mid-sentence. The look on Sir Orgen and Sir Redjon's faces said it all: This was no joke.

"Fantastical clothes?" the boy thought. He assessed his attire: black t-shirt with a moon shining over a castle and a single word written in calligraphy beneath: "Knight", torn blue jeans and tan Skecher sneakers.

"Sir McConnell you will address your king with the respect he is due!" bellowed Burton Redjon.

A grey-haired man wearing armor which had a golden hue, and a stag on its chest piece, stood and addressed the three newcomers. "Sir Orgen, you have kept us waiting all day with assurances that King Dominic would return. And yet here you stand with this, this, child. Is this some kind of joke?" asked Sir Thomas Albert Jameson.

"Exactly what I was thinking," thought Dominic.

"I assure you it is not, Thomas" replied Sir Orgen.

The men began to shout at Redjon and Orgen: "Explain yourselves!" "Where is King Dominic?" "Enough of this foolishness!" "What are you playing at Orgen!" The Knights of Munkelstein shouted. They were becoming uneasy and on the verge of riot.

Dominic was in a stupor. His parents and sister weren't here. Neither were his aunts or uncles, nor his best friend, Adam. The boy was lost deep in thought, his brain racing.

Sir Orgen took in a long deep breath and shouted, "ENOUGH!" The room shook for a moment and then fell silent. The giant now had everyone's total attention, including Dominic's. After a short pause, a more composed Sir Orgen addressed the confused group. "If you will allow me to explain the situation, everything will become clear, I promise."

"Finally," the boy thought. He *needed* to know what was happening and hoped the giant's explanation would end this awful prank once and for all. But as he awaited Sir Orgen's explanation, D had another strong feeling of familiarity. He had been in this room before; often.

"As you are all aware, our beloved king, his royal majesty King Dominic Philip Segarius of Munkelstein, departed our great kingdom twelve years ago with the promise that he would return," Sir Orgen started. "However, there is much you do not know about his departure. For decades, the tyrant Prince Mathias has waged war on our beloved land, and has failed at every turn; thanks largely to the brave men in this room and your loyalty to our King." Sir Orgen turned to look at Dominic with the word 'King'. The knights broke out in applause and cheers. Sir Orgen let them go for a moment and then raised his hand to silence them. "I think we can all agree," the Black Knight continued, "that we did not do this alone. Our ruler has provided us all with wealth, happiness and security. All King Dominic has ever asked of us in return, is our unquestioned loyalty to the crown and to the kingdom. Our king has fought by our sides at every battle, and has the scars to prove it."

As he stood there, trying to grasp the situation, Dominic felt suddenly at ease. "I have been here before," he thought. Then he spied something he hadn't noticed when first arriving to the War Room.

Hanging on the wall, directly across from where he was currently standing, was a large painting. The canvas covered most of the wall behind the empty chair at the head of the table. The depiction in the painting was of a handsome man on horseback. The man, a knight by the looks of the silver armor, was about forty-five years old, had striking blue eyes and light brown hair. He appeared to be in a battle, of some sort, and had a deep, three-inch cut below his left eye; which was seeping a bright red line of blood. Dominic instinctively ran his fingers across his cheek and a shiver ran through him. His parents had told him he cut himself while climbing out of his crib when he was a baby. "That looks like it could be me in thirty or forty years," he thought. The Silver Knight was atop a jet-black stallion, which was in mid leap as it bounded over a fallen tree. In his right hand, the knight held a large steel blade, ready to slice into something, "Or someone," the boy thought. This was the most beautiful piece of art Dominic had ever seen. But he *knew* he had seen it before.

"You will all recall the last time you saw King Dominic," continued Sir Orgen. "Twelve years ago, our king was standing in this very room, apprising us of Prince Mathias's plot to kill him. But what King Dominic could not tell you then, I must tell you now, lest I risk losing your loyalty to our beloved king." Sir Orgen paused for effect, then continued, "Do you remember the day King Dominic departed?" The knights nodded in unison. "He stood in this very room and asked only four things from us, the loyal Knights of Munkelstein. The men he trusts with his life. Do you remember?"

"Aye, Sir Orgen," shouted Sir Elijah Moren, the knight in the dark blue armor with the eagle on the chest piece. "Our king's first request was to trust in him fully, and without question."

44

"If there was another way he would have taken it," yelled Sir James Tobias Bastile, the knight in the forest green armor with a wolf's head emblazoned on it.

"Yes, yes James. That is exactly what the king said," replied Sir Orgen. "Next, King Dominic asked that you not question his motives for departing," the Black Knight continued.

"While retreat was best left to cowards, there are times where stepping back could prove to be more powerful than moving forward," yelled the man in white armor with the bear crest, Sir Michael Robert Krebow.

"Thank you, Michael. The king could not have said it better himself," Sir Orgen replied.

The men were hanging on the giant's every word now and Dominic was impressed. He could see that the Black Knight was a natural motivator. When they first arrived in the War Room, the knights were ready to riot, now they were nodding their heads in agreement and seemed on the verge of cheering.

"Thirdly, King Dominic asked us, his most loyal and trusted servants, to continue our unending devotion to the kingdom and to defend it with our lives while he was gone," Sir Orgen retold.

Without thinking, Dominic spoke, "For there is nothing more important, and nothing that tells the true measure of a man, than his loyalty to his kingdom."

Sir Orgen stopped and gazed at Dominic in amazement. A smile crossed the giant's face. "Yes, my lord. Those are the exact words you used!" he said excitedly.

The boy was stunned. "Did I just say that?" he thought. The knights looked around at each other puzzled. There were low murmurs, but nothing he could make out.

"And finally, who remembers the final request from our king?" asked Brenden.

Burton Redjon spoke up, "The king instructed us to tell no one that he had abandoned his kingdom…"

"Departed his kingdom," Sir Orgen corrected.

"…departed his kingdom," Sir Redjon continued, as he shot Sir Orgen a look which would have made a lesser man quake. "If word were to reach Prince Mathias that the king had *departed* his kingdom, we would find ourselves in a war which could destroy Munkelstein," the Red Knight said, correcting himself.

"Exactly. Thank you, Burton," replied Sir Orgen.

However, this small bit of politeness did not seem to quell the anger Sir Redjon felt for being corrected in front of the other men. At that moment, Dominic could see that the two knights were not friends. They had apparently fought together to defend their kingdom, but in Dominic's opinion, off the battlefield, these men might be enemies.

In the War Room

"Thank you for the history lesson Brenden, but we all remember quite well the king's final words to us. And I for one have spoken to no one of our last meeting with King Dominic. Nonetheless, I have heard whispers that Prince Mathias has devised a plan to take King Dominic's throne once and for all." Sir McConnell was standing now as he addressed Sir Orgen. "Brenden, we have been patient and have asked no questions as to the truth of why our king departed. However, now, now is the time for answers. I will no longer sit and wait until that bastard Mathias is at our front gate. For when the day comes, it will be the men in this room, and our families, and the citizens of this great kingdom who will suffer; not our absent king. Twelve years is long enough, now I demand you tell us where the king is hiding."

Brenden Orgen felt anger beginning to rise within him. How dare this man question his beloved ruler. He paused to allow his temper to subside before addressing the traitorous comment.

"You are right Stephen. Now is the time for answers. Let me tell you what I know," the giant replied calmly. Pausing a moment, as if in deep thought, he then continued. "For nearly thirty years, King Dominic Philip Segarius has ruled the Kingdom of Munkelstein, and for nearly thirty years,

Prince Mathias has attempted to take the throne for himself. Thanks to the brave men in this room, the prince has been unsuccessful.

"In the weeks leading up to his departure, King Dominic had become aware of an imminent threat to his life. The king believed a traitor had infiltrated Munkelstein and was sharing intelligence with Prince Mathias," Sir Orgen informed them. "Try as we might, we were unable to uncover who among us had betrayed Munkelstein. If the king perished, Prince Mathias would claim the throne for himself, and, well I'm sure I don't have to explain to you what would happen should he succeed."

"We know all this Brenden. Get to the point," shouted Sir Krebow. "Where is King Dominic?"

"This treacherous plot left King Dominic with few options," Brenden continued, not acknowledging Sir Krebow's rude outburst. The giant was beginning to lose patience with his brothers. "The king could stay and hope the assassin was discovered before he could complete his evil task. However, if this cowardice killer succeeded, and King Dominic had every reason to believe that he would, Munkelstein would fall prey to Prince Mathias's army. King Dominic trusts us, the men in this room, however, he was not willing to risk the lives of the citizens of this great kingdom unless he had no other choice.

This left our king with only two options: stay in Munkelstein and die, or take a step back and regroup." Sir Orgen paused again to let this point sink in. The room was dead silent as the knights contemplated this thought. "I ask you all to look inside yourselves and ask, 'What would I have done if I wore the crown? Would I stay and face certain death, or regroup and live to fight another day?' If you are honest and true of heart, you will understand the king's dilemma."

"Brenden," started Thomas Jameson, "where is King Dominic now? If it is as you say, and the king's life was truly in jeopardy, by someone within these walls, what has changed? If he returns, how will his safety be assured?"

"Unfortunately, Thomas, you are correct," Sir Orgen replied. "If it is as we fear, and there is indeed a traitor amongst us, then nothing has changed. However, I can say that if one of the men in this room is the traitor, then Prince Mathias would have known all along that King Dominic had left Munkelstein. This means that either our original information was incorrect and we do not have a traitor, or Prince Mathias is more interested in killing King Dominic himself, than simply taking the Munkelstein throne. Either way, the time for stepping back has finally ended."

"So, where is he? Where is the king, Brenden?" shouted Elijah Moren.

"He is right in front of you Elijah," replied Sir Orgen as he placed his hand on Dominic's shoulder.

"Brenden, are you saying this *boy* is our king?" Stephen McConnell laughed. "Well boy, are you our king?"

Brenden glared at the Grey Knight and said, in a low growl, "If I need to remind you once more to show your king the respect he is owed, you will not have to worry about Prince Mathias murdering you, my friend."

Thomas Jameson broke the awkward tension. "Brenden, you have yet to show us any proof of what you claim," he said, trying to divert Sir Orgen's attention from Sir McConnell. "However, I have seen dark magic with my own eyes and believe anything is possible. This boy may very well be our king and, if you are young man, I apologize for my tone. Is there anything you remember, or can tell us, which would prove you are indeed King Dominic Segarius?" the Gold Knight asked.

The boy could feel them all studying him as they awaited his response. He had only been in this place for a few hours and was still grappling with all which had occurred in that time. If he didn't tell the Gold Knight something substantial, he knew there was likely to be a riot. Before he could respond, fate intervened.

Knock…knock…knock.

In the War Room

"Sir B-B-Brenden, I have a m-m-message for the k-k-k-king," shouted a voice outside the door.

Burton Redjon turned, threw open the door and shouted, "We've asked to be left undisturbed. Your message had better be urgent or there will be hell to pay!"

Standing in the doorway, was a frail, meager looking redheaded boy, no older than Dominic. His outstretched hands were shaking as he handed the Red Knight a small scroll.

"What is this boy?" Sir Redjon demanded.

The redheaded boy was visibly frightened by the sight of the large man in red armor, glowering down at him. "Who could blame him?" Dominic thought. The small freckle faced boy was standing before a very large man who was demanding information from him.

"S-s-s-sir R-r-r-redjon, my l-l-l-lord," the boy stuttered. "A c-c-c-courier, has j-just arrived t-to the g-g-g-gates with th-th-this. I was t-t-t-told to deliver it to the W-w-war Room i-m-m-m-mediately," the boy struggled to say as he handed the scroll to Sir Redjon.

The Red Knight snatched the scroll from the boy. "And you've delivered it. Now GO!" he shouted as he slammed the door on the boy.

"What is it Burton?" asked Sir Orgen.

The Red Knight studied the scroll for a moment, then replied, "It's a message for King Dominic, from Prince Mathias."

"Prince Mathias? May I see it please?" the Black Knight asked as he snatched the note from Burton's hand.

The giant held up the scroll and examined its seal: the head of a jackal over two intersecting daggers and the words '*I am my brother's keeper*'. "Definitely Prince Mathias's seal," the giant muttered to himself.

"What does the message say?" asked Sir Jameson.

"Perhaps now is not the time," the giant replied, looking down at Dominic.

"Now is precisely the time," replied Stephen McConnell. "Perhaps this is the proof Thomas is asking for."

"Go on," Dominic instructed, "read it Brenden." "Maybe this is my birthday surprise," he thought, but didn't believe.

"Very well, sire," Sir Orgen said reluctantly, as he broke the seal, unrolled the scroll and read:

"Greetings my old friend. I've missed you these many years.

"Things have simply not been the same since you ran away from home. When we were boys, you were the bravest person I knew. I would have never believed that the great King Dominic Philip Segarius, would run and hide like a scared child, had I not seen it for myself. I was told of

your cowardice departure some time ago, and while I had many chances to take back what is rightfully mine in that time, I thought it would be much more fun to make you suffer first. After all, where's the fun in taking back an empty *throne. Finding you has cost me a fortune, but find you I did. I could have killed you the day I found you. But where's the sport in killing a defenseless child? Besides, I knew we would see each other again. I'm nothing if not patient. Please, don't thank me. I have something much more fun planned for us anyway.*

"That you are reading this, tells me you have indeed found your way back to Munkelstein. I only wish I could see the look on your pathetic subjects faces when they see that their 'almighty ruler, the great King Dominic Philip Segarius' *is nothing more than a scared twelve-year-old boy. I wonder, do you even remember who you were before? My guess is you do not; although, I have no doubt your memories will come flooding back to you very soon. Running and hiding from me has only prolonged your inevitable death. A death which, I assure you, will be slow and painful. You will suffer more than you could ever imagine. And, only when I am satisfied that you have learned your lesson will I relieve you of your pain. The magic you used to escape me was brilliant and expertly crafted. Thanks to you, I have magic of my own. How else could I have found you? The look on your face as you opened that bottle was priceless. Now, there is only one more look I wish to see on your face. Oh, I would give anything to be there when you read this and discover that I have taken*

your beloved family and locked them away in the dungeon deep below Sylvania Manor. Magg's and Randy say "hi". Unfortunately, poor Rose has just been too afraid to speak. Although, I'm certain she would send her love, if she could.

"So, you not think me heartless, I am willing to give you the opportunity to save your precious Bennett family. In exactly five nights, I will expect you to come to me and offer your unconditional surrender; (Three days from now I will send a messenger with instructions). If you refuse me, or do not comply with my wishes, I will return your family to you in pieces. If you harm a single hair on my messenger's poor old head, I will peel the skin from Randy's bones and wear him as a coat. I trust you understand my point. Please do not fret my boy, I will see your face soon enough; of that I assure you.

"Welcome back old friend!

The One and Only True King of Munkelstein,
Prince Reynaldus Wilhelm Mathias"

"We have to save them! We have to save them now! He's going to kill my family," Dominic shouted. "What are we going to do? We have to save them."

"Sire, we cannot simply attack Sylvania," replied Sir Redjon. "It is too heavily guarded. We would suffer massive casualties. Plus, Prince Mathias would see our troops approaching well before we reached his gates. Your family would be dead before we ever touched Sylvanian soil," the Red Knight explained. "Sire, your family was a means to protect your life, as well as our kingdom. We are in a war and there will always be casualties in war. Perhaps it is best to…forget them."

A flush of anger filled the boy. In the past few hours, Dominic went from being a twelve-year-old boy playing in his yard, to being told that he was the ruler of a kingdom he'd never heard of; a kingdom, by the way, which he'd ruled for thirty years. And, as crazy as it all sounded, part of him was starting to believe it.

The more Dominic thought about it, the more he came to realize how different he was from everyone he knew. There was the fact he bore no resemblance to his parents; something he was just now realizing. His mom was a demure woman no more than 5' 02", with green eyes, long red hair, and a pale freckled complexion. His dad was average height with dark, almost black, hair and brown eyes. At the age of twelve, Dominic was already as tall as Randy, and while the boy had never met his grandfather, he had seen plenty of photos of the man; Randy Bennett Sr. was a full three inches shorter than his son.

How had Dominic not noticed it before? He looked nothing like any of the relatives he'd ever met, or had ever seen in photos or home movies. His sister Rose, who would be sixteen in a few months, could pass for the younger sister of Mrs. Maggie Bennett. As crazy as the past few hours had been, in some way, everything was starting to make sense to Dominic and, to his surprise, he felt a sense of relief.

"Burton, hear me and hear me well," the boy growled, with the bravado of a king. "I, excuse me, *we*, will not leave my family to die in the dungeon of a madman. *If*, I am the king, then it was I who put their lives in jeopardy, and it is I who is responsible to save them. And, if I *am* the king, you all have known me for, according to your own admission, more than thirty years. I will not lie to you, I have no recollection of my previous time here, however, I can assume that we have fought many fierce battles together. I can also assume you would all give your lives for mine, as I would for you." A few of the knights nodded in agreement; others looked at him with skepticism. "I can also assume that the King Dominic you remember is a man of his word, yes?" the boy asked; although he hardly sounded like a boy any longer.

"Aye sire, you have always been so," replied Sir Orgen.

"Then you will all heed my words and know what I say is true. We will not let my family perish in that place," King Dominic proclaimed. "Sir Redjon says this is a suicide mission, and I should simply forget my family. How can I do that Burton? I ask you all, how can you expect me to simply forget the people who have kept me safe these past twelve years? I will not. No, WE will not abandon them now," the king insisted. "You must all ask yourselves this: Do I believe that the man standing before me is truly my king? If you believe I am not, then leave now. I will not stand in your way, because honestly, I'm not sure what to believe either. However, if you look at me and see even the smallest glimmer of the man you have known as your king, standing before you, then I implore you to stay and fight with me."

Dominic finished his speech, his heart racing. He hardly felt like the person he was before entering the War Room. Maybe he really was their king. After all, how else could he have given such an impassioned speech? Now the only question was: 'Do *they* believe he is the king?'

Without hesitation, Sir Brendon Fredrick Orgen knelt before Dominic, the King of Munkelstein, and asked, "What will you have me do, my lord?"

And then, one-by-one, the Knights of Munkelstein knelt in respect to their king.

Dominic Bennett stood in the War Room, seven men

kneeling before him. Knights kneeling before their king. Prepared to give their lives for king and kingdom.

"Please, rise," replied King Dominic. "We have work to do."

4

A Dungeon in Sylvania

Oh my God, please Randy, please. What is happening? Why are we here? What did we do?" Maggie Bennett pleaded as she bawled into her husband's chest.

"It's ok Magg's. I promise I'll get us out of here," her husband replied. Randy Bennett was doing what any good, loving husband would do to comfort his wife: trying to put her mind at ease by telling her what she needed to hear. He only wished *he* believed what he was saying.

When he first awoke, Randy thought he was dreaming. But after an hour of searching the room for an exit, and screaming at the top of his lungs for help, he knew it was no dream. They were in real trouble and he felt helpless.

"Daddy I'm scared," Rose whimpered.

Randy pulled his little girl close to his chest and rubbed her shoulder. "I know Rosey. Hey, you don't think your dad would let anything bad happen to you and your mom, do you?" He felt his daughter squeeze him tight. "I love you my sweet pea. I'll get us out of this, I promise. We'll be home before the street lights come on. Ok?" He felt Rose's posture relax a bit. She may not believe him, but she certainly felt safer with her dad there.

Randy sat, comforting his girls and trying to make sense of what was happening. He was smart enough to understand they were in real trouble. They were in a cold, empty room made of stone. "A dungeon?" he thought. "But why and by whom?" Then Randy thought back to a night twelve years ago. The night of the most bizarre storm he'd ever witnessed.

He remembered Maggie calling to him as he stepped outside to assess the damage, "Please be careful," she told him. There was something else too. He wasn't sure exactly what she had said. "Something about insurance," he said under his breath.

*　　*

(A Stormy Night, Part 2)

"Please be careful." Randy shot his wife a quick smile which was meant to calm her, but she could see he was worried about

60

what he might find. "And hey," Maggie yelled as he stepped into the night, "that's what insurance is for."

Randy stood on the porch of his four-bedroom brick Tudor, in anticipation of the damage caused from, what was in his opinion, the fastest moving storm in history. The air was warm and thick, and the wind was still. Taking in a deep breath, Randy let the darkness consume him. He breathed in, expecting to smell the damp odor of rain, but instead smelled only the sweet scent of Maggie's flower garden.

As his eyes adjusted to the light of his new surroundings, Randy had two immediate thoughts: the first, was how much he loved the smell of Maggie's flowers. The woman loved to garden.

When they first moved into their home on Gallen Drive, Maggie insisted on planting nothing but rows of various white flowers around the front of the house. Randy suggested she add some color to the garden, to which Maggie would reply, "Trust me, it'll look beautiful." And, of course, she was right.

His second, much more puzzled thought, was, "What the hell?"

As he stood there, alone in the darkness, Randy tried to rationalize what he was seeing. "Snow?" he thought. "How on Earth? I've heard of summer storms bringing hail but, snow?"

And then it hit him; hard. As the reality of what he was seeing began to permeate his brain, his heart sank. Scattered across the freshly manicured lawn, lay an almost perfect blanket of fresh snow, made entirely of Maggie's white flower petals. The scene was as beautiful as it was heart wrenching. The precision at which the petals had been removed from their stems and 'placed' across the lawn, seemed almost surgical to Randy. There was literally, not one petal left on any of the plants.

"This is going to crush her," he mumbled.

He stood there for a moment, collecting himself, the moon casting his shadow over the snowy ground, and heaved a heavy sigh. "Well, let's see how bad the rest of this is," he said as he stepped from the porch.

Randy turned to face the house and prepared himself for the damage the storm must have done. The roof looked unscathed as did the siding. "Looks like we got lucky," he said to the bushes.

Maggie had planted a row of green junipers at the front of the porch, just behind the rows of flowers. She felt the contrast of the deep green backdrop would make the white daisies and asters 'pop'. And of course, as always, in the matter of flora and fauna, Maggie was right. However, Randy had never noticed the mound which now seemed to be bridging the two shrubs closest to the porch steps.

"Now what?" he asked himself.

Stepping closer to the junipers to investigate the debris, Randy saw something lying on the bushes. In the darkness, it appeared to be an old tattered shirt. The cloth looked to be handmade, its edges frayed from years of use. He reached down to inspect the old garment more closely, but before he could grab it, the shirt moved. Randy startled as the cloth wriggled a second time. Remembering he was holding his flashlight, he flipped it on and aimed the light at the now visibly agitated piece of clothing.

Thinking that perhaps, a raccoon had gotten itself tangled in the cloth during the storm, and was now struggling to break free, he reached for the bundle. "There, there little guy, I've got you," he said gently.

He pocketed the Maglite, crouched low and with one quick motion scooped up the cloth, and its prisoner, into his arms. It was immediately apparent to Randy that this was no raccoon. Whatever it was, it was not happy. He gently pulled back the blanket to reveal the mysterious captive and was greeted with a very human face. Wrapped in the centuries old, tattered garment, was a baby.

Randy's brain began to spin, as he attempted to process exactly what he was seeing, when the front door opened. "Is everything alright out there, honey?" Maggie asked. She paused as she saw her husband standing on the porch holding something odd in his hands. Before she could ask him what he was doing, Maggie Bennett heard a baby crying.

"I, uh uh, it's um uh, I found it in the…uh…it's a baby," was all Randy could muster.

*   *

"Rose, it's time your mother and I tell you something," Randy said. He knew Maggie wouldn't be happy about it, but given the current situation, he didn't have a choice.

"What Randy? What do we need to tell…no, absolutely not," Maggie said, realizing what Randy meant. "We said we would never say anything to anyone, not even Rose."

"Listen Magg's, I think he might have something to do with why we're here. Don't you?" Randy asked. "I mean, it's the only thing that makes sense."

He absolutely knew how his wife felt. In fact, he was the one who implored Maggie to keep things quiet about where Dominic came from; not that he knew where the boy came from. All Randy knew for sure was Dominic wasn't theirs.

A Dungeon in Sylvania

*   *

"And when they ask, just tell them we've been planning on adopting a child for a while but didn't want to say anything until everything was approved. Tell them you're superstitious and didn't want to jinx it," Randy told his wife that night twelve years ago. They had worked on their story all evening; making sure to get every detail right. When the time came to tell their story, even Maggie was starting to believe it.

The following morning, Maggie phoned her best friend and neighbor, Stephanie Cole. "Stef, Stef, Stef!" she yelled excitedly into the phone. "Stef, we got him! Stef? Are you there?"

"Yes, Maggie I'm here what are you talking about? Got who?" the voice on the phone replied.

"I'm so sorry Stef. I wanted to tell you but I was worried that it wouldn't happen if I did but, he's here. And you just have to come over and see how beautiful he is." Maggie then told her friend the story she and Randy concocted.

Stephanie spent the entire day with Maggie, oohing and ahhing over the sweet boy. Stef, who herself was seven months pregnant, could not have been happier for her friend. If she doubted Maggie's story at all, she did not let it show.

65

Now that Maggie had an ally, convincing the rest of the neighborhood was easy.

From that point on, Dominic was part of the Bennett family. No questions asked.

*   *

"Randy, please, don't," Maggie pleaded.

He said nothing for a minute, and then, "Magg's I have to. She deserves to know the truth. Especially since it may have something to do with the situation we are *all* in. Ok?" Randy asked. Maggie said nothing, but he felt her nod her agreement on his chest.

"Rose? Do you remember when your brother was born?" Randy asked his daughter.

"Kind of. I mean, I was only three. I remember mom coming home from the hospital with him," Rose replied.

"Right. But do you remember mom being pregnant?" Randy asked.

"No. But I was only three how could I, I mean…what are you saying?" Rose asked. She was a smart girl and immediately knew something wasn't right.

"Rose honey, when you were three, there was a storm. It raced through the neighborhood faster than any storm I've ever seen," Randy started.

A Dungeon in Sylvania

"I remember that night," Rose interrupted. "Mom and I were upstairs and you came running in yelling for us to get to the basement. I also remember how scared you both were," she added.

"Exactly!" Randy said excitedly. "But what you don't know, is that all of the weather stations were calling for clear skies that night. There was going to be a meteor shower and they encouraged everyone to go outside and observe it. 'Once in a lifetime,' they called it. What's even stranger is that the storm hit only our street. More specifically just our house," he explained. "The next day not one of the news stations talked about the storm and, when I asked around, none of our neighbors had any idea what I was talking about." It was too dark in the dungeon to see her face but Randy knew Rose was contemplating what he was telling her.

He continued his story, telling Rose how, after the storm cleared, he went outside to check for damage, and what he discovered in the bushes. He told his daughter how they decided to tell everyone they had adopted Dominic and that no one knew the real story of what had happened that night. Until now.

They sat silent for a long time, when Maggie asked, "Do you have any questions honey?"

"It explains so much," the young girl replied. "A few months ago, my friend Connie was over and we were looking at pictures of our trip to the Grand Canyon. Connie mentioned how Dominic looked like he was adopted because he didn't look like you or dad. I laughed and said, 'Yeah he's definitely adopted' but I was only joking. Dominic has always been so different from the rest of our family. Not in a bad way," Rose said.

"I understand what you mean honey," Maggie assured.

"The only thing I want to know is, why?" Rose asked.

"Why?" Randy repeated. "Why what Rosey?"

"Why did you keep him? I mean, you find a baby in your bushes after a storm and you don't call the police. What if his mother has been searching for him for the past twelve years? You kept him from his real family! How could you?" Rose asked, a twinge of contempt in her voice.

Maggie jumped in, "Your dad left out one important part of the story honey. He told you that when we found Dominic he was wrapped in a blanket and that is true. However, pinned to the blanket was a note from Dominic's mother, asking us to protect him."

"A note?" Rose questioned.

"Yes, a note," Maggie replied, "It said, 'Dear Mr. and Mrs.

Weber, please watch over my son, he is in grave danger. I will return for him when it is safe. Thank you, Beatrix. His name is Dominic.'"

"So, you see Rosey, we had a choice to make: we could call the police and tell them what we found, or we could say nothing," Randy explained. "If the letter was a hoax, we would be in serious trouble; however, if we believed what the letter said, we would be protecting an innocent life. And yes, part of our decision was based on our selfishness to have another child. But Rosey, you have to understand, your mother and I felt that the circumstances surrounding his arrival were strange, to say the least." Randy paused as he gathered his thoughts.

"The storm seemed to be centered over our house. Every single leaf and flower petal on every flower and tree on our property had been blown from their stems and *placed* on the lawn. It was as if the sky opened-up over our house with the intent of delivering Dominic to us. I know this sounds bizarre, believe me I do. Your mother and I have agonized over our decision almost every night since your brother arrived." Randy finished and waited for his little girl to process the information.

How could anyone believe such a fantastic tale? It really boiled down to whether or not Rose could trust her parents to be honest with her.

"And you think that we're stuck in this, this place because of D?" Rose asked.

It was a good question. Randy certainly thought it made the most sense. "I don't know honey," he replied. "The night we found your brother, the thought had occurred to me that the storm had something to do with his arrival. I believed his mother used the storm to cover her tracks," Randy replied.

"You mean she conjured it? Like a witch?" the girl asked, mockingly.

"No, that's not what I am saying," he replied. "His mom was probably driving around the neighborhood, looking for a safe place to leave him. Maybe she saw the storm coming and thought it would be the perfect opportunity to drop Dominic off without being seen," Randy explained. "I never thought for a moment that your brother fell from the sky, or the storm was 'conjured' up by a witch. At least, not until we woke up in this place."

"Maybe she meant to leave him somewhere else. I mean, how do you know she wanted *you* to raise him?" asked Rose. "After all, you said the letter was addressed to Mr. and Mrs. Weber."

Maggie replied, "We checked into that as well. There are no family's named Weber living anywhere within five miles of us. I'm not sure why Beatrix thought we were the Weber family." Then a thought occurred to her, "Randy, do you think Beatrix is involved in this? That she's trying to get Dominic back?"

He could hear fear in his wife's voice as she spoke. "Magg's," Randy replied, "for the first time since we found that note, I don't believe Beatrix exists."

The Bennetts sat in the darkness of the dungeon; each processing the circumstances which brought them to this place.

"Dad?" Rose whispered.

"Yeah sweet pea?" he said.

"Do you think this has anything to do with the strange old man in I saw in our backyard this morning?" she asked.

5

Dyog Ronndewo

W hat are we doing, Sir Orgen? We need to get back to the War Room and figure out how to save them," Dominic was directing, not asking.

The king and his giant of a guardian were in a large bedroom. The room was rectangular and, judging by the large oak desk near the window, also doubled as an office. Opposite the desk, sat a large king-sized bed. "Of course, it's a king," laughed Dominic to himself. The bedding was emblazoned with the blue and yellow colors of the Kingdom of Munkelstein. Next to the bed sat a modest table, on which were a silver ewer, a drinking glass, and a candelabra. In the middle of the floor, lay a bear skin rug. Dominic would have guessed this particular beast had to have been at least nine feet tall.

"Sire, please listen to me," Sir Orgen pleaded.

Dyog Ronndewo

The boy could see the concern in the giant's eyes. As much as he wanted to get right to plotting the rescue of his parents and sister, Dominic knew he needed to listen to his "Friend?" he thought. The strange feeling of knowing and trusting the giant, in the matte black armor, returned and had burrowed itself deep within Dominic's brain.

"Go ahead Brenden. Tell me, what is so urgent," the boy blurted.

"Sire, you have only just returned after being gone for more than a decade. The Dominic Segarius I knew, twelve years ago, would not have needed more than a couple of hours to plan a rescue of this magnitude. You are not that Dominic and do not remember who, or where, you are," Sir Orgen explained. "You must be briefed on what has happened since you left, how many soldiers we have, our strength and standing with the other kingdoms and other information pertinent to planning an attack. Your transformation from man to boy seems to have erased the memories of your past. This is not an unexpected side effect. In fact, you yourself predicted this could happen," Brenden said with empathy. The knight understood how important the Bennetts were to the boy. In Dominic's mind, they were his *real* parents. How could you ask a man, or a boy, to turn his back on his family when they were in danger? Sir Orgen continued, "Sire, might I suggest we spend some time talking before we plan our attack?"

"Talking? We have been talking. That's all you've done since I got here is talk, talk, talk. My family is going to be killed by a madman. The time for talking is through," the boy shouted. He was on the verge of demanding they head for the Great Plains immediately; however, the look on Sir Orgen's face told the boy he should hear him out. "I'm sorry, it's just, I can't sit here and pretend that my family isn't being tortured or possibly even already dead," the boy said solemnly. "I mean how do we even know that this Mathis guy hasn't killed them already?"

"Sire, this is exactly why we need to talk before you make a decision which cannot be undone," the giant replied. Dominic's shoulders slumped. He didn't like what Sir Orgen was saying, but he understood it. "Before you left Munkelstein, you were one of the most calm, rational men I have ever known. That king would have plotted every part of a rescue as complex as this one, down to the last detail, until he found every flaw and weakness. And certainly, *before* ever stepping foot outside the castle. The man who took your family, the one you called Mathis, his name is Prince Reynaldus Wilhelm *Mathias*."

"So what? Mathis, Mathias. I ask you, does it matter what this man's name is? Do you ask what breed the dog is after it has bitten you?" Dominic retorted.

"Now that sounds like my king," thought Sir Orgen excitedly. "You are correct, sire. But the problem isn't that you did not know this man's name."

"Then what exactly is the problem?" Dominic quipped.

Sir Orgen continued, "The problem is, you do not remember that Prince Mathias is your older brother."

"Wuh, wuh, what?" the boy struggled to ask. He could hardly breathe. "My...brother?" The boy's legs buckled. "I have a brother?" He felt as if he had been hit in the solar plexus. "Why would my brother...?"

The room began to spin. He fought to stay on his feet but it was a battle the king was not going to win. The boy spun around, collided with the footboard of his bed, and collapsed on to the floor.

*   *

"That's it right there."

"Well go already."

"I'm going, don't rush me."

"Haha, I knew you were afraid."

The boy held his breath and walked slowly towards the makeshift tent. If you could call what he was looking at a tent. Whomever owned this place, must have taken the scraps from a dozen different garments and sewn them together to make the disheveled looking home. However, it wasn't the home's appearance which concerned Dominic; although he did wonder how a man could live in such a small structure. No, what worried Dominic was what was inside; or more accurately, who was inside.

The rumors, depending on who was telling them, were that the owner of the dilapidated hovel was a wizard. A man more powerful than Merlin and Dahagen combined. He could read your mind and tell your future. He could move from place-to-place in an instant. One story even had him bringing his cat back from the dead; a cat, by most estimations, who was now more than 300 years old.

Dominic never believed any of these stories. But now that he was standing only five feet from the man's home, the boy was starting to believe everything he'd ever heard about the one they called, Dyog Ronndewo.

"Well, go already," Reynaldus urged his younger brother again. Younger by a mere two minutes, Dominic would often say.

Reynaldus was born exactly two minutes before Dominic;

however, when you were talking about the rights to a throne, those two minutes were everything.

The twins looked nothing alike. Dominic was a handsome boy with brilliant blue eyes and a muscular build. Reynaldus's hair was auburn, which matched his eyes, and he had the build of a boy who spent most of his time reading. Dominic was faster and stronger than his brother and had a keener sense for strategy. Reynaldus, while not strong or fast, was smart; brilliant, actually. He could tell you everything there was to know about every species of plant and animal in the Munkelstein kingdom. He could track weather patterns and could predict the weather days before it came. The two boys working together would be a match for any army. But the hatred Reynaldus had for Dominic, made working together impossible.

It was pitch black in the tent as Dominic stepped through the flap door. His hands were damp and trembling. He could smell the mustiness of what had to be a lifetime of mold and mildew. He stood frozen in the darkness. Brave as he was, he didn't dare move further into the tent. The last thing he needed was to trip and fall, bringing the tent down on top of him.

"Why have you come?" a gravelly voice whispered from somewhere in the distance.

77

"I am Prince Dominic Philip Segarius, son of King Roland Miguel Segarius of Munkelstein, brother to Prince Reynaldus Wilhelm," Dominic tried to say this with the confidence of his title, but even he could hear the quiver in his voice.

"I did not ask your name boy. Why have you so rudely intruded into my home?" the voice asked.

Dominic felt a cold shiver run through him. The voice now sounded like it was just inches from his face.

"Sir Ronndewo, I am here because I have been told remarkable things about you," Dominic struggled to say. He was fighting the urge to run from the tent; but he'd come too far to turn back now.

"Have you now?" the voice asked. "What have you been told about this poor old man?"

"They say you are a great wizard; greater than Merlin and Dahagen combined," Dominic replied confidently.

The old man burst into laughter at this. "AAAHAHAHA. Is that what they say?" he cackled. "My, my, I had no idea I was so extraordinary. As flattering as you are, boy, I am a busy man and do not have time for you to fawn over me. I will ask you once more, why have you come?" the voice asked from behind.

The wizard was somehow standing directly behind Dominic. "But how?" he thought. The boy had been in the same spot since he entered the small space and, unless the tent had grown since he entered, Dominic's hind end was still against the door flap. "My lord, I have been told you are a great and powerful man. It seems I have been misinformed. I apologize for wasting your time." He felt foolish. Reynaldus had tricked him again. "I'm going to squash my brother!" he thought as he turned to leave the tent. He reached for the flap but it wasn't there. It may have been completely dark inside the hovel, but Dominic knew he was standing directly in front of the exit. He hadn't moved a muscle since entering. The boy reached forward to try again, and grabbed only a fistful of musty air. He could suddenly hear his heart pounding.

"Leaving so soon?" the voiced asked mockingly.

The wizard was only inches from Dominic's face and he could feel the old man's breath on his skin. "It seems I have been misled and I do not wish to waste any more of your time, Dyog, sir." Dominic did his best to keep his voice calm as he spoke.

"Misled?" asked Dyog. "By who?"

"Yes. My brother…" Dominic started.

"Reynaldus?" interrupted the wizard. "Yes, I know him. Did he not tell you we have met before?"

"No, sir, he did not," the boy replied. Anger had replaced Dominic's fear. "He brought me all the way out here and knew this man was no wizard," he thought. "When exactly did you meet my brother?"

"I do not recall. One cannot truly measure time, Dominic Philip, son of King Roland Miguel Segarius, brother of Reynaldus Wilhelm," the wizard said with all the nobility of a lord. "After all, what is time to the moon and the stars? However, unlike the moon and the stars, time is an illusion," Dyog was behind Dominic again, only now he sounded a world away.

"I do not understand. Where did you and Reynaldus meet?" Dominic asked, completely disoriented now.

"Why, in this very spot. Although, come to think of it, your brother is not aware of our meeting, yet. We will not meet until just before your twelfth birthday," Dyog replied, in a tone that sounded as though he found this information amusing.

"My twelfth birthday? Forgive me, sire, but my twelfth birthday was almost three years ago," Dominic said politely. The old man was obviously out of his mind and Dominic was not going to hang around when the man finally snapped.

"My apologies, Prince Dominic. I meant your second, twelfth birthday," Dyog replied. The wizard truly enjoyed these moments.

"Sir Ronndewo, I do not wish to offend you. Is it possible

that you are mistaken? A man is twelve only once. Once time has passed it has gone forever. You cannot relive what the past has taken," Dominic replied.

"I know what I mean, boy. As smart as you are, it seems you know very little. Time is a concept, an idea," the wizard explained. "If time were a river, the past would be down stream and the future up. Yet, is it not possible for fish to swim upstream to spawn, thereby starting life anew?" the wizard challenged.

"Yes, sir, it is, but as you have said, time is an idea. A river is tangible. I can touch and see a river. I cannot see or touch time so I cannot move through it. And the fish creates a new life. It does not start its life over," Dominic began to argue, then decided philosophy was best left to scholars. "If you will just show me the exit, I will leave you to your business."

"Nonsense. I am enjoying our conversation. As you can imagine, I don't get many visitors," the wizard mused. "You say you cannot see time, however, that is only because you lack the vision." As the wizard spoke, a warm blue glow appeared in the distance. It was the first bit of light the boy had detected since entering the wizard's home and it appeared to be coming from an orb which was floating in Dyog's hand.

The wizard stepped forward and the boy could now see that

the orb was not floating, but seemed to be the handle of a staff, or a cane. The old man continued to move slowly and effortlessly towards Dominic.

"Your brother and I met, or should I say, will meet, five days before your twelfth birthday," Dyog said. "He was worried for your safety and came to me for help. He said you had been lost and your kingdom was concerned. Although, to be truthful, he really came for the very reason you have come today."

"I came here on a dare from my brother," Dominic said defiantly. "He told me you were a great wizard and that men feared you. That is all." Dominic said the words, but knew they were not true.

"My boy. One does not travel for days to the edge of nowhere to prove he is brave. No, you came for another reason, one which requires much more bravery than merely intruding into an old man's home," Dyog replied.

Dyog Ronndewo seemed to know what was in Dominic's head but the boy asked him anyway, "Then why did I come?"

"For the same reason all brave men come here: You wish to know the answers to questions which have not yet been asked. You wish to know how it will end before it begins. To know what's in the box without ever having opened it." Dyog

82

paused, and said, "Men are never satisfied with today, so they seek tomorrow and end up pining for yesterday. I warn you my boy, your excitement in discovering your fate will pale in comparison to the regret you will have for hearing it. Few men can say they are thankful for what they learn within these walls. Your brother was no different." Dyog paused again, allowing Dominic to absorb this. "It's possible you will be the exception to a very painful rule," he added.

"What did you tell my brother?" Dominic asked.

"The same thing I will tell you, the truth. Your fate, if you truly wish to hear it. Although I must say, your brother did not react to what he heard as I would have hoped," replied Dyog. "Perhaps, you will prove to be the more...mature brother. But enough about Reynaldus. Let's talk about your future, King Dominic Segarius."

*   *

"Hahahaha. I knew you'd chicken out," Reynaldus cackled, as Dominic stepped from the tent.

It felt like he had been in Dyog Ronndewo's home for close to an hour, and his eyes needed to adjust to the intense sunlight.

"The deal was you were supposed to go in and have a conversation with Dyog, not turn right around and leave. I guess you're not so brave after all," Reynaldus said, beaming. He would be holding this over his little brother's head for years.

"What are you talking about?" Dominic replied, confused by what he was hearing. "I did speak with him. I was in there for at least an hour."

"You're kidding, right?" Reynaldus responded in disgust. "You walked in and came right back out. Look at you. You look like you've seen a ghost. Chicken. Bawk, bawk," the boy was now sniggering ear-to-ear and strutting around in a circle, flapping his arms.

"He has to be joking," thought Dominic. "I was in there for at least an hour. Maybe longer." Then an overpowering thought filled his head: 'Time is a concept, an idea.' He contemplated this for a moment, patted the satchel, and began the long journey home.

6

The Truth

It was the middle of the night and the room was dark. "The power must be out," he said. Dominic had never had a dream so vivid and real in his life. Sure, he was nervous about fighting the Black Knight today, but he'd been practicing and felt he had a decent chance to win. Besides, he was only twelve and the fight wouldn't be real. There had to be a law against a grown man beating up a little kid on his birthday. This thought put him at ease. Still, it was a strange dream.

"Sire? Are you awake?" a voice asked from the side of his bed.

Dominic's heart began to race. He heard the strike of a match and watched as the flame danced towards him, igniting the candle on his nightstand. In the warm glow of the candlelight, Dominic could see, seated in a chair beside his bed, the Black Knight.

The boy let out a scream, "Mom, dad help, he's come for me! Help!"

"Sire, sire, it's ok you are safe. You've just had a bad dream. It is I, your friend and loyal subject, Brenden," the man said.

The voice was familiar. It was the voice of the man in his dream. Then it hit him, 'it wasn't a dream'. The boy felt his heart sink as his new reality began to set in.

"My lord, you have been asleep for hours. How are you feeling?" Sir Orgen asked with genuine concern in his voice.

"I don't know what's real anymore," Dominic whimpered. The boy was on the edge of tears. "Have I lost my mind?" he asked.

"No, sire, you have not lost your mind. You have been through much in the past twelve hours. You are just struggling to make sense of all you have seen and heard since you returned to us. Shall I explain the situation again?" Sir Orgen asked with compassion; however, to Dominic it sounded as if the giant was talking to him like he was five years old.

"I understand the situation. I'm the king of a place I've never heard of called Munkelstein and my family has been kidnapped by a lunatic who wants me to surrender or...", he stopped as he thought of the last thing he remembered about this day. "Sir Orgen? Before I fain...passed out," the boy corrected, "you told me something about Prince Mathias."

The Truth

"Aye, sire. You have gone through much today and this may be difficult to hear again," Sir Orgen said.

"Just call me Dominic, ok? Please?" the boy asked. Being called 'King' and 'Sire' and 'Sir' was not helping matters. He just wanted to go back to being Dominic.

"Yes, sire...uhh...yes, Dominic. Prince Mathias is your brother," the giant stated directly.

A sudden flurry of questions sprung from the boy, "He's my brother? Then why would he do this to me? Why is his name Mathias and not Segarius? Did you say he was older than me? Does he hate me?"

"Your brother, Prince Mathias, is exactly two minutes older than you. However, you do not resemble your brother."

"Of course not, I'm twelve."

"Certainly. "But before your departure, you had similar features and looked somewhat like relations but not identical. You are what the doctors call *'fraternal twins'*. That means..."

"I know what 'Fraternal' means. I'm twelve, not an idiot," Dominic snapped. He was starting to feel like two separate people: the carefree boy from Clarkston and someone more, mature? Older? He couldn't define it, but he most definitely did not feel like a boy any longer.

"My apologies, sire, Dominic. I do not mean to offend you.

It's just, I am trying to give you as much information as possible," replied the giant. For the first time since Dominic's arrival, Sir Orgen felt like he was finally back in the company of the king, or at least partially. "Prince Mathias was born Reynaldus Wilhelm Segarius; however, when your father passed away, and bequeathed the throne to you, your brother left the kingdom and took your mother's surname name, 'Mathias'. Reynaldus was angry that you were to be king over him. After all, he was the eldest Segarius boy and in the history of Munkelstein, the eldest boy has *always* taken the throne upon the death of the king," Sir Orgen explained. "After your coronation, Reynaldus left Munkelstein and swore that he would return one day and take your throne. In the years since you've ruled Munkelstein, your brother has attempted countless times to overthrow the kingdom and steal your crown and throne. A throne he still contests. A throne I believe he will contest until he takes his last breath."

Sir Orgen watched as Dominic processed what he had just heard. There was an intensity in the king's eyes which Brenden had not seen in decades. He knew the look all too well. Dominic was processing this new information and beginning to formulate a plan.

As a master tactician, the King of Munkelstein processed

and stored every bit of information he could gather on his foes. The skill was what made the king a brilliant strategist.

"Do you remember how you got the scar on your face?" Sir Orgen asked.

Dominic gently stroked his left cheek. "My parents," he said, "my parents said I cut myself when I was a toddler trying to crawl out of my crib." He paused for a moment, thinking about his family, praying they were safe. "Sir Orgen?"

"Sire?" the giant replied.

"When I was in the War Room, I saw a mural on the wall. There was a man on horseback on it. It looked like he was in a battle. Below his left eye he had a fresh cut in the exact spot as my scar. It seemed familiar to me, like I had been in that battle. Is the man in the mural...me?" the boy asked. He could hardly believe he was asking such an outlandish question, but he could no longer deny how familiar everything was starting to feel.

"Yes, my lord, the man in the mural is you, sitting atop your favorite horse, Uriah," Sir Orgen replied. "This is excellent, you *are* remembering." The giant could hardly contain his excitement. His King had returned in the flesh this morning, and now it seemed that his mind was returning as well.

"Tell me about the battle. How did I get my scar?" Dominic

asked, as he watched Sir Orgen intently; like a boy waiting for his father to read him his favorite book.

"We refer to this as *The Oncor Gorge Battle*," Brenden began. "Prince Mathias had amassed an army of 10,000 men along our eastern border. We were outnumbered almost two-to-one and many of our soldiers were convinced that this would be their final battle. There were rumblings among some of the men that you had grown soft against your brother and you lacked the resolve to defeat him once and for all. The morning of the battle came and the unrest within the troops had come to a head. You had grown weary of their accusations, and you knew the only way to convince them we could win the fight, was for you to take matters in to your own hands. Standing in the center of the inner courtyard, surrounded by thousands of battle hardened warriors, you gave a speech unlike any I have ever heard. You told them that this was not the time for cowardice. That believing they couldn't win, was much worse than losing and that having a superior strategy was far more important than having greater numbers. To prove your point, you mounted Uriah and rode out to the edge of Oncor Gorge, alone. "At first, many of our soldiers thought you had turned coward," Sir Orgen said, speaking as if he were reliving that day.

"Why did they think I was a coward if I rode out to face the enemy alone? And why didn't you and the other knights follow me?" Dominic asked excitedly. His heart was racing at the thought of this epic battle.

"The brave Knights of Munkelstein followed you without question," the Black Knight replied. "However, Uriah was the fastest horse in Munkelstein and catching up to you proved to be an exercise in futility. The troops thought you a coward because you were heading *away* from the enemy."

Sir Orgen continued, "The enemy was along our eastern border. You mounted Uriah and headed west towards Mount Phi. But what your army did not know, as they did not grow up in Munkelstein, was that Oncor Gorge does not end at the foot of Mount Phi. Oncor Gorge has a hidden pass which cuts *through* Mount Phi allowing you to attack Reynaldus' rear flank. Once word of your plan spread through the camp, any hesitation or doubt of your resolve, vanished faster than Mathias's army when they heard the hoof beats of our steeds charging up their arse!" Sir Orgen laughed.

"When Mathias's army saw us coming, half of them immediately fled. His fighters were not seasoned warriors and were only in it for the reward Prince Mathias promised them. When they no longer felt they could win, most fled. This left Reynaldus with less than half his troops. Moments later our armies clashed and it quickly became evident we were the superior fighters. Most of what was left of Prince Mathias's troops were forced to retreat," Sir Orgen paused. His face was sullen and sad. "Almost 2,000 men died that day; 317 of them were our men," he said somberly.

"Were any of them your friends?" the young boy asked.

"I knew many of the those who fell that day, and while I did not know each man personally, they were all my brothers," Sir Orgen replied.

Dominic understood what Sir Orgen meant. Although he himself did not remember The Battle of Oncor Gorge, he understood that a group of men fighting and dying together, to defeat a common enemy, would only do so if they believed in each other.

"How did I get the scar?" the boy asked.

Sir Orgen gathered his composure, and replied, "The remaining enemy hoard soon understood they had no chance to win, so they turned tail and ran to join their cowardly brothers. This left Prince Mathias alone on the Great Plains. He was a hundred yards out from us, sitting upon his horse and facing an army of men who wanted nothing more than to peel the flesh from his bones," Brenden said with anger in his eyes. "You started after your brother's army, but when you saw Reynaldus alone on the Great Plains, you stopped Uriah and halted the men. We were 4,500 men against one coward. You never told me why you stopped your pursuit of the prince, perhaps you felt sorry for him or thought he might surrender. No matter the reason, your brilliant strategy had defeated him once again. Prince Mathias sensed you were not going to pursue him further. Being the opportunistic snake that he is, he knocked an arrow, drew his bow, aimed and let it fly. At the last moment, you recognized the arrow was on target and narrowly turned your head away in time. The arrow cut across your cheek and buried itself into the thigh of the unlucky bastard foolish enough to be at your side," Sir Orgen said howling with laughter, and rubbing his right thigh.

"Then what happened?" Dominic asked un awe. He could listen to this story all night.

"By the time the arrow had ruined a perfectly good pair of my trousers, the prince was riding full speed back across the Great Plains. You sent your 10 fastest riders after him…. but your brother escaped," Sir Orgen said, with what Dominic thought sounded like deep remorse.

"What?" the boy asked. "What's wrong? What happened?"

"The men you sent to pursue Reynaldus never returned. For weeks, we thought they had betrayed the crown and joined the prince. Then, one night, weeks later, a watchman spotted a cart approaching the castle gate. We surrounded the cart only to find it had no driver. In the back, however, were..." the giant stopped midsentence. There was a long silence as Sir Orgen remembered the event. "In the back of the cart, were the flayed corpses of all ten men, sire." Dominic could see a deep sadness in Sir Orgen's face. He placed his hand on the giant's shoulder. "The physician thought they were alive while it happened."

Dominic tried to think of something to say to comfort the man. It was decades later, but the boy could tell how painful this was for Sir Orgen. "Sir Orgen, you could not have prevented it. The prince is obviously a madman," was the best he could do. Then panic set in as Dominic realized what this could mean for *his* family.

"From that night, until the night of your departure, you never forgave yourself for what happened to those brave men. Sire, you felt that it should have been you who went after Reynaldus and you've lived with that guilt ever since. Perhaps it is best that you have forgotten," Sir Orgen whispered.

The two sat in silence. Together, but each alone with his thoughts. Sir Orgen remembering a dark, sad time. Dominic thinking of his family and imagining their screams as Prince

Mathias did unimaginable things to them. The boy king's initial thought was to assemble every person in the kingdom and ride as quickly as possible to Sylvania. However, as he contemplated this, calmness took over. His mind became thoughtful and strategic. It didn't make sense to sacrifice thousands to save three. What was it the guy with pointy ears said on Star Trek: "The needs of the many outweigh the needs of the few?"

They sat awhile in silence, then Dominic asked, "Brenden, what does my brother look like? Would I recognize him if I saw him?"

The Black Knight appreciated the change in subject. Even decades later, the pain of what they saw in the cart that awful night was too painful to bear.

"You knew that when you left twelve years ago, the prince would eventually learn of your departure," the giant replied. "We had no doubt he would search all the kingdoms for you. But you *knew* he would never find you. Your plan was genius and it would take more than a man to find you." The knight stopped in mid thought and then exclaimed, "Perhaps this explains the latest report," Sir Orgen pondered.

"What reports?"

"We have just received news that the prince may have been

involved in a horrible accident. I do not know the details, but from what I hear, your brother appears to have aged significantly, almost overnight."

"Aged significantly? What do you mean?"

"I am told he now looks to be hundreds of years old. His skin is sagging and cracked and he has trouble walking,"

A memory sparked in Dominic's head. "He was there," he mumbled. When I opened the bottle. Prince Mathias was there. Standing in my yard not ten feet from me!" the boy shouted. He then retold Sir Orgen the events of his departure from Clarkston.

"...and then just as the cork came out, I noticed an old man standing at the edge of the trees, watching me and...smiling. He was holding something in his hand. A blue crystal?" he questioned.

Dominic stopped again. The crystal. He'd seen it before in a...dream. Then a thought overwhelmed him, "If this was real, if what was happening right this minute was real, then it was also possible that the dream he'd had, of an old wizard, might not be a dream at all."

"That wasn't a dream," the boy said, "it was a memory."

7

A Dungeon in Sylvania
(Part 2)

Hello? Is anyone there? Please, someone help us!" Maggie Bennett's voice was becoming hoarse from what seemed like hours of yelling. "Please, just let my daughter go. She hasn't done anything to anyone. PLEASE!"

"Come now Maggie, you're going to hurt yourself if you keep yelling like that," the gravelly voice said above them. The Bennetts heard a 'whoosh' sound as though something heavy was being slid open above them. "Is everyone comfortable down there? Heh heh heh heh," the voice laughed.

The ceiling looked to be about ten feet above them and in the center, was a small scuttle opening. Looking up, Randy could see the first bits of light they had seen since waking up in their prison. As his eyes adjusted to the light, he saw the silhouette of a man sitting in a chair, peering down at them.

"What do you want from us? Where's my son!" Randy shouted, anger surging through him.

"Your son! Hahahahahahahaha! Very funny Randy. I'm sorry, may I call you Randy?"

Randy could hear joy in the man's voice and his anger boiled over. "You let us out of here now you son-of-a-bitch or I swear I will rip your heart out with my bare hands!" he screamed. Rose recoiled from her father. She had never heard him so furious.

"Randy, Randy, Randy. You should really watch your temper. You're scaring poor Rose." The man's demeanor had switched from levity to something much more sinister. "If you hear nothing else I say, hear this and hear it well: *If* you ever leave Sylvania alive, and with all your pieces, it will be because I am merciful. The only chance you people have of ever seeing the light of day again, rests solely on the shoulders of one man, or should I say 'boy'. Were I you, I would save my energy. Might I suggest you spend the time you have left praying, or having a meaningful conversation with your daughter, instead of making threats you have no chance of following through with. Do you understand me, RANDY?" the man asked, his tone harsh and direct.

A Dungeon in Sylvania (Part 2)

Randy was clenching his fists so tight, his nails cut into his palms. Escape was looking bleaker with every word this lunatic spoke. He took a deep breath and tried to calm himself. "What do you want from us?" he asked through gritted teeth.

"From you? Nothing. Your way out is dependent solely on your son's ability to follow instructions. Very soon we will see how much Dominic loves his mommy and daddy," the old voice said. "Oh, my apologies Rose, and his sissy."

Maggie had been holding back her emotions and finally blurted out, "Where is our son? Don't you hurt him, he's just a boy. Let us out of here, you monster!" she demanded through her tears.

"HA! A boy? Your son is no boy Magg's," the man replied; disgusted by what he was hearing.

"What does he mean Dominic's not a boy, daddy?" Rose asked, her voice quivering.

"My poor darling Rose. Have your parents not told you the truth about dear old Dominic Bennett?" the voice asked incredulously.

"We've told her everything," Randy shot back. "Dominic was left in our care twelve years ago because he was in danger. He hasn't done anything to anyone. Don't you lay a finger on him!" Randy demanded.

"Hahahaha. Oh, Randy, Randy, Randy" the man laughed. "I really should thank you. I haven't laughed like this in years. No, RANDY, your son is neither innocent, nor is he a boy. He may look twelve and may even act like a twelve-year-old, but the fact is, your *son* is much older and, believe it or not, he is a king."

"Now who's being funny?" Randy quipped. "Do you think just because you have us locked up in this, this, this dungeon, that we're idiots? We've raised Dominic from a baby. You've obviously lost your mind. Just tell us what you want, or let us go." Randy was starting to believe they would never see the outside of this room. The man sitting high above them was obviously insane and there was simply no negotiating with a crazy person.

"There you go Randy. It's nice to hear you lighten up," the madman replied. "Yes, Dominic was left in your care because he was in danger. Someone was trying to kill him, but for you to understand why anyone would want to kill your little boy, let me tell you a story:

"About seventy years ago, a great man named King Roland Miguel Segarius became ruler of the Kingdom of Munkelstein. In fact, the Segarius family has been the only ruling family of Munkelstein since its creation, more than a thousand years ago.

A Dungeon in Sylvania (Part 2)

King Roland married a beautiful woman named Beatrix Corinn Mathias who, on her twenty-fourth birthday, gave birth to twin boys. Sadly, she passed away due to complications during child birth. The poor sad king never remarried and had no other children. This left just the twin Segarius boys as potential heirs to the Munkelstein throne.

"Years later, after King Roland passed away, under very mysterious circumstances, his youngest son, Dominic, was crowned king and has ruled Munkelstein ever since. King Roland's eldest son, Reynaldus, being a great man, of superior intellect, contested his brother's claim to the throne. After all, Reynaldus was the eldest son and, by rights, the crown should be his. Unfortunately, King Roland had rewritten history before his death and had made it so his youngest son was to be king upon Roland's passing. There was simply nothing poor Reynaldus could do, except take what was rightfully his by force.

"The great Prince Reynaldus attempted many times to take back *his* throne; however, his barbarian of a brother, seemed to have luck on his side." The madman paused a moment and Randy could swear he was licking his lips.

"Dominic Philip Segarius's reign as King of Munkelstein is almost over. So, you see, as long as I have breath in my body, I will not rest until Munkelstein is mine."

"What a fascinating story. You should write a book," Randy chided. "Does this fairytale have anything to do with why we are here?" he asked.

"Fairytale? Awww, Randy. Don't you believe my story?"

"Not one word," Randy said defiantly. "My son has read almost every book ever written about kings and kingdoms. I think I would have heard of Munkelstein."

"You disappoint me Randy. Are you so arrogant to think your world is all that exists in the universe? Do you believe you know all there is to know?" the madman asked. He was becoming fed up with his prisoner's lack of respect. Obviously, he was wasting his breath with these simpletons. As much fun as this evening had started out, it was now quickly becoming tiresome.

The man rose from his chair, and was about to leave when Rose asked, "Are you working for Dominic's brother?"

He stopped mid-rise and reseated himself. "Perhaps the evening wasn't going to be a waste after all," he thought.

"You said Dominic's brother had contested the throne and then you said *you* would not rest until *you* ruled the kingdom. So, you are either working for his brother or you plan to steal the throne for yourself," Rose challenged.

"Oh, Rose my dear. It appears I have been wasting my time

talking with the wrong Bennett," the madman replied. "You are correct, my girl, that is exactly what I said. However, there is a third option which you seem to have overlooked." He was once again enjoying himself.

Rose replied, "You're either a lackey for Dominic's brother, a traitor or...or...or you're his brother." She stopped at this thought. Her dad was right this was a fascinating story but she couldn't shake the feeling there was some truth to it. She always knew Dominic was different but Rose just assumed her brother hadn't *found* himself yet. Surely when he was older things would be different for her brother. After hearing the truth about Dominic, and now that they were trapped in what was obviously a dungeon, she was starting to believe what the old man was telling them.

"Very good Rose! Very good indeed! You truly are the brains of the family and much more like your brother than your parents. Allow me to introduce myself, I am Prince Reynaldus Wilhelm Mathias and I am the ruler of the Kingdom of Sylvania; which is the place you currently find yourself," Reynaldus explained. He was starting to like this girl. It was a shame he would have to kill her. "You see Rose, like you, Dominic is my younger brother. And I ask you, when in history, has a younger son been crowned king over the elder,

103

far more intelligent, capable son? Hmm? TELL ME ROSE!!! WHEN!?! NEVER!!! THAT IS WHEN!!!" The dungeon echoed with Reynaldus' words reverberating in the air.

Randy pulled his family tight to him. With every word the madman spoke, Randy felt their chances of ever seeing the light of day diminish.

When the man, calling himself 'Prince Mathias', spoke again, he did so with such calm that if frightened Randy to his core. The turn from calm-to-anger-to-hatred and back to complete calm sent a chill up Randy's back.

"That's right Rose. Never. It has never happened. The eldest son has always been crowned king upon his father's passing, always," Reynaldus said with a calm, slow cadence. "However, our father, in his infinite wisdom, mistakenly chose the much weaker son as the heir to his throne. But don't you worry Rose, dear. I will correct this mistake very, very soon." Reynaldus seemed to be having a discussion with himself and it terrified young Rose. "Rose? Are you still there? You haven't left, have you? Hahaha, of course you haven't. After all, where would you go?" Prince Mathias asked, pausing to gather his thoughts. His memory wasn't as good as it had been only weeks ago. It was one of the more frustrating things about his new, 'condition'.

A Dungeon in Sylvania (Part 2)

"So, where was I? Oh yes, we were discussing *our* brother, Dominic," Reynaldus continued. "Rosey, did you know that when a king dies, his crown goes to his son and not his own brother. I mean, what kind of half-baked deal is that? But there is a silver lining my dear, don't you worry. If the king has no sons, the crown goes to the closest living, elder male. I guess that explains why so many royal uncles kill their nephews. Regicide, I believe they call it. Sadly, our poor, darling baby brother has no sons for me to kill. Unfortunate, wouldn't you agree, Rose?" The more Reynaldus spoke, the more Randy's hope of being rescued faded. "If Dominic were to die unexpectedly, say, by having his skin carved off and his limbs removed, the crown would go to me," the prince said enthusiastically. "Isn't that wonderful?"

"Here's another question for you, Rose, why do you suppose our brother never had a son? I mean, after all, he has known all along that if he died before he had an heir to the throne, that I would be crowned the King of Munkelstein. And yet, he still made the choice to not have children. Why do you suppose he did that? I think, deep down, he wants me to kill him and take the throne. What do you think Rose? Do you think our brother wants me to be king? Don't you think I'd make a wonderful ruler?" Reynaldus asked. "I'm just dying to hear your perspective on this conundrum." Prince Mathias went silent. This time he was actually awaiting a response from the poor frightened girl. "Come on Rose honey, don't disappoint me. You have proven to be the one bright spot in this cold dark place."

Reynaldus was mocking her little girl now and Maggie could not take any more of the lunatic's laughter at her daughter's expense. "We get it you're a genius and the rest of us are not worthy to be in your company," she shouted. "Leave my daughter out of your cruel game, you sadistic bastard. She's just a little girl." Maggie had tried with everything in her being to keep her composure, but she couldn't take anymore of the crazy man's games.

Randy was just about to unleash his own fury of idle threats and insults on his captor, when he heard his daughter's voice, timid and afraid.

"Because he knew…" she whispered.

"What's that Rose? Speak up my dear," Reynaldus said, reveling in the moment. "My hearing isn't what it used to be." "If only my dear brother were here," he thought to himself.

The girl paused to gather her nerves. Once she calmed herself, she said confidently, "Because he knew if he had a family, you would find a way to use them against him."

A Dungeon in Sylvania (Part 2)

Clap, clap, clap, clap.

"Bravo Rose. Bravo," Reynaldus said. The prince was now standing above them, applauding. "I may not kill you after all. It would be a shame to waste such a precious mind. You remind me so much of a girl I knew in school. She was..."

"He knew how much of a deranged coward you are and chose not to put innocent people at risk," Rose interrupted. "Dominic chose the more difficult path. His selflessness makes me proud to be his sister. It's funny, you act like you're the smart brother, yet, it sounds like Dominic has outwitted you at every turn." The girl was unleashing all the anger, fear and frustration that had built up in her since waking up in the prison. "Dominic made it so the only way for you to become king, would be to kill him; yet he's still alive. It sounds to me that you are afraid of our little brother."

The prince had been enjoying seeing the spark he had ignited in the girl, start to take flame. "And then she went and ruined it with her disrespectful attitude," he thought.

"SILENCE!!!" Reynaldus bellowed. "Make no mistake. I have killed for much less, my darling Rose." He was seething, and all due to a little girl. "Not that I owe you an explanation, you ungrateful brat, but I have tried to kill that son-of-a-bastard brother of yours for most of his life. I even had a full roof plan to kill him in his sleep, and make it look like natural causes, just like our dear father's death. Obviously, none of my attempts have been successful, until now. I was out of ideas and quite honestly, I was ready to give up on my quest when I realized there was one man who could help me find my brother," the prince explained. "I had truly hoped that this man would want to help me, but well, things didn't go exactly as I had hoped. Anyway, we eventually came to an agreement," Reynaldus said, now utterly exhausted.

When he first sat down to talk with the Bennetts, he only planned on staying for a few minutes; just long enough to put paralyzing fear into them. He had stayed much too long and needed to go and rest up for his big day.

"As I look down at your pathetic family, Rose, I can honestly say that the price I have paid for my victory was well worth it. You people, are the final piece I needed to make my darling brother suffer as I have suffered. You, my love, are the keys to the throne," the prince said as he loomed above the hatch to the dungeon. "I apologize for being a bad host, but I really must go now; there is much to do to prepare for the Bennett family reunion."

The room above them was dimly lit, but Rose could clearly see the man smiling down at them. In his right hand, he held a staff. As she sat gazing up at the crazy man, Rose saw a feint blue light appear in the prince's hand. Suddenly, Prince Mathias raised the staff high above his head and said, "Oh, and Rose, you really should be more respectful. Remember this the next time you even think to call me a coward," and then drove the staff into the floor.

The tip of the staff struck the ground with such force that it pulverized the granite floor. A bolt of brilliant blue light (later Rose would swear it was a lightning bolt), hurled out of the staff, split in two and struck Rose's parents in their chests. The impact from the blast hit with such force, Randy and Maggie were thrown across the dungeon and into the stone wall.

King Dominic's adoptive parents, collapsed to the floor, their clothes smoldering.

The last sound Rose Bennett heard, besides her own screams, was the sound of a cackling madman as he closed the door above them, locking them in their crypt.

And then...nothing.

Not the sound of her mother crying.

Not her father's voice telling her, "Everything will be ok, Rosey."

Not the strained breathing of her parents as they gasped for air, struggling to live. And sadly, with her ear held to their chests, not the sound of their beating hearts.

Rose sat there, begging to hear the heartbeats of the people whom she loved most: the women who gave birth to her and taught her about love, and the man who made her laugh with his silly jokes when she was sad. The people she knew would always protect her and keep her safe.

She listened, but heard...nothing.

For the first time in her short life, Rose Bennett was alone in the world.

8

Disposable Magic

It was dusk and the sun was setting over the painted rock walls of Oncor Gorge. As twilight approached, a lone man sat upon a jet-black stallion, gazing at the sky. He sat lost in thought, wondering if he would ever see this place again. Remembering back to when he was a boy and his father would take him out to this exact spot to watch the sunset. The boy would ride on the back of his father's horse laughing, arms wrapped tightly around his dad's waist. He loved this place and the memories it brought. Unfortunately, he had not observed this breathtaking view more than a handful of times since his father's unexpected passing. After all, running a kingdom demanded a man's full attention. He sat there knowing, at any moment, news would come which would forever change his life.

Disposable Magic

As the last bit of light disappeared over the horizon, he began to ruminate over his time as king. He had never married, nor fathered any kids. He was king of the greatest kingdom ever known and yet, there were times when he felt alone and powerless.

He thought back to a time, decades ago, when he and Reynaldus went to see Dyog Ronndewo. A man more powerful than Merlin and Dahagen combined. Or so it was said.

Dominic had gone to see the wizard on a dare from Reynaldus who had always known how to manipulate his younger brother. Although, when Dominic thought about it, it really wasn't too difficult to manipulate him back in those days. He always wanted to be like his father: the bravest man he knew. The only way to prove you were brave, or so Dominic thought, was to never back down from a challenge. He laughed out loud at this thought now. Bravery, he came to realize, was about what you were willing to do, or willing to sacrifice, to achieve something greater than yourself. As he sat there contemplating this, he wondered what his father would think of him and the job he had done as king. Would he be proud of King Dominic? Or would he be ashamed of how things had become between the brothers?

Dyog Ronndewo had been on his mind often lately. Everything the wizard had told Dominic had come true so far. Everything. In the spring of Dominic's twenty fourth year, he became King of Munkelstein; after his father had died suddenly in his sleep. That was the first major 'premonition' the wizard had prophesized. His exact words were *"In the spring of your twenty fourth year, King Roland Miguel Segarius will go to his final sleep."* Dominic would give anything to have believed the old man. If he had, maybe things would have turned out differently.

When he left the wizard's tent that afternoon, Dominic thought he had been in the presence of a lunatic. The closer he got to home, however, the less real his encounter with Dyog Ronndewo seemed. Ten years after meeting Dyog Ronndewo, King Roland passed away, alone in his room. The physician told the boys there was no evidence of foul play and, even though his father was still a young man in excellent health, he seemed to have died of natural causes. Exactly as the great wizard foretold.

At first, he wondered if he had somehow brought this tragedy on his family. If he had never walked into that tent, would his father still be alive? But in the moments following his father's passing, Dominic came to believe that no one could see the future and his father's death, while tragic, was simply a coincidence.

113

Disposable Magic

It wasn't until he was crowned as the new King of Munkelstein that Dominic began to believe that what he was told, was indeed his future. Almost every day since his coronation, King Dominic thought back to his meeting with Dyog Ronndewo.

* *

"Let's talk about your future, King Dominic Segarius. In the spring of your twenty fourth year, tragedy will befall the kingdom. King Roland Miguel Segarius will go to his final sleep. Foul though it may seem, none can be proven. The youngest will take his father's crown, leaving big brother all but forgotten. Alone, you will rule the greatest kingdom ever known; longer than any before, or after you.

"Your prowess in battle will never be disputed; however, when the arrow flies, stow your pride.

"As the eighteenth anniversary of your coronation nears, the prince will attempt to render upon you the same fate as your father. Your choice will be simple: accept your fate or abandon your throne and live to fight another day. I would love to tell you which you choose, but how can I, you haven't made your choice yet. If you choose to step back, you leave your kingdom vulnerable, the men who follow you may think you to be a coward. Without allies your kingdom could be lost. However, staying will mean your certain doom and the crowning of the eldest Segarius boy as king. Only you can decide if those at your table can be trusted.

"Stepping back will not be easy. If you survive, and return to your kingdom, you will not be the same. You will never be the same. In your absence, your brother will have become more powerful than imaginable; but at a cost. Upon your return, you will have to choose between your kingdom and the lives of your family, but choose you must.

"While I cannot tell you which path to choose, I can offer you aide should you require it." Dyog Ronndewo reached into the pouch he had slung over his shoulder, and pulled out three objects. "They are something of my own design. I call them: Disposable Magic."

*　　*

"Disposable Magic," Dominic said to himself.

He knew the decision, he was foretold he'd have to make, was finally upon him. Very soon, King Dominic would have confirmation as to whether there was a traitor in Munkelstein; if so, his life was most certainly in danger. While those around him had assured the king that a spy in the kingdom was no reason to panic, King Dominic knew something they did not: *"As the eighteenth anniversary of your coronation nears, the prince will attempt to render upon you the same fate as your father. Your choice will be simple: accept your fate or abandon your throne and live to fight another day."* These words, this omen, replayed in his head from the second he heard there may be a conspirator at his table. If the news, from his spy inside Sylvania, came back that one of his 'brothers' was indeed a traitor, the king would have to make the decision Dyog Ronndewo had prophesized.

The only part of the prophecy King Dominic could not make sense of, was the wizard's use of the term 'family'. "A choice between my life and that of my family?" he thought. The king had purposely not married, nor had children, due of this prediction. Yet, here he sat, faced with the decision he was told he would have to make. If King Dominic did have a family, his choice would be simple: he would always fight to protect his family. Was the wizard wrong about this part? By 'family', did Dyog Ronndewo mean the kingdom? If so, why not just say "kingdom"? Before he could ponder this thought any longer, he heard hoof beats approaching.

It was now full dark. Although he couldn't see the man riding up on him, the king knew from years of riding into battle, or racing across the Great Plains with him, that it was

Sir Brenden Orgen approaching. He turned Uriah to greet his old friend.

Sir Orgen's horse, Onyx, slowed to a trot then stopped at the king's side. "Happy birthday your majesty. You don't look a day past seventy," the man in black chuckled.

"Great night for a ride, eh Brenden?" the king replied.

"Aye, sire. Reminds me of our time hunting the giant bears of the Crescent Forest when we were boys. I believe that was the first time I ever saw you frightened," the knight joked.

"Frightened? ME?! Ha-ha, yes I may have needed to change out of me under garments after that night," the king replied. Both men burst out laughing at the thought. Reminiscing on old times. Simpler times.

When the laughter faded, they sat in the darkness, neither man speaking; as if not saying the words would make the truth less real.

It was the king who broke the silence, "Well Brenden. What have we learned?"

"Sire...", Sir Orgen started.

"Brenden, how long have we known each other?" King Dominic asked rhetorically. "I appreciate your loyalty and respect more than you could ever know, but under the circumstances I'd feel better if you would just call me by my given name. Can you do that for me, please?"

"Of course, Dominic," Sir Orgen replied. "There is a man arriving tonight from Sylvania. He claims to have information which will hopefully answer for certain if Prince Mathias has a spy in Munkelstein. This may tell us if the rumors of treachery are true. If there is a traitor within our ranks, your life is truly in danger. Normally, I would tell you not to concern yourself with what the prince does or does not know about our great kingdom. Hell, he grew up here and knows its layout as well as anyone. Our defenses have little, if any, vulnerabilities so if he wants a fight, let him come. But Dominic, with what you've told me about your meeting with the wizard and his premonitions, I'm worried for your safety. If what you say is true, your life may truly be in grave peril."

"I know Brenden. If what Dyog has foretold comes to pass, I will be dead by week's end if I stay. And if I leave, I not only abandon my throne, but risk the men thinking me a coward," the king replied. Then added, "Or worse, Reynaldus lays siege on Munkelstein."

Sir Orgen did not envy the decision his king would have to make. "Perhaps you can sit the men down and explain to them what the great wizard foretold," Sir Orgen queried.

"I do not think that is the right approach my friend. What do you think Sir Jameson would think of me if I told him that, when I was a boy, I went to see a wizard to hear my future and was told that one day my brother would attempt to have me killed in my sleep?" he asked sarcastically. As Dominic said the words out loud, he wasn't even sure he believed them. "No. While I appreciate your advice my friend, we must keep this bit of information to ourselves."

Sir Orgen felt foolish for even suggesting it. He loved his king and only wanted what was best for him, and the kingdom. "Dominic, I can assure you of one thing, as long as I draw breath, that coward brother of yours will not step foot inside our home. If you leave, I will make sure your kingdom is still here upon your return. However, whether you tell them the truth or not, you still need to address the men and apprise them of the situation. Give them just enough information as to keep their loyalty; but not too much where they think you to be mad. And should you choose to stay, I will guard your life with my own," Brenden said stoically.

"Thank you, my friend. But you cannot be with me every moment of every day. You cannot taste my food for me or watch over me while I sleep. If I am to believe what Dyog has foretold, and I do believe it, then the choice is to stay and die or leave and regroup," King Dominic explained. "The problem is, I do not know in this instance what regrouping would mean. If we have a traitor among us, we need to flush him out. However, what's to say there isn't more than one traitor. The only way Munkelstein will ever truly be protected, is with me as king and my brother in a box. I don't see any other way. Do you?"

"I've thought on this long my friend," Sir Orgen replied. "If what the wizard told you is true, I see no other alternative for you." Brenden spoke as if he were talking to a man on his death bed. "Where will you go?"

"I'm not sure yet, but wherever I go, it's better for us both if you do not know."

"When?" Sir Orgen asked, staring out into the cold blackness of the Great Plains as he spoke.

"Tonight, as soon as I speak with him. It's only a matter of days, or hours, before they know we're on to them. They'll make their move soon. It's best if I leave tonight."

"I will ready a fresh horse and supplies for you at once."

Dominic patted Uriah's neck. He had ridden into battle more times than he could remember on this noblest of animals. It pained him to think this might be their final ride together. "Let us not be hasty my friend. I will not be leaving until I hear the news from his lips. However, when I leave, I will not be going by horseback."

"How then? You can't leave Munkelstein on foot and expect to get further than the edge of the Great Plains. You may as well stay and take your chances," Sir Orgen said. He was becoming agitated and beginning to think maybe the king had lost touch with the real world.

"Brenden, I need you to trust me now more than you ever have." King Dominic knew his friend better than he knew himself and the giant would need to be assured that whatever the plan, Dominic would return home safe. "There's one thing I did not tell you. One important detail I left out about my encounter with Dyog Ronndewo. After he told me I would have to choose between my life and the life of...others, he gave me these." He reached into his coat and retrieved a brown leather satchel. He unclasped the buckles holding the bags flap shut, reached inside and held out the contents for Brenden to see.

"What are those?" Sir Orgen asked.

"Dyog called them: *Disposable Magic*," the king replied.

*   *

The young king sat by the fire; listening as the giant finished his story. "And then you told me what you needed me to do

121

for your escape to succeed. I must say, I thought you might be losing your mind when you first explained your plan to me." The giant paused, "But I never lost faith in you, sire. I have always believed you to be the smartest tactician alive and if you said a plan would work, it worked, always and without question. And here you are, back just as you said."

The boy sat absorbing the story of the night twelve years ago. He was beginning to believe everything Brenden had been telling him since he arrived. And now, as he contemplated this latest story, he felt as if it wasn't so much a story as it was a lost memory. The horse, the sunset, the watch, even the glass and the bottle.

The bottle! That was it. This was his chance to find out once and for all if this was a hoax. "Explain to me what the bottle looked like," Dominic blurted to the giant.

"Sire?" Sir Orgen asked, puzzled by the boy's request.

"Explain in detail exactly what the bottle looked like. The one you say I showed you before I left," the boy urged.

"I will never forget that bottle my lord. The bottle itself was really nothing special. In fact, you could say it was very ordinary, until you looked closely. The glass was flawless, no chips or air pockets from when it was blown. I have never seen a piece of glass as perfect. A cork had been shoved deep into the bottle's neck. At the time, I thought you would have to break the glass for the cork to be dislodged. But that is not why I remember the bottle so vividly; it was what was inside which I will never forget. Inside the perfectly created phial was, well it is difficult to describe my lord," Brenden drifted off.

"A purple...cloud which moved as if it were alive," Dominic said, lost in thought.

"Yes! That is exactly how I would describe it. It was one of the most beautiful things I have ever seen," Sir Orgen replied excitedly.

From the expression on Brenden's face Dominic could see that this man was being truthful. He not only described it perfectly, but Dominic could see in Brenden's eyes that the giant was truly moved by the beauty of what the bottle possessed.

"So, the bottle was meant as a means for me to return to Munkelstein?" the boy king asked.

"Aye. You told me that the contents of the bottle would return you home in an instant. Your plan required you to travel a long distance and, when the time was right, you could return without delay."

"What about the other items you mentioned, the glass and the watch? What do they do?" the boy asked. Dominic never really believed in magic but after what he had experienced in the past few days he was beginning to believe anything was possible.

"The piece of glass you called a 'Gazing Glass'. According to Dyog, whoever possessed the Gazing Glass could use it to travel anywhere, in any time."

"What does that mean, *in any time*?" Dominic asked.

"It means you could use it to travel anywhere, real or imagined. There was one catch, however: you could not travel to a place and time which you already occupied," the Black Knight replied.

"How does the glass work? I mean, how did I use it to travel to Clarkston?" Dominic asked, with the feeling of utter confusion creeping in again. Just when he thought he was starting to figure things out, he had to try and wrap his head around a new bit of craziness.

"When I saw you last, you told me that all you had to do was stare at a place on a map and, if you focused hard enough, you would 'lose' yourself in that place. I did not believe it was possible and thought perhaps you were under so much stress that you were going mad. Then you went into your chambers alone that night, and when I went to check on you an hour later, you were gone! Your windows were closed and locked, as was the only door leading into your room," Sir Brenden said.

"So, you're saying, the glass can teleport you? That it teleported me to Clarkston?" Dominic asked. He was starting to believe he had hit his head while playing in the yard and was most likely in a deep coma somewhere. How else could he explain it?

"I'm not sure what you mean by 'teleport', but I can tell you with certainty that you vanished that night. And there is no explanation for how you did it; at least not one that I could find," Sir Orgen explained. He could feel the boy's doubt creeping in again.

"How are you so sure? Maybe I snuck out when no one was looking?" the boy asked. He knew how this sounded but it made more sense than what the giant was trying to tell him.

"Sire, that is also not possible."

"Why? Why is that not possible but disappearing by staring into a piece of glass is?"

"Because, sire, I stood guard outside your door from the moment you entered your chamber. On your orders, I was to stand guard to ensure that you were not disturbed. There was only one person allowed in your chambers that night, besides me. When your guest arrived, you let him into your chamber's and the two of you spoke for about an hour. When he left, he handed me a note written in your handwriting," Sir Orgen replied. He tried to imagine himself in the boy's position. Would he believe such a fantastic story?

"What did the note say? The one you say I wrote to you," Dominic asked.

The giant reached into his pocket and pulled out an old, ragged piece of yellowed paper. On the outside of the note was written: 'Brenden, wait one hour before reading.' Sir Orgen opened the note and read:

"Brenden, my friend, it seems I will be departing tonight after all. This will be difficult for you to read, but I will be gone for quite some time. Look for me exactly twelve years from tonight, in the old dungeon below the castle. I am trusting you to keep things running smoothly while I am gone; there is no one I trust more. This is the path I must take. Please, do not lose faith in me my friend.

Until I return,

Dominic Philip Segarius, King of Munkelstein."

When he finished, Brenden folded and pocketed the note. There was more to the story but he wasn't sure exactly what had happened or how he could explain it to his king. And would it even matter now that Dominic had returned? The giant had lived with his secret for twelve years. Never knowing if his careless mistake may have killed the one person he was asked with protecting. "I don't even remember falling asleep," he thought.

"Brenden. Brenden! Are you ok?"

"Hmmm, oh yes. Where was I? Oh yes, an hour later, after I read the note, I entered your room and, you were gone," Sir Orgen said sullenly.

Dominic sat silently, contemplating what he had just heard. He had indeed awoken in a dungeon. On his twelfth-birthday, no less. After a few minutes in thought, Dominic asked, "What about the watch? What does the watch do?"

The knight did not answer at first. Dominic couldn't tell if it was because he was trying to remember what the watch did or because he didn't think Dominic would believe him. Then he got his answer. "Sire, perhaps that is enough for one night. I know this all sounds too fantastic to believe and maybe if you get some rest it will make more sense to you in the morning," Sir Orgen replied.

"Brenden, in the last two days, I've been told that I am not a boy from Clarkston, but the king of a kingdom I've never heard of. I was told that my parents are not my parents and that they have been kidnapped by a madman; who, by the way, is my brother and wants to kill me so he can take my place as king. Now you're telling me, there are magical items that can transport you to and from places AND times. What could possibly surprise me at this point? Honestly, just tell me and get it over with. Please," Dominic pleaded.

"Very well," Sir Orgen agreed reluctantly. "If by 'watch' you mean the 'Piece of Time', that's what you called it, you told me the *watch* could be used to alter time; but only for the person possessing it. Once you got to your destination, you were going to use the watch to become very young, thereby disguising yourself." The knight waited for the boy to process this new information. "Do you understand sire?"

"So, I used the glass to leave Munkelstein and travel to Clarkston. Once there, I used the watch to become a, to become a what, to become a baby?" It was all too surreal, but a thought occurred to him. If he believed he was the King of Munkelstein, and he was starting to believe it, then he had to believe that, at some point, he was a man. If it was also true that he was once a man, then his age must have been altered by someone, or something.

He replayed everything in his mind, for the thousandth time since he awoke in the dank dungeon, little more than a day ago: FACT: He had been playing in his yard, on his birthday. FACT: While playing in his yard, he found an old bottle. A bottle Sir Brenden could describe perfectly.

FACT: He grew up in Clarkston. From what he could see outside, not only was he no longer in Clarkston, he may no longer be in Michigan.

FACT: Right before he opened the bottle, he saw an old man standing in his yard smiling at him holding what appeared to be a blue crystal.

All of these facts were true, prior to his awaking in the dungeon, he couldn't dispute it. And if he did indeed believe that these things were real, then wasn't it possible that the 'Disposable Magic' Sir Orgen described to him, was also real? After all, it did explain everything.

Then a thought occurred to him. How could he have forgotten, after all, it was there the whole time. "Brenden?"

"Yes, sire?"

The boy reached into his pocket and pulled out an old piece of brass. "Is this the Piece of Time?" he asked.

The giant was stunned. "Yes sire, it is the very one. Have you had it with you this entire time?" the giant asked.

The boy went on to explain to Brenden how he found the Piece of Time and how he could not figure out what the dials were for.

"You told me that you had to set the dials to the number of years you want to travel either forwards or backwards. The top button will move you forward through time and bottom button will move you backward," Sir Orgen explained.

"Then it must be broken. I've tried a hundred times to get it to do something, but I could never figure it out."

"No sire, it is not broken. Remember, this is *Disposable Magic*. The person possessing it can use it only once. You used it twelve years ago, now it is simply a memento," Sir Orgen explained. He studied the boy sitting in front of the fire and felt for him. It must be difficult to accept all he had heard in such a brief period of time. The boy looked exhausted. "Sire. Perhaps you should get some rest. This is a lot of information for you to process and I worry it may be too much for you. Let us talk some more in the morning."

He thought about arguing with the giant, but Dominic knew Brenden was right. The boy was exhausted. Maybe sleep was exactly what he needed.

"You're right, Brenden. We have a big day tomorrow. Have the knights assembled in the War Room at noon to discuss our plan to save my family."

"Very well, sire. Sleep well," Sir Brenden Fredrick Orgen said as he bowed and left the king's chamber.

Dominic knew very well that the man he was starting to

think of as his only friend in this place, would be standing guard outside his door while the boy slept.

"Goodnight Brenden," he whispered to the giant.

And within seconds, the King of Munkelstein was sound asleep.

9

The Treachery of Repelzen

The night of his departure from Munkelstein, King Dominic sat alone at his desk contemplating the most dangerous quest he would ever undertake. A few hours earlier, he had returned from what he thought might be his final ride with Uriah. Upon the king's return, the brave Knights of Munkelstein gathered in the War Room for one final meeting before he departed.

King Dominic explained to the men that what he was planning was necessary if they were to rid the world of Prince Mathias once and for all. The king told the Knights of Munkelstein he would be leaving on a journey of epic proportions and assured them he would return when the time was right. Finally, he convinced the loyal guardians of

Munkelstein, that this victory would bring peace to all the Kingdoms for a thousand years.

As he spoke, King Dominic hoped the knights would cheer, bang their fists on the table and hail his name; however, he heard none of this. This lack of enthusiasm, while disappointing, was not surprising. What King Dominic Philip Segarius, admired most about these men, besides their bravery and loyalty to the kingdom, was their honesty. Above all, King Dominic respected those who told him the truth. The king felt their truthfulness assured him they could be trusted. And, in the king's opinion, trust between men was paramount.

He grew up hearing stories of rulers who would imprison, torture or kill, any subject who did not agree with them. Even at an early age, Dominic was smart enough to understand that any king who did not trust his citizens, ended up becoming tyrants who ruled with fear, and intimidation. Dominic swore to himself that, should he ever become king, he would rule his kingdom with kindness and respect. Then he reflected back to a story his father had told him many years ago. The story of King Repelzen.

*   *

Disposable Magic

King Repelzen had ruled Oakfursten for only three years, when he started hearing murmurs from his spies about the king's council. The king's council, it seemed, were beginning to have their doubts about the king's sanity. "They were concerned that Oakfursten was on the verge of a revolt against the throne," their father explained.

"You see," King Roland Miguel Segarius told his sons, "King Repelzen had recently imposed a tax on the kingdom's poorest citizens. He thought that charging a stiff tax on the homeless, and less fortunate in his kingdom, would either force them to leave Oakfursten or give them an incentive to work harder; which in-turn would give them a better life. King Repelzen believed he was helping his poorest citizens and that they would love him for it. However, because the king had lived his entire life in a castle, coddled by servants, and did not understand that poverty is very rarely a choice. In the king's deluded mind, he thought he could rid Oakfursten of squalor and thereby make the Kingdom of Oakfursten a model society for all kingdoms to envy."

"That is a brilliant idea father! Did his plan work? Or did his council go behind his back and ruin his plans?" asked young Prince Reynaldus Wilhelm Segarius; who seemed delighted by the story.

The Treachery of Repelzen

King Roland loved both his sons very much. His youngest, Dominic, seemed fearless for a boy so young. He was constantly asking his father questions on strategy; whether it be for hunting or fighting. The boy had a strategic mind which would serve him well on the battlefield and in life; however, what King Roland admired most about Dominic was his genuine compassion and empathy for his fellow man. The boy truly cared about the wellbeing of others. King Roland's eldest son was another matter.

Reynaldus was brilliant, that much was true, but to King Roland it seemed that his eldest boy used his intellect only in deceitful ways. The boy was constantly getting into trouble for tricking the less fortunate out of what little money they had. Reynaldus would devise schemes in which he promised some poor soul a return of more than double his initial investment. And when the poor fool inquired as to the status of his investment, Reynaldus would explain that the money was gone. He would concoct a story so complex that the greatest scholars in the Munkelstein could not comprehend it. And if that same poor fool became angry and demanded his money back, the prince would simply threaten to have them thrown in the dungeon, or hanged. After all, he was next in-line for the throne.

When King Roland first heard of Reynaldus's scheming he

sat him down and explained that stealing from people was wrong; especially from those less fortunate than himself. Unfortunately, Reynaldus did not hear his father. The boy tried to justify his actions and talked in circles trying to confuse his father. This saddened King Roland deeply, for he knew his son could not see how unkingly his actions were. He began to fear for the future of Munkelstein, were Reynaldus to become king.

"Well dad? Did his plan work? Was King Repelzen able to get rid of those filthy vagrants?" Reynaldus asked again.

King Roland looked down at his son with sadness. "No Reynaldus," he replied. "King Repelzen's plan did not work. "The council of Oakfursten approached the king to inform him that many of his subjects were upset with his new Poverty Tax. The citizens told the council members 'if something didn't change soon, King Repelzen had better start sleeping with his eyes open'."

Dominic could see in his father's eyes that this story was an important lesson. He wasn't sure why he was telling them the story of King Repelzen, but he had his suspicions, as he glanced at Reynaldus in disgust.

"Did King Repelzen repeal the tax father?" Dominic asked naively.

"Unfortunately for Oakfursten, King Repelzen was too arrogant to see the faults in his new tax," said King Roland. "Men like King Repelzen do not understand the real world. He did not understand that some men need a helping hand from time-to-time and that aiding those in need is one of the greatest things you can do for your fellow man." Reynaldus let out a guffaw which was quickly met with a look so menacing from King Roland that the boy recoiled for fear of being slapped. "You should pay special attention to this story my son," the king said, eye's locked on Reynaldus.

"Early one morning, the citizens of Oakfursten were awakened by the blaring sound of trumpets. King Repelzen had established years earlier, that the sound of trumpets was a signal for the people to assemble in the courtyard for an urgent message from his majesty. King Repelzen, true to his nature, used these horns frequently. I have been told he used the horns to inform his citizens that he had 'heard the funniest joke' or he had 'just eaten the most exquisite strawberry'. Needless to say, the people of Oakfursten had come to disregard the urgency of these trumpet blasts; however, this particular morning was different.

"King Repelzen was a notorious narcoleptic. There were rumors he slept sixteen hours a day and that he never awoke before noon. So, when the trumpets sounded at first light that morning, the people of Oakfursten were understandably concerned.

"The citizens of Oakfursten arrived at the courtyard that morning and found their king waiting for them. King Repelzen was a large sloppy man who very rarely arose from his throne, except to retire for the evening. But on this day, as the townsfolks assembled in the courtyard, they were greeted with his majesty standing at the top of the castle steps, grinning like a cat with a full belly."

"When all had arrived to the courtyard, King Repelzen spoke, 'Citizens of Oakfursten,' he said. 'It has come to my attention that many of you are unhappy with some decisions I, your loyal and gracious majesty, have recently made. My trusted council has expressed to me your concerns, which is why I have called you all here at such an early hour.'

"The king went on to talk about how understanding and merciful he was. As he spoke, the people noticed a strange banner draping the castle wall to the king's right, which had not been there the night before. That is when the good people of Oakfursten saw just how merciful and understanding their ruler was.

"'I ask you, who among you are unhappy with my new tax

plan?' King Repelzen asked. The crowd remained silent. They knew their king well enough to keep their tongues still, lest they become separated from them. 'No one? Really?' he exclaimed. 'Well, well. Could it be my trusted council members have been untruthful to their most merciful king? Let us find out together, shall we?'

"King Repelzen then motioned to a sentry standing near the banner and with one pull of a rope, it fluttered to the ground. But the king did not watch it fall. He was transfixed on the horrified expressions of the Oakfursten citizens gathered before him. Their shrieks and screams pleased King Repelzen."

"What was behind the banner father?" asked Dominic. The boy's expression was one of worry and concern.

"Behind the banner, seated at a long table, were the king's royal council…"

King Roland was cut off mid-thought by Reynaldus. "What's so horrifying about a bunch of dusty old men sitting around a table?" the boy snarked.

"Well, Reynaldus, King Repelzen had assembled his council and seated them at the council table. But you see, first he had ordered the council members to be 'disassembled'. The king had his council members limbs and heads removed and sewn back on; however, they were sewn on to each other's torsos. The horrified expressions on the council members faces told the people that this ghastly act had been committed while they were still alive. The sight was gruesome and wretched. The flesh of the dead had begun to turn blue and purple. A few of the faces had swollen and seeped a thick greenish fluid. The flies began to circle the corpses and the smell of death permeated the courtyard. Many of those gathered there that day fainted. Those who tried to flee, or turn away from the horror, were met with beatings from the king's army; who had surrounded the courtyard during his speech.

"After a few minutes, once King Repelzen was certain everyone understood his message, he spoke again, 'I was recently made aware that my council had been telling me lies about you wonderful people. This,' the king said, pointing to the council table, 'is what happens when we cannot trust each other. Do you see my council? Look at them sitting there all…disorganized.' King Repelzen laughed as he said this. 'I simply will not abide treachery in MY kingdom! Let this be a lesson for those of you who believe me to be mad, or choose to disobey my laws. I will not tolerate disobedience.'

"King Repelzen turned to leave then stopped and turned back to readdress the crowd, who were still completely silent (except for the occasional sound of retching). 'One last item if you will indulge me. As of today, there will be a 30% tax increase for all in the kingdom. Let's call it the: King Repelzen is Merciful Tax,' he said. And with that, he spun on his large heels and headed into his castle."

King Roland sat silent for a moment, studying the boys and letting them absorb what they had just heard. Dominic looked somber; he could not believe that such evil could occur in the world. Reynaldus also wore a sad expression; however, King Roland could see a slight up-curl at the corners of his son's mouth, as if he were holding back a smile.

"What happened to the King?" Dominic demanded. "Did the people of Oakfursten overthrow him? Please tell me he didn't get away with it," the boy pleaded.

"Son, it's best you know now that the world is full of evil men who do not always pay for their crimes," King Roland explained. A tear of anger streaked down Dominic's cheek. The king brushed it from his son's face with his thumb, and said "But in this case, King Repelzen got exactly what he deserved.

"The King of Oakfursten, told the people on numerous occasions that he was a merciful man. What he meant by this was, he was merciful because he only punished those he deemed had done him wrong. He did not punish their families, their friends or their friend's families.

"To further drive his point home, King Repelzen left the corpses to rot in the sun for weeks. At the end of the second week, as the maggots slithered in and out of the corpses and the ravens had little left to pick from, one of the king's servants snuck into the king's chambers, through an open window, and slit Repelzen's throat while he slept. The servant, it turns out, was the son of one of the council members. The boy could no longer bear seeing his father's mutilated corpse rotting and being devoured by all manner of vermin, so he did what others would not."

King Roland allowed his boys to digest the story before asking, "Now I want you both to tell me what this story has taught you. Dominic, you first. What is the morale of this tale?"

"The morale is, you should treat others with respect and dignity; especially if you are their king. Also, if you are truly a just king, you should be able to listen to your advisers and not take everything as an attack on the crown. I mean, King Repelzen was obviously deranged, but had he listened to his council when they approached him to inform him that the citizens were on the verge of revolt, he may have lived long enough to actually create a great kingdom," Dominic replied. King Roland Segarius had never been prouder of his boy.

"Reynaldus? What about you? Do you agree with your brother?" King Segarius asked his eldest child, preparing himself for disappointment.

Reynaldus sat silent, contemplating his response carefully. 'Daddy's-favorite-child' just spewed a mouthful a crap that almost made Reynaldus vomit. He knew what he should say; what his dad wanted him to say. But he realized if he was ever going to prove himself worthy to rule Munkelstein, he needed to speak his mind. After all, wasn't that the true morale of the story?

"King Repelzen should have followed his instincts," Reynaldus replied. "He was killed by a council member's son. Had the king shown less mercy, and also punished the council members families, he might have lived longer. Had he done as Dominic suggested, and listened to his council when he had never done so in the past, they would have seen him as weak. If a king shows weakness, he loses the respect of the people. A king who is not respected, is useless."

By the time he finished his thoughts, any chance Reynaldus had of becoming the next King of Munkelstein were dashed.

*   *

King Dominic sat alone in his chambers thinking about his father and the story of King Repelzen. He swore after hearing the story that, should he ever sit in the throne, he would rule with true mercy and compassion.

Even though Dyog Ronndewo had foretold it years earlier, Dominic was as surprised as anyone when he was coronated after his father passed away. Well, maybe not as surprised as anyone. Reynaldus was furious and swore to lay waste to anyone challenging him for the throne and was immediately arrested and locked in the Munkelstein dungeon.

In Munkelstein, as in most kingdoms, threatening the life of the king was punishable by death. As if to prove a point, King Dominic Philip Segarius's first merciful act as king, was to free and pardon his brother. A decision he would regret for the rest of his days.

10

I Spy

I'd like a few minutes alone if you don't mind," the king asked.

"Aye, sire. I will let you know when he arrives," the Black Knight replied.

Brenden Orgen exited the king's chambers and closed the door behind him. He had spent more hours standing guard outside the king's chamber door than he could count; something he didn't mind at all. In fact, Sir Orgen felt honored to serve as his king's protector. He had known Dominic Segarius for more than thirty years and respected the man from the day they met. In the knight's mind, giving his life in service to his king would be the highest honor he could achieve.

His orders tonight were simple, he was to allow only one person into the king's chamber this evening. From what Dominic had told him, the man they were expecting was not a threat to the king so the giant needn't worry. Still, Brenden didn't plan on taking any chances. Especially tonight.

*　　*

King Dominic was alone in his chambers, preparing for the long journey ahead. He had just finished addressing the Knights of Munkelstein. He told his loyal brothers the news of the treachery in Munkelstein and his plan to rid the world of Prince Mathias once and for all. In his speech, the king had asked the knights to trust him, unconditionally, and to tell no one that he was leaving the kingdom. It was truly an inspired speech.

Dominic had always been calm and level headed in stressful situations. This, however, was unlike any situation he had ever been in, and for the first time in his life Dominic Segarius was afraid. He feared not for himself, but for his brothers and his kingdom. The king knelt in front of his bed, closed his eyes and began to pray. He prayed that his departure would not mean the end of the kingdom his forefathers had entrusted to him. He prayed that the bond he had with the Knights of Munkelstein was strong enough to endure the most difficult test he could ever imagine putting them through.

When he had finished his prayers, King Dominic went to

his desk, sat down on the hard chair and removed the satchel from his jacket. Nestled inside the small brown sack was a pale blue blanket, wrapped around three items given to him by an old wizard. The king unfurled the blanket and carefully laid out its contents. Lying there, in the dull flicker of the candlelight, were the keys to King Dominic's plan. 'Disposable Magic', Dyog Ronndewo had called them.

When he was a boy, Dominic traveled with Reynaldus to see Dyog Ronndewo and ask the wizard what the future held for the youngest Segarius boy. All of Munkelstein knew Reynaldus was destined to be their next King; however, Dominic did not know his destiny, and there were days when this lack of information consumed him. When Dyog referred to him as 'King Dominic', he decided that the man must truly be crazy. After all, Reynaldus was first in line for the throne. And if he was being honest, Dominic was relieved to discover the wizard was a lunatic. Because if the man was crazy, none of what the wizard had told Dominic, in the tent that day, would be true.

Years after his encounter with Dyog Ronndewo, he had all but forgotten he had ever gone to meet the wizard. But then his father died unexpectedly in his sleep and, even more unexpectedly, Dominic was crowned King of Munkelstein. It wasn't until the initial shock of his coronation had worn off that Dominic began to reflect on his meeting with Dyog. The man said many unbelievable things, most of which had come true. Now as he sat alone at his desk preparing for his journey, King Dominic thought back to Dyog Ronndewo.

*   *

"While I cannot tell you which path to choose, I can offer you aide should you require it. They are something of my own design. I call them 'Disposable Magic'."

The wizard held up a beautiful piece of emerald green cut glass. Its edges were jagged yet smooth. "This I call, 'Gazing Glass'. Use it to take yourself anywhere you would like to go. All you need do is gaze through it and focus on the place you would like to travel to. You must focus your entire being through the glass," Dyog explained. Dominic wasn't sure what the wizard meant, but he was pretty sure the man was not of sound mind.

As if sensing, or hearing, his skepticism, Dyog Ronndewo pulled the next item from the brown leather satchel. "What good would a trip to 'any-place-you-would-like-to-go' be without a way to get back home?" Dyog asked as he pulled a small clear bottle from the satchel.

148

I Spy

It looked like an ordinary bottle; although Dominic had never seen a bottle as perfect as this. He peered into the vessel and saw one of the most beautiful things he had ever seen in his life. Inside the bottle was what appeared to be a purple storm cloud; which moved as if it were alive.

"This is the most beautiful thing I have ever seen. What do you call it?" Dominic asked.

"What you are holding, my boy, is the 'Homeward Nebula'," Dyog replied. "All you need do is remove the cork and you will be brought immediately back to your home; regardless of where you are." Dominic was mesmerized by the contents of the bottle and only half heard Dyog as he spoke.

"…in a protected area such as a cellar or a locked room," the wizard explained

"Wait, what did he just say?" Dominic thought to himself.

"Finally, and perhaps most importantly, my best creation yet," Dyog Ronndewo said, as he held up a round brass object. "With this, 'Piece of Time', you will be able to move *through* time," the wizard explained and handed the magic to Dominic.

The boy studied it closely. Whatever it was, it was expertly crafted; Dominic could see that much himself. On the back of the timepiece was carved an 'All Seeing Eye' adorned with a hand carved filigree design. There were two buttons on the side of the watch and a gold crown at the top.

Dyog explained to Dominic, "Use this to move through time, however, keep in mind, only you will be affected by its use. To use it, simply adjust the crown. Once you have decided how many years you wish to travel, depress one of these buttons," Dyog said, stroking the side of the Timepiece. "The top button will advance your age forward the numbers of years you have selected, and the bottom button will reverse your age. But be careful, traveling too far through time could have devastating consequences."

"Devastating consequences?" Dominic asked. "What do you mean?"

"Setting time back too far would result in a 're-do', of sorts. You simply cannot exist in time before your birth; but start over you would. Moving too far forward in time, however, would be very, very bad indeed," Dyog replied.

As Dominic contemplated the wizards warning, Dyog wrapped the Disposable Magic in a pale blue wool blanket and placed them back in the satchel. "Do you have any questions before you depart Dominic Philip Segarius?"

"Why are they called Disposable Magic?" Dominic asked.

"Heh heh. Is it not obvious, boy? Because they are disposable.

Each item can be used only once by its owner; which is you. So, make sure you use them wisely," replied the Wizard. "Is there anything else? Your brother has been waiting patiently for you for almost an hour. I'm sure he must be quite worried about you by now. Wouldn't want him to think the old crazy wizard is in here doing unspeakable things to his baby brother," Dyog joked.

Dominic thought for a moment then asked, "When do I use them? I mean, how will I know when it's time?"

"That is for you alone to decide. I suggest you wait until you have no other options. Until then, keep them safe. This is powerful magic and in the wrong hands they would be very dangerous."

The great wizard's warning were the last words Dominic would hear Dyog speak. Before he knew it, the boy was standing in the bright sun.

"Hahahaha. I knew you'd chicken out."

*   *

With the Disposable Magic laid out in front of him now, there were only a couple things left for King Dominic to do. He pulled open the top drawer of his desk and removed a map. The map was of a place he had never seen before. A few years

151

ago, when he realized the old wizard may not be so crazy after all, King Dominic decided to prepare himself. He did not know when he would have to leave, only that, when the time came, he would need to find a safe place to hide. A place Reynaldus could never discover. Dominic spent months pouring through ancient books in the castle library, when he happened upon a map of a very strange land. The king wasn't sure if this place was real or imaginary, but according to Dyog, it wouldn't matter.

Now, the time had come and he was out of options. Although, if he was being honest, that wasn't entirely true. Had he not gone to see Dyog Ronndewo, at the behest of Reynaldus, everything would have happened the same way. His father would have still died far too young, Dominic would have still been crowned King and Reynaldus would still be plotting to kill him. The only thing that would be different, and Dominic knew this to be true, was that had he not met Dyog Ronndewo that fateful summer day, he would be staying and taking his chances with the assassin.

It seemed the wizard was right yet again when he told Dominic: *your excitement in discovering your fate will pale in comparison to the regret you will have for hearing it.*

Regret was exactly what he felt as he sat alone plotting his retreat. Regret for not warning his father, regret for not killing his brother when he had the chance and regret for leaving his kingdom without a king. He let himself feel the pang of regret in his gut for a moment longer, then forced himself to push it aside and focus on the task at hand.

He had everything he needed and was almost ready to go. "Just one more thing to address," he said to no one in particular.

Then, right on cue, there was a knock on his door.

Knock...Knock...Knock.

"King Dominic, my lord, he has arrived," Brenden said through the door.

Dominic strode across the room, unbolted the latch and pulled open the heavy oak, slab door. Standing in his doorway were Sir Orgen and an old, frail looking man. The old man was at least a foot shorter than King Dominic, had grey hair and pale blue eyes. His back had a severe arch as if he had a spinal condition which would not allow him to ever stand upright again.

"Seamus my old friend, thank you for coming on such short notice. Come in," greeted King Dominic. The old man ambled through the doorway and into the king's chambers. "That will be all Sir Orgen. Thank you," he said and shut the door behind him.

"May I sit, sire? My journey has tired me greatly," the old man struggled to ask. His breath was labored and he looked exhausted. "I do not believe I am long for this world my lord. Why have you summoned me on this cold evening?"

If you didn't know him, you would assume that Seamus Breitling was a weak feeble old man. You might also assume that this weak old man was in the twilight of his life and very near death's door. But you would be wrong.

In truth, Seamus Breitling was only two years older than King Dominic, one year, eleven months and two weeks older to be exact. They had met years ago when they were only boys, and had been friends ever since. His real name was Kelin Richard Semtun and only he and King Dominic knew of his mission.

"You can stop the charade Kelin. We're alone," Dominic replied.

The old man gave the king a sly grin, straightened his posture and wiped the make-up from his face. "Thank the Gods. My back is killing me. I don't know how much longer I can keep this charade up, your majesty. So, tell me my friend, why am I here?" Kelin asked.

Kelin was a master of disguise and manipulation, and was King Dominic's most trusted and successful spy. It had taken him nearly two years from the time he arrived to Sylvania to fully infiltrate the prince's inner circle. Now he was one of Reynaldus's most trusted advisers; although Prince Reynaldus knew him as Seamus Breitling.

"Please Kelin, sit," Dominic said, motioning to the chair at his desk. When his friend was seated, Dominic sat himself on his bed and asked, "Can I get you something to drink? You must be thirsty from your long journey."

Kelin was an expert at reading people, and what he saw in his friend's face, worried him. "No thank you, sire. When I got word that I was urgently needed in Munkelstein, I rushed back as quickly as I could. Tell me, my lord, why I am here? How may I serve my king?"

"Tell me, were you able to avoid suspicion with your hasty departure from Sylvania?" Dominic asked. "The last thing I want, is to put your life in danger. If you think for a second Reynaldus suspects anything, we need...." The king was cut-off in mid thought.

"Sire, trust me Prince Mathias suspects nothing; however, the longer I am gone the more likely I risk blowing my cover. Let's discuss the reason I am here. It is a long journey back to Sylvania," the spy urged.

"There have been many rumors swirling around the

kingdom that we have a traitor in our ranks," the king started. "Normally this would not be concerning, however, I..." Dominic stopped himself. Brenden was the only person he had confided this information too. Telling Kelin would only put his friend's life in greater danger. "Let me just say I have other information which makes this situation very troubling for me," he explained. "What I am about to ask you is much too important to trust with a messenger; which is why I have called you back to Munkelstein in the middle of the night. I need to hear this from your own tongue: Are the rumors true? Is there a traitor within our walls?" Dominic asked. "Before you speak, understand that your information has the power to put things in motion which cannot be undone."

Any worry Kelin had seen earlier in his king's face, was now gone. His king now had the stoic resolve of the man Kelin would follow to the ends of the horizon.

"Dominic, I will be blunt, as I know time is critical," the spy began. "No doubt you have read my reports and you know I have been a close advisor to the prince for almost a year now. In that time, he has asked for my council; which I have provided to him. Quite recently, the prince has taken to have all of his personal advisors watched. I am certain this means he suspects that information has been leaking out of Sylvania.

"Prince Mathias has also begun to make decisions without the advice from his council or advisors. About a week ago, the prince eluded that you would soon be dead." The spy paused for a moment, watching for King Dominic's expression upon hearing his. True to his nature, Dominic did not flinch at the news. "Reynaldus has always cursed your name and told his people that it would not be long before he is the King of Munkelstein. But something he said recently sounded more like he *knew* something," Kelin recounted.

"What did Reynaldus say?"

"We were in our weekly council meeting, discussing the day-to-day issues of running Sylvania. As you know, Sylvania is more of a town than a kingdom, but Prince Mathias insists we refer to it as the 'Kingdom of Sylvania'. The council meetings rarely last more than an hour or two. Anyway, we had just finished our meeting and I was gathering my papers and preparing to head back to my quarters. The other council members had already left, leaving just Prince Mathias and I in the meeting room. I am an old feeble man, after all, and move much slower than my colleagues." Kelin shot his king a sly smirk.

"I was just stepping outside when the prince called me back. He walked over to me, laid his hand on my shoulder and said, 'Seamus, my good man, I wish to thank you for your sage advice since you joined my council. As a token of my gratitude, I would like to bring you with me when we take Munkelstein.' I told him I was honored and asked if he was bringing all his advisers to Munkelstein. The prince looked at me with his evil grin and said, 'You are a very wise man Seamus. Even with your aging eyes, I am certain you can see we have more than a few council members who would make better hog food than advisers to the King of Munkelstein.' I thanked him for his trust in me, told him I was honored and left." Kelin explained.

"King Dominic, you must understand, Prince Mathias has always been confident that he would one day sit in the Munkelstein throne; but this was different. Before he closed the door behind me he said, 'And Seamus, between you and I, you may want to go home and start packing.' Reynaldus said this as confident as a man telling me the sky was blue."

"That is excellent information Kelin, and obviously very troubling," the king began. "However, as I stated earlier, the information you give me here tonight will have ramifications which will reverberate for decades. What I just heard you say is not proof enough for me to make my decision. Please tell me you have something more substantial," the king urged.

Kelin knew Dominic would not take this bit of information as acknowledgement enough that his life was in danger. "I do my lord. Much more substantial," he replied. "Reynaldus only eluded that you would soon be dead. Before I could come to you with this, I needed to verify his plot. And I knew exactly where to get the details of the prince's plan.

"Over the past six months, I have made it a point to become very close with Prince Mathias's head of council, Selvin Ferguson; Selv to his friends. Selv has known the prince since Reynaldus fled Munkelstein, after your coronation. Apparently, Selvin was the first ally the prince made, and Reynaldus has trusted Selv ever since. Fortunately for us, Selv has a weakness for spirits and women. Put him in the proper environment and he'll sing like a bird.

A few days after my brief conversation with Prince Mathias, I invited Selvin out for a night of frivolity. We had just uncorked our second bottle of 'lubricant' when Selv said 'Very soon the war between the two kingdoms will be over'. I asked what he meant and he proceeded to tell me that 'King Segarius would soon be dead and Prince Mathias would take his rightful place as ruler of Munkelstein.' I asked him how the prince was going to kill King Segarius. Selv said the prince had someone within Munkelstein who was close enough to the king that he could move about without suspicion. And, that the king's death would look like natural causes.

"I tried to press him further but by this point he had spotted a lovely brunette across the pub and he was gone," Kelin said. He had given his king all the pertinent information he had on the plot to kill him. It was now up to Dominic to decide if it was enough.

"What is his plan? How will I be killed?"

"My guess is that, within the week, you will go to sleep and not awaken. He will make it look like natural causes. From what I could derive, you will be poisoned," Kelin replied bluntly. "There isn't a man or woman, in Munkelstein, brave enough to attempt to kill you any other way," he added.

King Dominic sat, processing all that he had just heard. He was replaying every detail of information his friend had acquired and searching for flaws in the prince's plan. When he was finished, he looked to Kelin and said, "Close enough that *he* could move about without suspicion. Let us look at the facts of what you have recounted for me, shall we my friend?" he asked rhetorically. "First, my brother has devised a plot to kill me within my own walls. Second, he will attempt to kill me, most likely in my sleep, within the week. Finally, and most troublingly, we do indeed have a traitor in our midst."

Kelin could see his king's brain working on a strategy. It was at times like these that he understood why King Roland chose his youngest son to rule Munkelstein. The man truly had a gift for strategy.

"Sire, who among your men have access to your chambers? If we can narrow the list of suspects down we can have them followed and thwart Mathias's plot," the spy rationalized.

"That is an excellent observation my friend, but unfortunately it will not work," King Dominic politely replied.

"Why not? They do not know that we are on to their scheme. We have the advantage, and if you have taught me anything about battle it is this: exploit every advantage you have to the fullest," Kelin urged.

"Yet again, you are correct, my friend. However, I have information which you do not," Dominic replied.

"What information? What are you not telling me?" Kelin snapped. He had been risking his life to get the king this vital information and did not have all the facts.

Dominic was about to tell his friend, "You'll just have to trust me," then thought better of it. He knew Kelin deserved to hear the truth. No, that wasn't it, he *owed* Kelin the truth. Years ago, his friend had volunteered to infiltrate Sylvania and learn all he could about its inner workings. He had put his life in danger every day protecting Munkelstein and withholding information from the man at such a crucial juncture was unfair.

"Kelin my friend, before you came to me this evening, I had addressed my council of knights. What I told them, in short, was that there was a plot to kill me and that the information was credible," Dominic explained. I also told them that because of this, I would be leaving Munkelstein for a while to regroup and when I returned, we would crush Reynaldus once and for all," Dominic explained. "I did not tell them I was awaiting proof of this plot from you, because you and I are the only ones who know of your mission." The king paused for a moment; now he was the one assessing his friend's expression. "What I did not tell them, as they would have thought me mad," he continued, "was why I was so sure that leaving was the best course of action; only that they needed to trust me."

"How did they react?"

"That does not matter. They are loyal Knights of Munkelstein and will do as I have instructed; regardless of their feelings on the matter," the king said dismissively. "What does matter is that you know the truth. You have done more for Munkelstein then anyone will ever know. You do it selflessly and for no other reason than your love of this great kingdom. Kelin, I have very few people I trust absolutely. You are one of those few so I will tell you what I know and when I knew it, because you deserve to hear it. When I am finished you can decide for yourself if I am mad."

I Spy

King Dominic Segarius recounted his meeting with Dyog Ronndewo and the prophecy the wizard foretold. He told his friend how the wizard had called him 'King Dominic'. How Dyog predicted Dominic's father would die unexpectedly, and that Dominic would be crowned king over Reynaldus. Finally, he told Kelin the last part of the wizard's prediction: *As the eighteenth anniversary of your coronation nears, the prince will attempt to render upon you the same fate as your father.*

"Sire, that's in two days!" Kelin exclaimed.

"Yes, it is. Now you see my predicament," Dominic replied. "I would not blame you if you thought me mad. Hell, there are days when I wonder if I have lost my mind; but I can assure you I am as lucid as I have ever been. Now I must ask you, do you believe what you have heard? Do you believe a man's fate can be foreseen?" the king asked.

Kelin understood why Dominic asked him this question. The king was asking Kelin's opinion because Dominic knew he would die for him. The spy lived in a world of lies and deceit and knew when he was being lied to. Also, he was not afraid to tell his king the truth, something King Segarius valued above all else.

"Sire, I can see in your eyes that you believe what you have told me here tonight," the spy started. "And while I do not

163

know if what you say is true, I do know this: you are the bravest man I have ever met. Your bravery is matched only by your ability to strategically assess every situation and uncover the flaws in any plan. In all the years I've known you, you have never backed down from a challenge, especially as it relates to your brother."

"Thank you for the kind words Kelin but this is not the time. The hour is late and you must be getting back," the king replied abruptly. He did not mean to be short with his friend but Dominic knew they were running out of time. "I need to know whether you believe what I have told you. If you do not, then do not return to Sylvania tonight. Reynaldus will detect if you harbor so much as a sliver of doubt about your task." King Dominic was stern in his response to Kelin, and the King's emissary knew this came from a place of genuine concern.

"My lord, please, allow me to finish," Kelin said. "Yes, you are brave and strategic, but most of all you are loyal. Loyal to your friends, loyal to your people and loyal to your kingdom. I would never believe for a moment you would abandon your birth place unless it was the best and only strategy. So, you ask me, do I believe what you have told me? Yes, sire, I do believe you. In fact, I would stake my life on it." With that, Kelin

164

I Spy

Semtun rose from his chair, knelt before the King of Munkelstein and asked, "What will you have me do my Lord?"

"We do not have much time so listen closely..."

11

A Dungeon in Sylvania
(Part 3)

ose Bennett had just experienced something so traumatic, a weaker person may have curled up in a ball and withdrawn from the world. Her parents had been brutally attacked by a madman wielding some sort of device capable of shooting electricity. The bolt of energy had struck her parents with such force, they were thrown out of their shoes and into a nearby wall.

Only a few moments prior, Rose had been verbally sparring with their captor, a man who claimed to be the brother of the Bennetts youngest child, Dominic. The girl knew she was pushing it when she called the man a coward; but she never thought it would lead to...to...this.

When the initial shock of seeing her parents brutally

attacked had worn off, she rushed to their side. She heard Prince Reynaldus close the hatch to their prison and knew that help would not be coming for them.

Rose felt for a pulse on her mother's wrist and neck but found none. Then she checked her father; nothing. She then held her face tightly against her mother's chest praying for a heartbeat, but could only hear her own heart pounding with adrenalin. She did the same with her father, but again, nothing.

Fortunately, for Randy and Maggie, the Clarkston Community School system requires all High School students to take one semester of first-aid their Freshman year. Rose's class had just recently finished the section on CPR, and she sprang into action.

She gently lifted her mother's chin to ensure her airway was open, located Maggie's sternum and began chest compressions. After twenty quick compressions, the girl placed her mouth over her mother's and blew twice into her lungs. Rose then checked for a pulse; nothing.

The one thing they did not cover in her first-aid class, was how to do CPR on two patients simultaneously. "And, why would they?" she thought.

Deciding it would be better to alternate between her parents rather than deprive one of them of oxygen for too long, Rose moved to her dad. She quickly gave Randy chest compressions, thirty this time, and three quick breaths, then checked for a pulse.

Thump...........thump............thump.

"A pulse!" she thought. It was very feint, but it was there. Unfortunately, there was no time to celebrate. Rose turned back to Maggie and began chest compressions and breathing again. As she was blowing her second breath into her mother's lungs, Maggie let out a deep cough and then quickly projectile vomited into her daughter's face. They told her in CPR class that this could happen, but nothing could prepare you for it when it did. She quickly turned her mother onto her side, to prevent her from choking and listened again for a pulse. When Rose was certain Maggie's heart was beating, the girl turned back to her father.

By the time she checked on Randy a second time, his heart was beating strong, or at least much stronger than it had been a minute ago.

For the next ten minutes, Rose continued to monitor her parent's pulse and breathing. In her non-medical opinion, everything seemed normal. She sat, her back against the wall, legs bent, arms wrapped around her knees and quietly sobbed into her shirt. "Mom, dad, wake up, please," she begged quietly. She began to rock back and forth, praying her parents would be alright. Hoping they would not suffer any permanent damage and that her need to show a crazy man, she wasn't afraid, would not leave the people she loved most, permanently injured. "I am so, so sorry," she wept. "Please be alright mommy, please, please, please. Daddy, please forgive me. I didn't know he would…"

"Rosey, what's the matter," a raspy voice asked.

"Mom, is that you? Are you OK?" she asked excitedly. Rose was at her mother's side in an instant, hugging and kissing the women's pale face, stroking her long red hair.

"No honey, it's dad. What happened? Are you ok? Where's your mother?" Randy labored to ask. He was now sitting up, leaning against the stone wall.

"Daddy! You're alive," she exclaimed. The little girl wrapped her arms around her father's neck and squeezed him tightly, tears streaming from her eyes. Randy tried to return his daughter's hug, but he was still too weak.

"Rose honey, it's ok. I'm ok. Where's mom?" he asked.

Then Rose proceeded to tell her dad what had happened and how she managed to use CPR to bring them both back to life.

"Oh Rosey, I am so proud of you," Maggie struggled to say.

Disposable Magic

Randy, with his daughter's help, crawled over to his wife and lay next to her. He kissed her cheek and held her as close as he could. It was an embrace that told Maggie, 'he would never let her go', and they all began to cry.

Rose let her parents have their special moment to themselves. She sat quietly, thanking God and Buddha and anyone else she could think of, for giving her parents back to her. After some time had passed, Rose asked, "Are you ok mom?"

"Yes, honey I'm fine. Thanks to you," her mother said in an almost normal voice.

"Dad?" she whispered.

"Yeah, sweet pea?"

"I'm so sorry. It's all my fault. If I hadn't been so…" Rose started to say, but Randy stopped her.

"Rose my angel, you did absolutely nothing wrong. None of this is your fault, you have to know that. You didn't bring us here and you didn't lock us away like prisoners," he explained. "You did nothing wrong. I am so proud of the way you stood up to that monster, and then to top it off you saved our lives," he said touching Maggie's face. Tears were welling up in Randy's eyes, "You are much braver than I could ever be and I couldn't be prouder of you." His words were cut-off by

170

a hug so tight he thought his little girl had broken at least one of his ribs.

"I love you guys so much," Rose cried.

"We love you too honey," Maggie said as she hugged her little girl.

The Bennetts huddled together, holding each other tightly. Thankful to be alive. The room was still pitch black and, other than the occasional sniffle, silent.

"You do not belong here," a feint voice whispered.

"Did you hear that, dad?" Rose asked.

Maggie sprang up and shouted, "HELP! Let us out. Please help!"

"Lower your voice. If he hears you we will all be dead," the voice whispered urgently.

"Who are you? Can you help us, please?" Randy pleaded.

"Who I am is inconsequential, and yes, I can help you; when the time is right. When I return you must do what I say, when I say it, and do not ask questions. I will return for you soon. Until then, try not to die again," the voice faded away as he spoke.

"When will you be back? Please, we're so thirsty," Maggie begged.

But there was no response from the mystery voice. Just as they were giving up hope, came the sound of something sliding across the floor.

Disposable Magic

In total darkness, Rose worked her way around the room to where she heard the noise. After a few seconds of searching, she found a large plate lying on the floor. She ran her hands across the platter and felt three large mugs filled with stale water and three lumps of dried bread. The girl picked up the platter and slowly brought it over to her parents.

"No need to rush and spill our last meal," she thought.

12

A Stormy Night
(Part 3)

Seamus Breitling, had left the king's chambers only moments ago, on route back to the Kingdom of Sylvania. Dominic felt good about the plan he had concocted with his old friend, or as good as he could feel under the circumstances. Now it was time to execute it.

He studied the strange map he'd found in the library years earlier; searching for a place which would afford him safe haven. Having planned many battles, maps were not new to King Dominic. He had studies maps of all the known kingdoms, as well as vast areas explored only by the most courageous cartographers. However, this map was much different. The level of detail on this unique chart astounded the king. Sure, he could see similarities to many of the maps hanging throughout the kingdom, but nothing which could match what he was currently surveying.

On one side of the chart, was an area which looked like a large boot kicking a bird. On the other side, was an area which looked like one of the fingerless gloves worn by the people living in the northern Kingdom of Glacerius. (Glacerius was a place so cold and miserable, that in its history, no enemy had ever attempted to conquer it.)

After a few minutes of studying the map, Dominic's eyes became heavy. It had been a long day and he was exhausted. The more he stared at the map the more he became transfixed on the mitten. He thought to himself, "If this place is as cold as Glacerius, Reynaldus would never think to look there." Then the king held the Gazing Glass up to his eye and stared through its emerald hue, transfixed at the area labeled 'Michigan'. He patted his satchel one last time, to ensure everything was safe. Now was not the time to be careless.

As he peered through the glass, the tiny mitten began to turn; slowly at first. With each passing second, it spun faster. After a few moments, the map was spinning so fast, Dominic could feel his stomach churning as if he had eaten rancid meat. His mouth began to water and he was on the verge of losing what little food he had eaten that day. However, no matter how hard he tried, he could not break his gaze. Just as he thought he would vomit, Dominic's uneasiness quelled. The spinning had ceased and, although he was still in his room, he was no longer looking at a map. He was now staring into a wooded area which looked as real as if he were in the Munkelstein forest itself. The king suddenly smelled the sharp scent of pine needles and the sweet floral smell of fresh flowers. He could feel the cool, fresh, night air against his face. It was nighttime in this forest. The moon was full and lit the area around him with such intensity, King Dominic could see every toadstool and pebble with complete clarity.

Dominic closed his eyes tight, trying to clear his head and make sense of what he was seeing. He rubbed his eyelids and held them closed for a few seconds, trying to comprehend what he had just seen. The trees and foliage were as real as if he had been standing in an actual forest, and not sitting at his desk imagining it.

When his stomach had settled, and he had collected his thoughts, the king opened his eyes. He expected to be in his room, sitting at his desk. To his surprise, Dominic now found himself standing in the middle of a small grove of trees.

His heart immediately began to race and his breathing quickened. "What the...?" he said. "I must be dreaming." But he had never had a dream so vivid, or so real, in his life. Never had King Dominic dreamt in smells and sounds with such intensity. He quickly surveyed his surroundings and realized he was not in a forest, but in a small yard surrounded by trees; three trees to be exact.

At first glance, the trees seemed identical. They were the same size and had the same unique branch structures; they even appeared to be evenly spaced from each other.

The ground cover around the trees was a type of exotic grass which King Dominic had never seen in Munkelstein. He spied an errant raspberry branch jutting from beneath the strange grass and crouched to pluck an unripe berry. Dominic yanked his hand back in pain. A thorn had punctured the king's skin and a small spot of blood began to bloom from a hole in his right index finger. He brought his finger to his mouth and immediately tasted a familiar iron taste. At first, the shot of pain and taste of blood were not enough to convince him that what he was experiencing was not a dream. Reality hit Dominic when he looked beyond the tree line.

Sitting only a few yards from the grove, was a structure. "A dwelling most likely," he thought, but unlike any structure he had ever encountered. The building was two stories tall and constructed from brick, or stone, as well as a material which did not look familiar to Dominic. The lower level had more windows than he had ever seen in any home. His immediate thought was, "How cold and drafty the place must be."

Attached to the home was an elevated wood platform which resembled the stage in the Munkelstein courtyard. "This must be where they gather for their festivals," he thought. Atop the wooden platform were some very odd items. Near the largest window, was a strange metal object with a domed top and small wheels mounted to its base. On this strange little cart, was a sign which read: 'Weber'. "Weber," he said out loud. "This must be the Weber home." The more he assessed the structure the less he understood. "I need a closer look," he thought, and crept towards the home.

King Dominic slowly approached the dwelling; like a thief raiding a neighbor's crops. He approached the closest window and peered inside. The house was pitch dark and he strained to focus inside. Before his brain could make sense of the things his eyes were seeing, he was suddenly blinded by an intense light. The light was so bright and brilliant, it seared King Dominic's eyes and he recoiled in pain. The king turned and sprinted blindly back to the grove of trees, ducking behind the first oak he came upon. The light illuminating from this one small room was as, "Bright as 1,000 candles, burning all at once," he thought. "Impossible."

With the room illuminated, the king could now see inside the home. There were far too many fascinating and unbelievable objects for him to comprehend all at once. However, to Dominic, the most amazing object was the tiny orb attached to the rooms ceiling, which appeared to be the sole source of the light.

"Impossible!" he declared.

As he stood transfixed by the *impossible* sight, a small child ran past one of the large windows, screaming as if she were being chased by a monster. Dominic readied himself to take action. "She's in trouble," he exclaimed and immediately wished he had brought a weapon with him. Just as he started for the house, the 'monster' came into view.

Chasing after the little naked girl was a woman, who appeared to be in her early thirties. She had red, shoulder length hair, a pale complexion, was of average height and had a beautiful smile. King Dominic knew at once that this was the girl's mother. As he studied the woman, he was amazed at her resemblance to his own mother, Beatrix Corinn Mathias.

He was so mesmerized by what he was seeing, he didn't realize he was standing out in the open. The little girl suddenly spotted him. She ran to the window and pointed at Dominic. The girl appeared to be speaking as she pointed at him but he could not make out what she was saying. King Dominic immediately snapped out of his stupor and ducked, once again, behind the large oak tree nearest him. The girl's mother stepped to the window and peered out. She surveyed the area for a moment and then reached down, picked up her little girl and tossed her into the air. Even at this distance, and with the windows shut, the king could hear the little girl's infectious laughter. The mother began to tickle her daughter and soon both girls were laughing hysterically. The display of a mother's love filled King Dominic with a joy he had not felt in years.

"This is it. This is the place," he said, and pulled the satchel from his pocket.

Careful as to not draw further suspicion, the king hunkered down in the middle of the grove and laid the satchel on the thick grass. He unclasped the two metal buckles, pulled out the blanket and laid it atop his bag. The king carefully unrolled the cloth, exposing its contents, "Disposable Magic," he said as he reviewed his escape plan once more.

*   *

"You must go to a place where Prince Mathias would never think to look and at an age that, even if he discovers where you went, he would not recognize you," Kelin advised.

"Then I will go back to the very beginning," King Dominic replied. "I do not know what this may do to me, or if I will remember who I was before, but I truly believe this is the best course of action."

Kelin gave him a skeptical look and asked, "Are you suggesting you will go back to when you were a child? That's ludicrous!"

"Yes, it is," the king agreed. "When I met Dyog Ronndewo, he told me that he had met Reynaldus before my second twelfth birthday. I did not know what he meant, and quite frankly I just assumed he was mad; but it makes sense now! This is what he meant. It will take Reynaldus twelve years to discover my whereabouts," he explained. Dominic saw a look on his Kelin's face which told the king his old friend was starting to have his doubts. "I know what you are thinking Kelin, believe me I do. And I can't tell you why this is the correct plan, all I can say is, with every morsel of my being, I know this is what I must do.

"Everything Dyog Ronndewo foretold has come true, everything. However, I have struggled with this one piece of information. I was fifteen when I encountered the wizard. Since that meeting, I have been unable to make sense of how Reynaldus would meet Dyog before my second twelfth birthday. It makes perfect sense now!"

A Stormy Night (Part 3)

"Sire, perhaps Dyog simply misspoke," offered Kelin.

"That is what I thought at the time. I even challenged him on this point and he snapped back at me saying that 'he knew what he meant'. He was telling me that he and Reynaldus would meet when I was twelve," the king explained. "It is all so clear now. This is the path I am destined to take. I know this is difficult to understand my friend, but please believe me, this is what I must do."

Kelin allowed King Dominic's words to hang in the air for a moment, then he asked, "Ok, so you go back to the beginning of your time. Where will you go? How will you leave the Kingdom?"

"This part I cannot tell you, for your own safety. If you were to be found out, Reynaldus would do whatever he felt was necessary to get information from you," Dominic replied. "The less you know about this, the better."

The spy understood what his king was saying and he was right. The less Kelin knew about the specifics of Dominic's escape, the better it would be for the king. However, if Prince Mathias ever discovered that Seamus Breitling was actually Kelin Semtun, not knowing where the king was hiding would not keep the spy safe. He also knew it was best not to mention this to Dominic. The king already had enough to worry about.

"So, you travel from the kingdom to an unknown location, somewhere Prince Mathias would never look, then you use the Piece of Time to go back to when you were a...a baby and hope the people who discover you are good and honest. Then what?" Kelin asked sarcastically.

"Before I use the Piece of Time, I will need to hide the Homeward Nebula in a place which only I will be able to find it, or I may never return home. However, what if I have no memory of my current life and I never find where I have hidden the Homeward Nebula?"

"Then you have bigger problems to worry about then where you left your magic. Look, even if you have no recollection of anything prior to your using the Piece of Time, you will always be Dominic Segarius. Correct?" Kelin asked. Dominic nodded. "So, stash the bottle in a place where only a young Dominic Segarius is likely to find it. When you get to where you are going, look for a place that seems familiar in some way. That is where you will hide it," Kelin said confidently.

"Excellent idea!" the king exclaimed. He was immediately thankful he had decided to trust his friend. The man truly was a genius when it came to espionage.

Kelin continued, "Once you have found a family and stashed the magic, write a note asking the family to watch over 'your baby' for you. This will make it seem as if you were left with them intentionally, and quite possibly that you are in danger. If you are lucky, someone will take you in."

"It seems I will need quite a bit of luck if I am ever to return to Munkelstein," Dominic replied somberly.

"Luck! Ha! I've never once met a man as lucky as you. I do believe, my lord, that thou hast been born with a golden horseshoe up thine arse," Kelin replied with a heavy accent. Levity had once again begun to fill the room. "You'll be back home before you know it," his friend assured. "Besides, I'm the one who needs the luck. I've been trying to get rid of you for years, you crazy bastard." Both men burst into laughter.

They went through their plan a few more times, making sure they had covered every possible angle and uncovered every flaw. When they finished, Dominic thanked his friend for his help, and for not thinking him crazy.

While Kelin was reapplying his disguise, the king walked back to his desk, took a piece of parchment and a quill from the drawer and wrote a note. He folded the paper, handed it to Kelin and asked, "Will you please give this to Sir Orgen on your way out?"

Kelin took the note and said, "Good luck my friend. God willing, I will see you again very soon." He shook the king's hand and gave him a quick hug. "You'll be back in Munkelstein before you know it my lord." The spy adjusted his posture and in an instant, Kelin Semtun was gone; replaced with a much older looking Seamus Breitling.

"Truly amazing!" Dominic exclaimed.

"Thank you, my lord," strained the old gravelly voice. "If it pleases thee, I will take my leave now." The king nodded and Seamus Breitling ambled out the door.

*   *

Dominic Segarius held the Homeward Nebula to his eyes and peered inside. "Now where would young Dominic Segarius uncover you?" he said. Carefully, he wrapped the Homeward Nebula in the wool blanket and set it aside. The king surveyed the area and spotted a small tool lying near the edge of the wood platform. It looked to be a miniature version of the tools the stable boys used to clean the horse dung from the stables. "Perfect," he thought as he grasped the small garden trowel and snuck back to the grove. Once there, he could not help but notice how perfect the area was. The trees were almost identical to each other and were perfectly spaced apart. "This cannot be a coincidence," he said and began to dig a small hole in the center of Eden. The hole was just wide enough for the bottle to fit and deep enough that it would not be accidentally discovered. He then placed the Homeward Nebula in the hole, carefully covered it with soil and patted it flat. When he was finished he replaced the grass and stepped back to assess his work. "Perfect," he said.

With the bottle safely hidden, King Dominic placed the Piece of Time in his pocket and worked his way around to the front of the home. The light was no longer shining inside and the mother and daughter had gone; although this did not put the king at ease. "A woman that beautiful is bound to have a husband," he thought.

As Dominic crept around the side of the house, he heard a faint sound. The noise had a melody similar to the music his minstrels played, but it was unlike anything he had ever heard before. This 'music', if you could call it that, was much too grating for King Dominic's liking.

"Is this some sort of torture?" he thought.

As he crept around the house, the king spotted a small building; which seemed to be the origin of the obnoxious music. When he was within a few yards of the structure, he lay flat on his belly and began to crawl. He reached the building and positioned himself under a small window. The music was loud now but he could barely understand what the singer was saying.

"...he's learning to catch the heat of the third world man, he's a New World Man, he's a New World Man...", the voice shrilled.

Dominic peered in the window to assess the origin of the noise. Sitting there alone, next to what appeared to be a carriage of some sort, was a man drinking something out of a small metal can. Hanging from the ceiling above the man, was another of the glowing orbs. Scattered about the room were numerous other items which King Dominic could not comprehend. "Impossible," he thought again.

The music stopped and was replaced with a man's voice, *"That was Rush with, 'New World Man'. Coming up next, we'll hear from Bruce Springsteen and The Cult. I'm Mike Powers and it's 9:45. Here's Wendy Raines with the latest weather forecast on Detroit's best place for rock, WDTR."*

"Thanks Mike. We're looking at clear skies and a temperature of sixty-five degrees tonight. Perfect weather to get outside and watch the Perseid meteor shower. So, grab a blanket and some popcorn because it should be one heck of a show. Tomorrow's forecast calls for partly cloudy skies with a high of eighty-two degrees and a slight chance of....."

The man in the building suddenly rose from his chair and approached the window. King Dominic dropped to the ground and held his breath. "This is it. I'm caught before I ever got started," he thought. When he did not hear the man yelling, the king began to crawl to a more secluded location.

When he reached the front of the home, he spotted an entranceway. "Perfect," he thought. The area was dark and secluded. As he was assessing the area, clouds rolled in and blocked the moonlight. "Now was the time," the king thought.

He removed the Piece of Time from his pocket, set the dials to □4∃ and set in on the home's stoop. Dominic then pulled a small piece of parchment, a quill and a small sealed ink well from his satchel, wrote a note and placed it next to the Piece of Time. He looked around one last time, making sure he was alone, then stripped off his clothes. He laid his shirt carefully across a small bush close to the entryway and bundled the rest of his clothing into a ball. "What to do with these," he thought. Disposing of his garments was the one item he and Kelin hadn't planned for. Then he spotted a large bin only a few yards away. It was leaning against an adjacent dwelling and had the words 'Giovanni Waste Removal' written on it. Dominic sprinted to the bin, tossed his bundle of clothes inside, then raced back to the stoop. Next, he pinned the note to his shirt.

"Just one last thing to do," he thought.

Lying naked in the bushes, King Dominic Segarius took a deep breath. He held the watch in his hand and, at exactly

9:47 p.m. that night, the King of Munkelstein pressed the bottom button on the Piece of Time and shoved it as deep into the bush as he could reach. An instant later, a violent storm erupted. The wind gusted so aggressively, Dominic could see the petals of the nearby flowers being ripped from their stems.

As he lay there, perplexed as to what was going to happen next, he heard someone inside the home, shouting. Although the king could not make out what was being said, he assumed it had something to do with the storm.

He lay in the bushes, a violent storm erupting around him. Whatever was happening to Dominic had completely taken away his ability to move. An intense feeling of pressure began to squeeze his body, as if Uriah were suddenly lying across his chest. The pressure continued to build and his head began to pound. Every muscle in his body contracted at once, as if he were being electrocuted. His nerve endings seared with pain like a man being flayed and burned alive at the same time. The pain was so excruciating, Dominic howled in agony, but the king's vocal chords no longer worked. He lay there begging for mercy, willing the pain to stop.

When he had given up hope for relief, the storm abruptly ended, and with it, his pain subsided. Dominic tried to stand and stretch his sore body, but he no longer possessed the strength. The best he could do, was flail his arms and legs. King Dominic attempted to cover himself with his shirt, lest someone find him lying naked and paralyzed in a stranger's shrubs. However, all he managed to do was entangle himself in the cloth.

The king lay there, unsure what was happening to him. Worse yet, he could no longer remember why he was there, or who he was. Then, suddenly, he was being lifted into the air, his shirt tangled around him. Struggling to try and free himself, he kicked his legs and flailed his arms in an attempt to escape his prison. Panic set in and Dominic Philip Segarius, the King of Munkelstein, let out a cry.

The last thing he remembered was a man's voice saying, "I, uh uh, it's um uh, I found it in the...uh...it's a baby."

13

In the War Room
(Part 2)

E xactly three days ago, I stood in this room, trying to make sense of who I was and what had happened to me," the boy said. He was addressing the Knights of Munkelstein for the second time since his return, and even the skeptic Sir Thomas Albert Jameson couldn't argue that there was something very familiar about this boy. They were all listening intently to what Dominic was saying. Some of them had seen some type of magic before and therefore could believe anything was possible. However, a few, Sir Thomas Albert Jameson most notably, doubted what they had been told in their last meeting. They needed to hear, or see, something unequivocal if they were to risk their lives by taking the battle to Prince Mathias.

In the War Room (Part 2)

"As I stood before you, surveying the room," the king continued, "I can honestly say many things seemed familiar to me; but I simply could not believe it was possible for a man to turn back time and become a boy once again." There were grunts and head nods of agreements with this. "Since my return, I have strolled the grounds of this great kingdom and spoke to many of our loyal citizens. This truly is a wonderful place."

"Sire, pardon me for interrupting," Sir Thomas Albert Jameson said respectfully.

"That is quite alright Sir Jameson. Please, continue," Dominic replied.

"Thank you, my lord. You must forgive me but I am not yet convinced you are our King, Dominic Philip Segarius. I do not say this out of disrespect. I simply have trouble believing what you claim is possible." He knew what he was saying had the potential to throw the meeting into disarray, but he needed to say what he felt, and get some answers, before he would agree to risk his life.

"Sir Jameson, men," King Dominic said with a voice much more confident than his first meeting with these men. "I do not take your skepticism as disrespect. On the contrary, I would have trouble if you did not question me. Let this be a forum for you to ask what is on your minds. After all, it has been twelve long years since we have spoken honestly. From what Sir Orgen has told me about the night I left, and from what I remember, I was not able to tell you everything about why I had to leave the way I did. Thomas, let me first explain to you what I could not twelve years ago, then you may ask me anything you like."

Sir Jameson nodded in affirmation.

The king proceeded to explain everything that had happened, from the time he met Dyog Ronndewo to his arrival to Clarkston and his return to Munkelstein, three days earlier. When he was finished, King Dominic sat and took a sip from the chalice in front of him.

Sir McConnell broke the silence, "My lord, what you have told us here today is an unbelievable tale of magic and great courage. I understand Sir Jameson's skepticism as I too am a skeptical man; I believe all great thinkers should challenge what they hear and see. However, sire, in this case I do not need to challenge what you have told us here today," the Grey Knight said. "When I was boy, my father, Sir Stephen Francis McConnell, told me a very similar story.

"It seems when my father was a young man," Stephen recited, "he, and his best friend, went to visit an old wizard who, it was said, could tell your future. According to my dear departed father, the wizard told him he would have three sons. Dyog warned my father that his youngest son would die of disease in his fifth year. His second child, he was told, would be killed on the battlefield in his twenty fifth year." The Grey Knight paused, a solemn expression on his face.

"What is it Stephen?" Elijah Moren asked. "What happened?"

"My brothers died exactly as my father was told," he replied. "My father did not tell me of his meeting with the wizard until after my brother Jakobe died, during the battle of Arcadian. I begged my father to tell me who the wizard was and how I could find him; but he refused to say. All he would tell me was: *'Son, your excitement in discovering your fate will pale in comparison to the regret you will have for hearing it.'* He made me promise I would never pursue an encounter with the man you have called Dyog Ronndewo. As difficult as it has been, I have honored my father's wishes." Sir McConnell reflected on his father and brothers. It was apparent to everyone in the War Room that he missed them greatly.

"Sir McConnell, I thank you for retelling such a painful memory," Sir Jameson replied. "But I must ask, is it not just as likely that the things your father was told, the events which occurred after his meeting Dyog Ronndewo, were merely coincidence? Perhaps simply knowing the future somehow caused these terrible events to occur and were not preordained?"

"Absolutely, Thomas and exactly what I thought, at first," replied Sir McConnell. "When my youngest brother David passed away in his fifth year, my father thought it was nothing more than a sad coincidence. You may all recall the devastating outbreak of Shake Fever which broke out that year." Many of the knights nodded solemnly. Others looked down in reflection. "However, my father had not told Jakobe of his encounter with Dyog for fear Jakobe would meet his fate while trying to avoid it. All he did was to plead with Jakobe to avoid the fight in Arcadian. He told my brother that the battle was pointless and one not worth fighting; but Jakobe refused to leave his brothers-in-arms to fight without him," Stephen said. "On the eve of the battle, my father placed Jakobe under house arrest and paid a small squadron of men to keep him confined to his quarters. Regardless of how it happened, Jakobe snuck out that night and joined his brothers on the battlefield."

Michael Krebow asked, "I mean your family no disrespect Sir McConnell, but could your brother Jakobe's death not also be a sad coincidence? You also said your father did not tell you of his encounter with Dyog until after Jakobe's death so he did not actually tell you anything that had not already happened." The White Knight was the youngest of the knights and an only child. Since he had not suffered any great losses in his life, it would have been easy to dismiss his question as simply a young man with a lack of perspective.

"Again, I must agree with what you say, Michael," replied Sir McConnell. "Many of what happens in this life truly is coincidence. Perhaps having knowledge of what we are told *will* occur, only pushes us towards those things being realized. However, it is not what the wizard told my father which has convinced me of what our beloved king has told us here today. It is what Dyog Ronndewo told my father's friend which has convinced me...."

*   *

"I will not ask you again, tell me why you are here. What is it an old man can do for such a noble man as thee?"

For the first time in the young man's life, he was afraid. His friend Stephen was as white as a ghost when he stepped from the tent and now, standing here in this eerie place, the man started to question why he had come.

"Heh heh. I did not take thee to be a coward. Well, if there is nothing I can help you with, I will ask you to leave my home. As you can see I am a very busy man," the cackling voice said.

There was one thing this young man was not, and that was a coward. "I wish to hear my destiny," he blurted.

"Do you now? Why do you wish to hear your future? It is going to happen whether I tell it to you or not," the wizard replied. "Perhaps you should go home and learn some patience." The wizard's voice was fading as he walked away from the young man.

"That's odd. This place is so small. How could he have moved so far away from me?" he thought. "Please, sir. I have traveled far to meet you. I shall not leave until I get what I have come for," he said defiantly.

"Very well," the creepy voice was very close now. So close, the young man could feel the wizard's breath on the back of his neck. He felt a chill run through him as he prepared to hear what he had come for. "You seem like a man who knows what he wants. Who am I to argue with you?" With this comment, a blue orb appeared in Dyog Ronndewo's hand, and it appeared to be floating. The wizard shut his eyes and said, "You will be blessed with two sons: one will be both brilliant and cunning. What he lacks in empathy and compassion he will make up for with determination and hate. The other boy, will be blessed with a strategic mind; which will only be matched by his prowess as a warrior.

"In your forty-fifth year, you will have to choose between your sons. Your decision will have ramifications which will last for decades. If you do nothing, your kingdom will suffer at the hands of a tyrant. Should you choose to change history, your family will be torn apart. Simply put, you must choose between your family and your kingdom," the wizard said.

"What about my sons?" the man asked.

"What about them?"

"Will they live long lives? Do they marry? Will I become a grandfather?"

"That my lord, I cannot say. You asked me for your future, not your sons future," the man could hear the joy in Dyog's voice. "And it goes against wizarding protocol to divulge what happens after your death." Dyog never tired of these encounters; it was the only real fun he had these days. 'Wizarding protocol.' He'd have to remember that one.

The man thought for a moment. He knew arguing with a man as powerful as Dyog Ronndewo was futile. Instead, he asked, "What else can you tell me? Will I become king? What about my fate? How will I die? How old will I be when I finally meet my end?"

"So many questions my boy. Are you certain you wish to hear these things? Few men ever leave this place happier then when they entered," Dyog warned.

"Yes, my lord I am certain. I will hear what you have to tell me," the man replied.

"Ha-ha. My lord? Please, Roland Segarius, I am no lord. Let's start at the end, shall we?" the wizard asked. "You will pass in your sleep, alone" Dyog started.

Roland could think of much worse ways to go. "If I die in my sleep, then I must be an old man?" Roland questioned.

"When is Beatrix due to deliver, Roland?" Dyog asked, ignoring Roland's question.

"She…how do you know my wife is with child? We have told no one." Roland felt another shiver of fear shoot through him.

"Come now, I know much more than you could ever dream. Isn't that why you are here: because I know?" Dyog Ronndewo was truly having fun now. "Exactly two-hundred-twenty-eight days from today, your wife will deliver a pair of healthy baby boys into the world."

"A pair? You mean, were going to have twins? This is fantastic news. Twins are very good luck in my family," Roland replied, elated with the news. For the first time since Roland Segarius entered the tent, he was feeling glad he had come to see the wizard.

In the War Room (Part 2)

"Allow me to finish before you get too excited. As I was saying, your beautiful wife will deliver two healthy baby boys. Unfortunately for her, twins are unlucky in her family. Two months after you bury your wife you will bury your father and become king," Dyog said coldly. "As for how and when you will die, after twenty-five years as King of Munkelstein, you will be murdered in your sleep. It seems twins are bad luck in your family after all, King Roland."

* *

Sir McConnell finished retelling to the Knights of Munkelstein, the story King Roland had told his father's that day.

"Why is this the first we are hearing of this Sir McConnell?" the Black Knight demanded. "When King Roland passed away, unexpectedly, many of us thought foul play was involved, yet you said nothing. You knew he was going to die yet did nothing!" Sir Orgen's voice echoed through the War Room as he rose, knocking over his chair in the process.

"I did NOT know our beloved King Roland was going to die that night. I was as surprised and saddened by his death as anyone. Yes, he told my father what Dyog predicted that day, but he also told me that, the further they got from the wizard's tent, the less they believed what they had heard," the Grey

Knight explained. "My father said it was almost as if Dyog cast a spell with his words which made the entire encounter with the wizard feel like nothing more than a dream. They left Dyog's home, consumed with what they were told. By the time they had returned to Munkelstein, Dyog Ronndewo was like a distant memory. It wasn't until his beloved Beatrix passed away, from complications during child birth, that King Roland confided in my father that he was starting to believe what the wizard had told him," Sir McConnell stopped. He could see the look of loss on Dominic's face as he heard this new information. "I am sorry my lord. My father had sworn me to say nothing of what he told me about his meeting with Dyog."

"Is that all Stephen?" Dominic asked, ignoring the knight's apology.

"Yes, sire. That is all I know of my father's encounter with Dyog Ronndewo. I only brought this story up to explain to you, and the rest of the men at this table, why I believe what you have told us about your reason for leaving Munkelstein. And that I believe you truly are King Dominic Philip Segarius. Welcome back, your majesty," Sir McConnell said, as he knelt before his king.

"Thank you, Stephen. Please rise," King Dominic instructed. The Grey Knight rose and reseated himself at the table, staring solemnly down at his feet. "But you are not being completely truthful, are you?" the king asked.

"Sire? I assure you I have not left any of the details out of my father's retelling of his story to me," Stephen replied. "How could he possibly know?" he thought.

"There is one part of the story you have neglected to tell us," the boy began. "Under normal circumstances I would not ask you to divulge this information; however, I sense there may still be some skeptics among us. Stephen, please, tell us, what else did Dyog Ronndewo tell your father? Surely he must have told him of your fate?" King Dominic asked. The longer Dominic remained in this place, the more he felt like the man he once was.

"Why do you believe my father told me my fate? He never told Jakobe that he encountered Dyog, and he refused to tell me where to find the wizard to ensure I would never seek the man out," Sir McConnell said convincingly.

"I believe what you have told us here today, Stephen, and again, I thank you for your honesty. But I know your father told you of his encounter with Dyog. You told us he did not tell you of his encounter with Dyog Ronndewo until after your brother Jakobe's death, correct?" the king asked. Stephen nodded. "I'm convinced your father told you this story as a warning. Perhaps he felt that if he had told Jakobe, your brother would still be alive." King Dominic paused, studying the Grey Knight's reaction. He may look like a twelve-year-old boy, but he most certainly felt like a much older, wiser man. "Please Stephen, tell us what your father told you of your fate," the king urged.

Stephen McConnell sat and contemplated his king's request. What his father told him had not made sense, until today. Now he was being asked to explain something he himself had been struggling to fully understand for most of his life. "Sire, the conversation with my father happened more than twenty years ago. In that time, I have seen much of what he told me, come to pass, including his own death. However, what he told me of my fate did not make sense to me, until now," Sir McConnell replied. "Yes, you are correct, my father indeed told me of my fate. And yes, he did blame himself for Jakobe's death. He felt things might have turned out differently, had he told Jakobe the truth. But who among us would believe that someone could predict their future. Regardless, my father felt it imperative to warn me so I might avoid a…premature death."

"I know this is difficult Stephen; but the sun is setting on another day," the king interrupted. "Time is running short and

In the War Room (Part 2)

we still have much to do. Please, this information is important to us all."

Stephen McConnell's eyes focused on his feet. He had never told anyone this before and felt if he did not say the words, they would not come true. He took a deep breath and slowly exhaled. "Dyog Ronndewo told my father I would be killed attempting to rescue King Dominic Segarius's family from a madman," he said bluntly. Stephen McConnell sat silently and contemplated whether he should tell his king the rest of the wizard's tragic prediction, and decided against it.

"He'll find out soon enough," he thought.

14

The Proposition
(One night before King Dominic's return)

BOOM. BOOM. BOOM. The sound of a large object being struck against the solid oak door awoke Seamus from a dead sleep. "Pity," he thought, "girls never do that sort of thing in real life."

"Seamus Breitling, Prince Reynaldus Wilhelm Mathias demands your presence in his chambers at once," the voice bellowed.

"And does the prince wish for the entire kingdom to know of this meeting?" quipped the old voice as he unbolted the door.

"You are to come with us at once, sir," the voice declared.

Seamus opened the door to find four large men, clad in armor, waiting on his stoop. The old man went flush. For an instant, he thought he would faint. "This is it. They've found me out," he thought.

The Proposition

"Allow me to change out of my bed clothes. I won't be but a moment," Seamus replied.

"There is no time sir. We have been given strict instructions to bring you to the prince without delay." The largest and ugliest of the men had stepped across the threshold into Seamus's home and was now towering over the weak looking old man.

"Do I at least have time to put on my sandals, or does his lordship wish me to enter his chambers with dirty feet?" Seamus sniped, with the kind of sarcasm only a frail only man could get away with.

The uninvited soldier strode across Seamus's living room in two long steps, bent to pick up a pair of sandals he spied near the fireplace, and tossed them at Seamus. "Put them on and come with us," the soldier demanded.

A moment later, with sandals on, Seamus stepped out into the warm night air. He descended the small stoop and passed between the three soldiers standing in his front yard. Once past the large armor-clad men, he saw the other council members, their figures blocked by the gargantuan guardians of Sylvania.

"Selvin, what is this about?" Seamus demanded.

"I wish I knew," replied Selvin.

"No talking," instructed one of the guards.

The six council members walked the half mile from Seamus's front door to Prince Mathias's manor in silence. "Apparently, the fear of being disemboweled by four beasts is the cure for excessive conversing," thought Seamus.

Twenty minutes after leaving Seamus Breitling's home, the prince's council entered his chambers and took their seats around the council table. Prince Mathias was standing facing a large window, his back to the door.

They had been in his chambers for almost five minutes without Reynaldus acknowledging the council's presence. As if sensing Seamus was about to speak, Prince Mathias said, "My apologies for summoning you at such a late hour, but this could wait no longer." He remained facing the window as he spoke.

"There is something different about him," thought Selvin.

Prince Mathias had left Sylvania ten days earlier, without warning, and had only just returned. "There seems to be something different about him now," Seamus thought.

"I have known each of you loyal men for many years," Reynaldus said. "Your heads would not still be attached had I not trusted you all with my life. What I must tell you now will remain within these walls. Do you understand my words?" Prince Mathias demanded. His voice sounded raspy and his posture, at least from what Seamus could tell from where he was seated, looked like that of a much older man.

One-by-one, the council members answered affirmatively.

"Good. That is good. Should I discover you have betrayed my trust, you and everyone you hold dear will suffer the consequences. Do you understand my words?" the prince asked calmly.

The council members answered affirmatively, but with much hesitation.

"Excellent. I am certain you are all wondering where I have been these past days," Reynaldus started. "Allow me to explain. Ten days ago, I left Sylvania on a quest to find an old, shall I say, 'friend'. I have recently come to realize that this friend, was the only person alive who could help me find my dear brother, Dominic. You have all been extremely patient with me these past twelve years and I thank you for that. During this time, there have been many rumors regarding my brother's disappearance: Dominic died and Munkelstein is hiding it so we will not attack, he fled and is amassing an army larger than any the world has ever seen. But, my favorite story is the one from my man inside Munkelstein who told me Dominic vanished into thin air. Regardless of his fate, I simply could not take back my throne without first seeing the pain in my little brother's eyes."

"Who is this friend my lord?" Seamus asked.

"Seamus! I'm so glad you asked," Prince Mathias replied, his gaze still focused out the window. "Many, many years ago my brother and I went beyond the Great Plains to visit an old wizard. It was said this man was the most powerful wizard whoever was; greater than Merlin and Dahagen combined. We were young, only fourteen or fifteen. My future was set, or so I thought. Everyone in Munkelstein knew I was to be named king upon my father's passing; but my pathetic brother could not bear the thought of not knowing what the future had in store for him. So, after much convincing, my dear sweet brother agreed to travel with me to visit Dyog Ronndewo," Reynaldus recalled.

Seamus listened intently as Prince Mathias recounted his perspective of King Dominic's encounter with Dyog. Of course, Seamus had heard a similar, more detailed, story the night King Dominic fled Munkelstein. But it was somewhat reassuring to him that Prince Mathias's story matched so closely to that of his friend and king.

"I have no idea what the crazy old man told my brother, as the boy refused to tell me. All he would say was 'the man is a lunatic' and we had 'wasted our time going to see him.'" Prince Mathias paused in thought, eyes still transfixed to something outside in the blackness. "And I believed him; that is, until my father passed. When the declaration was read, my worthless brother seemed to be the only person in the kingdom not completely surprised that he was to be crowned the next King of Munkelstein; although I didn't see it at the time. It wasn't until he had been in hiding for almost a decade, and I had searched every corner of every land looking for my coward brother, that I realized there was only one man alive who could have helped the false King of Munkelstein disappear without a trace: Dyog Ronndewo!" Reynaldus growled.

His breathing was become heavy, either due to anger or exhaustion, Seamus could not tell. All he knew was the prince was becoming very agitated, and an agitated Prince Mathias had proven to be someone to truly fear.

Reynaldus remained facing the window, hood pulled over his head and face. Anyone who knew the man, as well as this group of followers did, could see there was something very wrong with him. His posture slumped and his voice was raspy and strained. Seamus thought Reynaldus must have been in a terrible accident. This would explain where he had been for the past ten days and why he seemed so, 'different' now.

"Ten days ago, I set out to find the greatest wizard ever known," the prince continued. "After a day's journey across the Great Plains, I arrived at the tiny hamlet of Villa La Trux', the town where Dyog Ronndewo was said to live. The place where my brother and I had traveled to, many years ago.

"I arrived to Villa La Trux' and found Dyog's hovel in the exact place and condition as it had been forty years prior. I entered his tent and before I could utter a single word, a frail voice called out from the darkness, 'Reynaldus my boy, I have been expecting you!' it said. The tent was so dark I could literally not see my hand in front of my face, yet this man knew who I was. And worse, he had been expecting me. I knew at that moment I was right. It was this man, the one they say was the greatest wizard to ever have lived, who helped my brother escape me and was the only person who could help me find him..."

* *

"You have been expecting me? How can that be? I myself did not know I was coming here until only a night ago. And I told no one," Reynaldus said, puzzled.

"My boy, I have been expecting you your entire life," the wizard replied. "In fact, I told your brother, King Dominic, you and I would meet, or more accurately that you and I had met." It sounded to Reynaldus like the old man was smiling as he spoke.

The Proposition

Reynaldus stood in the darkness of the tent, trying to get his bearings. Although he could not see Dyog, he could feel the wizard behind him. "Which is odd," he thought, "his voice is coming from directly in front of me."

"What do you mean you told Dominic we had met?" Reynaldus asked. "Why would you lie? You do not need to tell lies. You are supposed to be the greatest wizard ever. Or is that a lie as well?"

"While I cannot, and would never, say I am the greatest anything ever, I can assure you, what I am not my boy, is a liar," Dyog Ronndewo replied. "I told King Dominic Segarius you and I had met because we had met. Granted, I was referring to your arrival here today." Dyog paused allowing Reynaldus to speak, but when he did not, the wizard continued, "Of course not, you never do," he mused. "I can see you do not understand, just as King Dominic did not understand, so allow me to explain my meaning."

Reynaldus could not help but think that the wizard's continued referral to his brother as 'King' was no accident, and he could feel anger slowly start to build.

"I have met everyone I would and will ever meet when I was a boy. One of the many curses which come along with some of my, gifts, I suppose you would call them. So, while technically, you and I had not 'physically' met the day King Dominic came to me, in my memories, we had indeed met."

"Are you saying, you know everyone you are ever going to meet, exactly what they are going to say to you and how you will respond? Or are you saying you have already lived the experience of meeting them?" Reynaldus questioned. "Because either sounds ludicrous."

"Both," Dyog replied. The wizard had a knack for pushing a man's buttons. Sometimes he did it to frighten them, other times it was to test their resolve. After all, he had to make sure they were worthy of hearing what he had to tell them. But when he told Reynaldus, "I have been alive for more years than I care to count and of all my encounters, yours has been the one I have cherished most of all," he was being sincere.

"Really? And why is that? I mean, you knew I was coming and when. You also know why I came here and every word of our conversation; a conversation, by the way, which we have not actually had yet," the prince recounted. As much as he wanted, no...needed, to find his brother, Reynaldus was beginning to regret coming here. The wizard was either crazy, or worse: he wasn't. If Dyog wasn't a madman, then what he was saying was true and what Reynaldus was about to hear was going to answer a lifetime of questions.

The Proposition

"Yes, I knew when you would come here, and why. But try as I might, I have been unable to see the outcome of our conversation," Dyog replied sincerely. "I have met hundreds of men within these walls. I can tell you the names of every man who has entered my home as well as the day and time they came to me. I can recall every word of every conversation and the expressions on their faces as they heard what they came to hear," Dyog said. "But you Reynaldus, yours is the only meeting I do not know the outcome of. That has never happened before! This is a very exciting day. Don't you think?"

Reynaldus could hear true excitement in the old man's voice and he wasn't about to stay and be mocked any longer. "This is a waste of time, you're a lunatic," he snapped as he turned to leave Dyog's home. Reynaldus reached for the tent flap but grabbed only a fistful of air. "That can't be. I have not moved from this spot," he thought, confused as to what was happening.

"Please, sit my boy. Don't you want to see how it ends?" the voice asked from behind him. As Dyog spoke, a faint blue object began to glow in front of Reynaldus. It appeared to be floating as it moved slowly toward the prince. When the blue orb was no more than a foot from Reynaldus, it moved to his right, illuminating an old wooden chair. He could now see the

213

orb was not floating. It was attached to a staff which was being held in the oldest hand Reynaldus had ever seen.

The prince did as instructed and sat in the chair. Although he still could not see Dyog Ronndewo, it appeared to the prince that the old man was now seated as well. "Tell me why I am here," Reynaldus said confidently. "Tell me this and I might actually believe what you have told me isn't completely absurd."

As if reading from a script, at least that's how it sounded to Reynaldus, the wizard replied, "You have been searching for your poor lost brother, Dominic, who disappeared twelve years ago without a trace. You have been heartbroken ever since and have come here as a last resort. You are here for closure."

Reynaldus felt his throat tighten. He had been practicing that speech throughout his journey to Villa La Trux' and although it was utter nonsense, the wizard had repeated his words back to him exactly.

"However, we both know that is not truly why you came here today, is it?" Dyog paused awaiting a response from Reynaldus. After a few seconds he said, "That's ok. I've asked you that question a thousand times and you have yet to answer. How about I just tell you, hmm? You came to me because King Dominic Segarius vanished seemingly into thin air twelve years ago. Your brother, the king, the man you feel stole your crown, the man who you have tried time-after-time to kill, so you could claim what you feel is yours, but to no avail. King Dominic, the man, your brother, who has outwitted you at every turn leaving you to look like a fool," Dyog said, antagonizing the prince. "Push, push, push, poke, poke, poke," he thought.

Reynaldus felt an anger rising the likes of which he had never felt before. He leapt from his chair bellowing, "I KNOW WHO AND WHAT MY BROTHER IS! IF YOU WISH TO KEEP YOUR TONGUE, I WARN YOU, DO NOT MOCK ME!"

"My dear boy, sit. It is not my wish to anger you," Dyog said with a smile. "I only say these things to prove to you I know the truth of why you journeyed to see me. Your brother vanished into thin air twelve years ago did he not? You have scoured the globe looking for him so you could take back what you feel is yours; is this not also true? But I ask you, why have you not simply stormed Munkelstein and taken the throne by force? With the king absent, I would think it would be an easy feat to accomplish."

"If we have already met, and if you have lived this conversation for a lifetime, then why ask me questions you already know the answers to?" Reynaldus asked defiantly.

"Hahaha. My boy, a conversation requires both parties to speak. Yes, I could simply tell you all of this, but you have not lived our meeting yet. Have you?" the wizard replied. "And so, I will speak and ask questions and you will answer, and that is how a conversation works," Dyog quipped.

Reynaldus dug his nails into the hardwood of the chair. "Now he speaks to me like a child," he thought, "he does not know how easily I could slit his throat."

"But if you slit my throat, how will you get the answers you have come for?" Dyog asked. "Please, humor an old man. Why have you not taken Munkelstein by force? The king has been gone for more than a decade, and the throne has been just sitting vacant."

"Have you any idea what it feels like to know for your entire life that you were destined to be something special? And when the day finally comes for your destiny to be fulfilled, to have it ripped from you like a limb?" Reynaldus asked with pain in his voice. "That throne was, excuse me, IS, mine. I do not know what my brother did to turn my father against me, but I shall not rest until his head is hanging above my mantle like a trophy stag." Reynaldus stopped to calm himself. He was not about to let this man see him lose his composure once again.

"You are right Reynaldus, I have no idea how that must

have felt; but that does not answer my question. You could have taken the throne by now and then just waited for your brother to return and, if he did, you could easily dispatch him."

The prince waited a moment to respond. He knew Dyog already understood the answer to his own question. It seemed strange to Reynaldus that he should explain reasons which the wizard obviously already understood. When he finally spoke, it was so that he, Reynaldus, could hear the words for himself. After all, he had never uttered the words aloud.

"You are right, I could have taken back my throne a thousand times since my cowardly brother's departure, and on several occasions, I had the men amassed to do just that. However, I knew deep down that taking the throne without defeating my brother was like reeling in a trophy fish which someone else has hooked. Yes, the reward is the same either way, but deep down you know the victory is hollow and unearned. My brother has made a laughing stock of me every day since he stole my throne. He even came up with a way to turn my father against me. I don't know how he did it, but he did. All I have imagined, since his coronation, is watching him suffer. In that time, I have devised a million ways to inflict pain upon him. To just saunter into Munkelstein and take the throne without destroying him would not taste as satisfying.

The only way for me to right that wrong is to defeat my brother and take from him what he took from me," Reynaldus explained.

"What makes you think I can help you find your brother? I haven't spoken to him in decades," Dyog lied.

Reynaldus could hear the disingenuousness in the old man's words. "Come now, Dyog. We have had this conversation for a thousand years. Have I ever believed you had nothing to do with my brother's departure?" Reynaldus asked.

"Hahaha. I suppose you have not my boy. But I honestly cannot tell you where to find your brother, because I truly do not know," the wizard replied.

"I thought you were not a liar," Reynaldus said. "It recently occurred to me that Dominic was the only person in Munkelstein who was not utterly surprised when he was crowned king after my father's death. I used to think it was because my father had told Dominic he would be the next king. But when, after more than a decade of searching, I could not locate even the smallest trace of my brother's whereabouts, I remembered his meeting you, Dyog Ronndewo. If you didn't help him, you at least would have told him his future and his disappearance must have been a part of that future," Reynaldus challenged.

The Proposition

"You truly have a brilliant mind my boy. You never cease to amaze me," Dyog replied. No matter how many times the wizard lived this moment, he was always impressed with Reynaldus's intellect. Under different circumstances, Dyog would love to have a philosophical conversation with the prince. "However, you are not entirely correct. Due to wizarding protocol, I cannot disclose what I told your brother. All I can tell you is that I told your brother he would have to choose between staying and dying, or fleeing and returning to live another day."

"LIAR! Dyog the Great, sees the futures of men and knows all things!" Reynaldus shouted.

"Again, you are only partially correct. I can see the futures of those men who seek it out, but even my vision is limited. I can foresee major moments in one's life and the perils they may face. However, all men have free will and must determine their own paths; regardless of what they hear from me," Dyog explained. "I told your brother he would have to make a choice. I did not see which path he would choose. All I did was prepare him to make the decision once the time came..."

*   *

"…and then, after much coaxing, Dyog Ronndewo told me how he provided my brother with what the wizard called 'Disposable Magic'," Reynaldus recalled. "I will not get into all the details now, however, one bit of magic would allow him to travel to anywhere he could imagine. All my brother would have had to do was stare at the place he wanted to go with this," Reynaldus said, holding up what Dyog called a 'Gazing Glass', "and he would be taken there. Now, you men must discover where my pathetic brother has gone."

"Sir, how did you convince Dyog to help you?" asked one of the council members. "I had heard that he only conveyed information about the person with which he was speaking."

"That is true Cornelius. As you are all aware, I had put a plan in motion to kill my brother on the night he disappeared. When the time came to execute the plan, my man inside Munkelstein gave Dominic's brutish guard, Sir Orgen, a drink which was laced with the root of the Steifle plant. Sir Orgen was asleep within minutes of ingesting it, leaving Dominic alone and vulnerable. When my man entered my brother's chamber, all he found was an empty bed and some strange items on his desk," Reynaldus recalled.

"What items, sire?" asked Seamus. The spy could not believe what he was seeing. His friend King Dominic had showed Seamus this very piece of glass twelve years ago, during their last meeting.

"Other than some parchment and a quill, we recovered this Gazing Glass, as Dyog called it, and the most peculiar map I have ever seen." Without breaking his gaze from the window, Reynaldus pointed to a roll of paper lying on the table in front of his council. "Before you, lies the location of my brother. You are going to help me find where he has gone as if your lives depend on it," the prince said as he slowly turned to face his followers. Then, he lowered his hood and stood before his council, preparing himself for their gasps; which immediately followed.

Selvin Ferguson was the first to speak, "Sire! My God, what has happened to you?"

Standing before the Sylvanian council was a face unrecognizable from that of the man they knew just ten days earlier. Reynaldus now wore the face and posture of a man much, much older than anyone Seamus had ever seen. The prince appeared to be hundreds of years old with deep long lines running through his face and hands. His skin sagged as if years of extreme gravity had begun to pull it from his muscles and tendons. The prince's hair was now bright white, sparse and had grown so long, it hung below his shoulder blades. Seamus was dumbstruck by the prince's transformation.

The prince ambled slowly towards the council table, laboring for each step. As he approached them, the council members could see a faint blue light emanating from the prince's right hand.

"Sire, is that…is that the staff of Dyog Ronndewo?" Seamus asked.

"So many questions," replied Reynaldus. "But where to begin. Well, Dyog refused to tell me where Dominic had fled to; either because he did not know or because he was simply a stubborn old man. However, while he could not tell me where my brother went, he did explain how he helped my brother escape. The wizard gave Dominic what he called Disposable Magic." Prince Reynaldus explained each item to the council, and how the magic worked. "I asked Dyog Ronndewo for a similar magic, to allow me to find my brother; however, he claimed the magic he gave Dominic was unique and he had nothing else as powerful." Reynaldus was now laboring with each word. "He had no magic to give me and he did not know my brother's whereabouts; but he did offer me a proposition.

"It seems the staff of Dyog Ronndewo is the source of his

powers. If I was willing to accept the staff as his gift, all would be revealed to me. I asked him what the catch was. Why he would be willing to bequeath onto me something as powerful as this," Reynaldus said, holding the staff up for them all to see. "He told me that the staff, while powerful, was a burden he no longer wished to bear. That he had been waiting for me in anticipation of the moment his burden would be lifted from him. I asked him what would happen to me if I agreed to ease his burden, he said he could not tell me. At the time, I thought he meant he could not tell me because he did not know. Now I'm not so sure," the prince said, his mind wandering.

"The last thing he said to me was that mine was the only meeting in which he had not foreseen the outcome. After some deliberation, I agreed to his terms..."

*   *

Dyog rose from his chair and approached Reynaldus. "Kneel my boy and bow your head," the wizard directed.

Standing over the prince, Dyog Ronndewo raised his arms in the air and looked to the sky. The wizard muttered, what sounded to Reynaldus to be a chant; but not in any tongue the prince was familiar with. Dyog waved his arms in a circular motion and with every movement, the chanting became louder. After a minute, the wizard was screaming his incantation. Reynaldus cocked his head upward to sneak a peek at what Dyog was doing and could not believe what he saw. The wizard's arms were moving so quickly, Reynaldus could not see them. All the prince could see was a blue glow, which was no longer an orb of light, but a streak of light in a shape which the prince did not recognize: ∞. Dyog suddenly directed all of his energy at Reynaldus. There was a loud 'CRACK' as the blue light shot directly into Reynaldus' chest, knocking him to the ground.

The last thing Reynaldus remembered before losing consciousness was the smell of roses.

*   *

"I awoke some time later at the edge of a creek. How much time had passed, I do not know. It felt as if every bone and muscle in my body had been beaten with a club. My joints ached and I had trouble standing. I pulled myself to the water and rinsed my hands and face. Looking down into the stream I spied my reflection. What I saw, well, is what you see before you now, a 200-year-old man." Reynaldus paused to catch his breath.

"Sire, what happened to Dyog Ronndewo?" asked Claudius. "Did you seek him out and ask him to reverse this, this affliction?"

"After I composed myself, and the shock of what had happened began to wane, I set out to find the mad wizard and end his life. As you can imagine, I was a little disoriented and confused by what had just occurred. After a couple day's travel, I arrived back at Villa La Trux'," Reynaldus said, and let out a long sigh. "Only, Dyog Ronndewo was no longer there. I went to the exact spot I had been twice before, expecting to see the disheveled hovel of the most powerful wizard who has ever lived. What I found instead was…was…it wasn't there."

"Sire?" said Selvin. "Are you ok? Would you like some water?"

"Thank you, my friend. That would be nice," labored Prince Mathias.

Selvin rose and quickly went to the small table near the fireplace. He filled a glass with water and raced back to deliver it to the prince.

"Here you are my lord," Selv said, handing the glass to Reynaldus. When the prince had taken a few sips, Selvin asked, "What did you find, my lord? When you returned to Villa La Trux', what did you find there?"

225

"In the exact spot where I had stood twice before, where I had seen with my own eyes, the home of Dyog Ronndewo, now stood a great stone gristmill. The mill must have been hundreds of years old," Reynaldus said, lost in thought. "I entered the building but it was empty. Dyog Ronndewo was gone; if he was ever there at all." Reynaldus looked exhausted. It was apparent to the council that their leader had gone through a very traumatic event and needed to rest.

"Sire, you look exhausted. Perhaps you should lie down. We can finish this in the morning," Seamus proposed. "Nonsense. I have come too far and sacrificed too much to rest now. I need you to find the place my brother has fled to," Reynaldus instructed his council. "Only then will I rest."

Selvin stood and grabbed the map from the center of the table. He unrolled it and placed small stones at each corner to keep it flat. For the next few hours, the council members huddled around the strange chart, studying its every detail.

"It is very much like trying to find a single needle in a world of haystacks," Selvin thought.

"This seems like an impossible task. We're just going to have to make a guess as to where King Dominic went," thought Claudius.

Just as Claudius was having this thought, Selvin Ferguson exclaimed, "I've found it, sire! I've found where your brother has gone!"

The Proposition

The prince, who had nodded off watching the flames dance in his fireplace, jumped at Selvin's cry. "What? Where? Where is he?" the prince exclaimed, looking frailer than ever.

Selvin snatched the map off the table and hurried over to Reynaldus' side. "Here my lord. I believe he is here," Selvin said, pointing to an area of land that looked like a fingerless glove. "Look at this area here," he told the prince.

Reynaldus studied the map for a second, confused by what he was supposed to be seeing. "I do not understand. What am I looking for?" he asked.

"This map, while very old, is in almost perfect condition," Selv replied. "Its edges show no signs of wear and its corners have no dog ears or creases. The cartographer who drew this map used only basic natural brown tones for the land masses. Do you see?" Selv asked Reynaldus.

Reynaldus studied the map again, then replied, "Yes, my friend, I see. The map is pristine. As if it were drawn only days ago. But I do not under…" The prince stopped mid-sentence. "Selvin my friend you have done it!" Reynaldus exclaimed. "You've found him!" The prince was smiling with a delight that few had ever witnessed.

"What is it, my lord? Where has he gone?" queried Seamus.

"Come, see for yourselves," the prince beckoned.

Disposable Magic

The council members huddled around Reynaldus, their eyes following his finger as the prince pointed to a spot on the map which was shaped like a glove.

"But, sire," Cornelius said, "what makes you think he is there?"

"Look closely," Reynaldus whispered. He moved his finger and allowed the men to inspect the area labeled 'Michigan', more closely.

Just as Seamus was about to question Reynaldus, he saw it. It was subtle, but unmistakable. As Selvin had astutely observed, the map was drawn using only inks with brown hues. Darker browns were used to illustrate higher elevations such as mountains, while the lighter shades were used for flatlands. However, there was a very small spot, in the Michigan land mass, which was not brown. In fact, one could say it was emerald green. And if one were truly observant, one would say it was the exact shade of green as the glass recovered from King Dominic's chambers the night he departed.

"This is the place I will find my brother," Reynaldus said confidently and tapped the map. The prince seemed to have gained much of his strength back at realizing that twelve years of searching was about to pay dividends. "I will be leaving at once."

"But how, sire?" asked Seamus. "How will you get there? And how will you get back?"

228

The Proposition

"Yes, sire. How will you do it?" asked Selvin. "You told us the magic could only be used once."

Prince Mathias looked at his council with a sneer and said, holding the wizards staff up for them to see, "It seems my old friend has provided me with everything I will need for my trip."

"That is excellent sire," exclaimed Selvin. He studied Reynaldus and could see how utterly exhausted the man looked. The prince had waited a lifetime for this moment. What was one more night? "You look tired, my lord. Perhaps you should rest now. You'll want to have all of your strength for your reunion with your brother."

As much as he hated to admit it, Selv was right. Reynaldus nodded in agreement. He had never felt so exhausted in his life. "Perhaps you are right, my friend. I will leave at first light," he said. The prince then turned to the rest of the council, and with a gleam in his eyes said, "It won't be long now my friends. Ready yourselves for the trip to Munkelstein. All we have suffered for, will soon be ours."

15

I Spy
(Part 2)

The boy made his way across his bedroom, unbolted the latch and pulled open the heavy oak, slab door. He had recently returned to his chamber's after addressing the Knights of Munkelstein, for the second time since his return.

Standing in his doorway were Sir Orgen and an old frail looking man. The old man was shorter than Dominic, had grey hair, pale blue eyes and his back had a severe arch. Dominic thought the man must have a spinal condition which would not allow him to ever stand upright again. The boy could not help but think that he had lived this very moment before.

"Sire," Sir Orgen announced, "allow me to introduce you to, Seamus Breitling of Sylvania."

I Spy (Part 2)

"From Sylvania!" Dominic gasped. "Brenden what is this man doing here?" The king grasped the old man's robe and shouted, "Where is my family? You bastard's better not have harmed them."

"My lord, please allow me to explain why I am here, before you kill me," Seamus replied weakly. Dominic released his grip from the old man and did his best to regain his composure. "Thank you, sire. I have a letter from your brother which I am to deliver only to you," the old man said as he patted the pocket of his robe.

"Well let's have it then," Dominic said dismissively.

"I beg your pardon, sire, but this is for your eyes only. If we can just speak in private for a moment..."

"Are you mad?" Sir Orgen interrupted.

"I assure you I am not, Sir Orgen. If you recall, I met with your king twelve-years ago, and he trusted then that I wished him no harm," Seamus said calmly. "King Dominic, as you can plainly see, I am old and feeble. My fighting days are clearly over. I am here merely as a messenger."

There was something about this man which seemed familiar to Dominic. The boy couldn't shake the feeling he had met this man before. And in this exact place. "It's alright. I think I'll be safe," Dominic assured the giant.

The old man shuffled into the king's chambers. Dominic turned to close the door behind them and whispered to the giant, "But just in case, don't leave this spot." When the boy turned back, the old man was seated on the king's bed, his eyes transfixed on the boy.

"I do not think I would have believed it had I not seen it with my own eyes," Seamus said, bewildered.

"Believe what?" That I am the king of the greatest Kingdom ever known? That I am a great and powerful warrior in the body of a twelve-year-old boy? What? What is it?" Dominic snapped at the old man.

"No, sire, it is none of those. I cannot believe that you...have returned," the old man replied. "I have endured twelve long years in that hell, with your lunatic brother, awaiting this day. And finally, you have returned; just as you said you would."

"Wait. What? Do we know each other?" asked Dominic, confused. Confusion was a feeling the boy was unfortunately starting to get used to.

"Yes, my lord. We do know each other. Allow me to reintroduce myself, I am Kelin Richard Semtun." As he spoke Kelin straightened his posture and removed the make-up covering his more youthful complexion.

232

I Spy (Part 2)

"But…Sir Orgen said your name was Seamus something," Dominic replied.

"Breitling, Seamus Breitling. Yes, that is the name I use outside these walls, and the man your brother believes me to be," Kelin explained. "However, in reality I am, and have always been, your friend and loyal subject." The spy proceeded to retell the king of their first encounter as boys, and how, after Prince Mathias grew in power, he volunteered to infiltrate Sylvania. Finally, Kelin recalled the last time he had spoken to his king, and the plan he and Dominic concocted; with a little magical help, of course.

"At first, I thought you had turned coward my lord," Kelin explained, "but once you explained your plan in detail, I knew without question, that you would return. And here you are. Damn you look good!" he joked.

"What can you tell me of my family? Have they been harmed?" Dominic asked frantically. While the boy found Kelin's story fascinating, he had only one thing on his mind at that moment. "Have you seen them?"

"My lord, your family are being held in a dungeon deep below Sylvania Manor," Kelin replied. "Yesterday, I snuck my way down to the catacombs, and located their cell. They are alive, but very frightened." He opted not to tell his king of the brutal attack his parents had suffered for fear it would distract the king from plotting their rescue.

"Why didn't you help them?" the boy demanded. "You could have set them free!"

While Kelin could see the resemblance to his king, the boy before him was clearly no longer the same brave warrior. "I have provided them with food and water and assured them I would return to help," he replied.

"What are we waiting for? Let's get them out, now!" Dominic urged.

"Sire, we cannot just storm the gates and attack Sylvania. Even if we had the numbers, Prince Mathias would execute your family before we ever stepped foot on Sylvanian soil," Seamus explained.

Dominic was distraught. Kelin could see how hard it must be for the boy. Knowing his family was being held prisoner by a madman.

"There may be a way to get them out undetected; but it is dangerous," Kelin added.

Dominic thought about this for a moment. "How dangerous?" he asked. "It can't be worse than leaving them with a psychopath."

"Dominic, there is something else you should know,

regarding your brother. Prince Mathias has…changed," Kelin started. "He was involved in some sort of accident, which I am unclear as to the details of. As a result, Reynaldus seems to have aged more than 100 years." Kelin thought for a moment about the extreme transformation Prince Mathias had undergone. "He claims to have exchanged years of his life for powerful magic. For powers which I did not know existed." Dominic could see in Kelin's face that the spy was concerned with Prince Mathias possessing such powerful magic. "Dark magic indeed," Kelin mumbled.

"What do you mean, 'exchanged' years of his life?" Dominic asked.

Kelin Semtun then told his king how Prince Mathias encountered Dyog Ronndewo. How he traded years of his life for the staff of the great wizard and how the prince planned to use those powers to kill Dominic.

"This staff, does it have a blue crystal for a handle?" Dominic asked.

"How did you know?" the spy asked, dumbfounded by the question.

Ignoring Kelin's response, Dominic asked, "Why have you come here tonight? Anyone of Reynaldus' squires could have delivered a message to me. You have put yourself at significant risk, so it must be important." The voice Kelin heard utter these words sounded like his old friend, King Dominic Segarius.

"I am one of the few people in Sylvania Prince Mathias truly trusts. He asked me personally to deliver this message to you." Kelin reached into his pocket and handed the king a small scroll. "I am to await your response and then return immediately to Sylvania."

Dominic unfurled the roll of parchment and read:

"Hello again BROTHER. I can only assume that, by now, you've been made aware of what brought you to this unfortunate position. As time is of the essence, at least for your family it is, I will keep this brief: You have only two days remaining in which to surrender yourself to me, and save your family from a horribly painful death. Now is not the time for heroics baby brother. All you need to do is come to Sylvania at sunset, two nights from now, kneel before me and relinquish your crown. I will do the rest. It's very simple. So simple, even a child could follow my instructions (good thing huh?). Do you see how accommodating I can be?

My good friend Seamus will await your response.

I would be lying if I said I wasn't absolutely giddy at the thought of seeing my dear brother again.
Best Regards,
Reynaldus Wilhelm Mathias, True King of Munkelstein"

236

I Spy (Part 2)

Kelin studied the young boy's face as he read the contents of the message. The man he had met with in secrecy, twelve years ago, was no longer there; however, the face now before the spy was unmistakable. This was the face Kelin had known most of his life. The face of the boy he had met more than forty years ago. He watched as Dominic read, and reread, the message, studying every word. If he was frightened or upset, the boy did not show it.

When he had gleaned all he could from Prince Mathias's message, Dominic walked over to his desk, pulled out a small piece of parchment and composed a message of his own. When he was finished, he rolled up the paper and tied it with a thin piece of hemp cord. "You mustn't keep the Prince waiting," he said as he handed the small scroll to Seamus. "Hurry back to Sylvania. If Reynaldus truly does have spies within Munkelstein, it will look suspicious if you are here too long."

Seamus pocketed the king's message and reapplied his disguise. When he was confident he had resumed his Seamus Breitling persona, he slowly ambled his way towards the door.

Dominic thanked the man and gently embraced him. Then a thought occurred to the boy. He hurried back to his desk and quickly jotted down a second message and handed it to the spy.

“There’s something else I need you to do for me.” Then Dominic Segarius explained his plan to rescue his family.

16

A Dungeon in Sylvania
(Part 4)

R ise and shine Bennett family! This is an exciting day and I wouldn't want you miss a second of it," shouted the voice in Randy Bennett's dream. He was dreaming about the day his daughter was born. The young nurse was placing his baby girl into his arms for the first time when the voice shouted again, "Wakey, wakey Randy. I want you to be wide awake the last time you see your 'son' alive."

The door in the ceiling above, was flung open with such force, it shook the prisoners awake. Randy recognized the voice. It was a voice which would haunt the elder Bennett's dreams for the rest of his days. Although, judging from the current state of events, Randy suspected they didn't have too many days left. All he could hope for, was that the end would be painless, and his family would not suffer.

Maggie sat up and stared into the hole in the ceiling above her. The light shining through the opening, was the only light source they had, and it had been days since she had seen it. "What do you mean the last time we'll see Dominic alive?" Maggie shouted.

"Leave our boy alone," Randy demanded. "Take me instead. Please, I'll do anything you ask," he begged.

"Ha-ha. Take you? Randy, Randy, Randy, you never cease to make me laugh," Reynaldus said snidely. "I have already taken you. The only thing you can do for me now, is watch your son die," he laughed. "Once Dominic has died, painfully, and I become King of Munkelstein, I will send you back to your Clarkston. Not all of you of course. Dominic will not be joining you, I'm afraid," Reynaldus said with joy. These past days with his prisoners had been most memorable. "Almost worth the wait," he thought.

In the dungeon below, Randy sat huddled with his girls. As he listened to the lunatic laughing and bragging about killing Dominic, in excruciating pain, Randy became convinced his family was never going to leave this place. He squeezed his girls tight, closed his eyes and prayed for a miracle.

A Dungeon in Sylvania (Part 4)

"I wish I could stay and chat with you some more, but there are preparations to be made. King's don't just kill themselves you know," Prince Mathias cackled.

In the room above her, Rose heard a door opening, and then the soft shuffling of feet heading away. An instant later, the Bennett family was alone again. However, this time, the prince had left the trapdoor open and the candles burning. The light was soft and feint, but for the Bennetts, it might as well have been the sun. They had been in absolute darkness since their arrival, and while they were still sad and afraid, this little indulgence gave the family a small glimmer of hope.

Randy sat and studied the opening above him; calculating the distance from floor to ceiling and wondering if he could boost Rose and Maggie up and out. "I can't let them die in this place," he thought to himself. But before he could give an escape plan too much thought, he heard the familiar scratching sound, of something sliding across a stone surface.

The light emanating into the room, while not bright, was enough to allow Randy to make out the rooms outline. He scurried to the place he heard the sound come from and found another platter. Like the one they received two days earlier, this plate had three small mugs of water and three lumps of stale bread on it. Randy picked up the plate and hurried over to his girls. He handed each of them a mug and a lump of bread, and then he noticed it. Neatly folded under one of the lumps of bread was a piece of paper. Paranoia set in as Randy snatched up the small note.

"Is this a trick? Are we being watched like rats in some sick science experiment?" he thought.

"What is that?" Rose asked as she watched her dad pocket the note. Even in such a dim dank place the girl didn't miss a thing.

"I'm not sure," Randy whispered. "It was under a piece of bread. I think it may be a note. Or a trap."

"A note?" Maggie exclaimed.

"Shhh. Lower your voice Magg's. I don't know what it is. What if he's trying to trap us into doing something stupid?" Randy said, motioning his head towards the trapdoor.

"What could he possibly be trying to trap us into doing? If he wanted us dead he'd have done it already," Maggie said defiantly. "Here, give it to me." Feeling like a scolded child, Randy took the note from his pocket and handed it to his wife. Maggie unfolded the note and burst into tears. "It's from him! It's from Dominic! He's alive!" she shouted.

"SHHHHHHH. Maggie lower your voice," Randy urged. He waited a moment, and when he was certain they were alone, Randy asked, "What does it say?"

A Dungeon in Sylvania (Part 4)

Maggie did her best to gain her composure, tears streaming down her cheeks. She cleared her throat and whispered:

"Hi mom and dad, and Rose. I am so sorry this is happening to you. I don't have a lot of time so I'll keep this short. The man who has taken you is very dangrous so please do what he says. I have something he wants and, as soon as I give it to him, you will be freed. However, because I do not trust him, I have a plan to get you out of there. When the time is right, a friend of mine will free you from your prison. His name is Kelin Semtun and when he comes for you, do as he says without question. Do not hesitate, for there will only be one opportunity for you to escape. I promise this will be over very soon. Don't worry, I know where you are at. I promise I will be there shortly. In the meantime, try to stay calm. I love you more than you will ever know.
Love your son, Dominic."

"How do you know Dominic wrote it? That was a pretty vague message. Anyone could have written it," Randy said. It seemed too good to be true and he didn't want to get his hopes up if the note wasn't really from his boy.

"Can I see the note mom?" Rose asked. Maggie reluctantly handed the paper to her daughter. It was the first sign her son was alive and her instinct was to guard it with her life. After a minute of reading and rereading the note, Rose exclaimed,

"That's his handwriting! I'd recognize his sloppy chicken scratch anywhere," Rose whispered excitedly.

"Are you sure Rosey? Anyone could forge his sloppy handwriting," Randy replied. "I mean, he said, *'for there will only be one opportunity for you to escape.* That's way too formal to be D's writing." He genuinely wanted to believe his son had written the note. If only D had put something personal in the message which only the they would understand. "I mean, it does look like his writing," Randy added, trying to convince himself his boy was alive.

"Dominic definitely wrote this dad," Rose said confidently.

"How can you be so sure?" Randy asked.

Rose let out a little chuckle and replied, "It's simple, look. He spelled dangerous, d-a-n-g-r-o-u-s, he forgot the *e*. I've told him a million times, 'it's pronounced dan-ger-ous, not dan-grous'. And see here," Rose said, pointing to the note, *"Don't worry, I know where you are at.* Where you are 'at'. I swear he ends his sentences with prepositions just to drive me bonkers. Mom, dad, this note is definitely from D," she said handing the note back to Maggie.

Randy looked into his wife's eyes and felt something he hadn't felt since waking up in this strange place: hope. "Magg's our boy is alive," Randy said as he grabbed his wife and squeezed her tight. "We're getting out of here Magg's. We'll *all* be back home before you know it and this will all be just one bad dream."

Randy Bennett believed what he told Maggie to be true, however, he couldn't shake the feeling that the worst was yet to come.

17

The Road to Destiny

I t's time to go, my lord," Sir Brenden Orgen said as he peeked his head into the king's chambers. He hated that Dominic would not take his advice. Going to Sylvania was suicide, but no matter what the giant told him, the king refused to listen.

The boy was at his desk, lost in thought. He was cleaning the only memory of his home he was fortunate enough to have had with him the day he departed Clarkston. When he first found it, the watch seemed ancient. Now, sitting in his room, in a seemingly ancient time, the watch suddenly seemed quite modern.

"Sire? Are you alright?" Sir Orgen asked, now standing beside Dominic. "You don't have to do this. I can have a small army assembled within a few hours. We can storm

Sylvania and kill that bastard once and for all." The Black Knight knew what the boy's response was going to be before he said it, but he'd never be able to live with himself if he didn't at least try to change his king's mind.

"Thank you, Brenden. I appreciate you trying to protect me, but I have to do this," Dominic replied. "I know you think this is suicide but it's not. I can't explain why, I just know that this is what I must do."

"As you wish," Sir Orgen said reluctantly. "When you are ready, the others are waiting for us at the stables."

When his watch was cleaned and polished, he placed it into a small sack along with an apple, a chunk of bread, a rock and a small vile. Dominic looked up at the giant, threw the sack over his shoulder. "After you," the king instructed.

*   *

The sun was only moments from setting behind the band of riders as they approached the edge of Sylvania. From where he sat atop his horse, Dominic could see only a handful of main buildings in Sylvania. Compared to Munkelstein, Sylvania looked more like a small village than a kingdom.

In the center of the town stood a large stone structure which looked, to Dominic, to be a cross between a cathedral and a prison. The building's main entrance had an ornate façade with a series of marble arches over its grand entranceway. Bookmarking the main doors were windows made of hand-laid pieces of beautiful colored glass, arranged in a haphazard, mosaic style. Above the doorway, carved in stone, read: 'Sylvania Manor'. On the right side of the building, the only side Dominic could see from his vantage point, were what appeared to be several large windows; however, they were currently closed off with metal shutter coverings.

"That's where they'll be," Dominic said, pointing at Sylvania Manor.

Before proceeding to its gates, the riders from Munkelstein sat surveying the kingdom for a few moments. If there were any chance of getting the Bennett family out alive, the knights would need to understand the lay of the land.

Surrounding the main building were five rings of large structures. "Those are most likely supply buildings, guard barracks, a general store and the like," Sir McConnell explained.

Encircling the rings of supply buildings were more than a dozen more rings of smaller structures. Each of these rings consisted of dozens of buildings.

"And those," Sir Jameson said, pointing at the outer rings of buildings, "would be homes."

"Judging by the number of homes I would guess no more than a thousand people live here," said Sir Orgen.

The king studied the layout of the city a moment longer, when he noticed something. "Look," he told the knights, "the buildings and homes are laid out in a series of circles surrounding Sylvania Manor. It's actually an ingenious layout," the boy said. "Reynaldus put Sylvania Manor at the center of his kingdom and then surrounded it with rows of buildings for protection. The more important the structure, the closer to the center it is. And look, see how none of the streets travel straight through to Sylvania Manor. Anyone trying to attack the prince would have to traverse row-after-row of buildings."

Sir Orgen wasn't sure how he had missed it, but the boy was right. "Her roads are more like alleyways than streets," the giant acknowledged. The alleys ran only from building-to-building. The distance the structures were spaced from each other meant each alley was no more than forty or fifty feet in length. "It must be a nuisance to live here," he said. But he had to give it to Reynaldus, any siege would require the attacker to zig-zag his way around structure after structure before reaching the kingdom's center. And to make matters worse, the alleys were only wide enough to allow one horse to pass through at a time. This left the attacker vulnerable with every twist and turn. "It's a death trap," he sighed.

To make matters worse, the lands surrounding the Kingdom of Sylvania were even less welcoming. Sylvanian was bordered on three sides by the Sylvasatanian mountain range. The vast land between the mountains and the town was rocky and had very little foliage. It was certainly not an ideal location to live, but defensively speaking, it was almost perfect. The only way in or out of Sylvania, was the road they were currently on.

"Ingenious indeed," said Sir Jameson. "This changes things, sire. Your plan accounted for a stealthy extraction of your family. I don't see how we maintain stealth now."

Dominic turned to Sir Jameson, then turned back to Sylvania. He hadn't thought of asking Kelin about Sylvania's layout when they met two days ago, and now his plan to rescue his family was thwarted before it began.

The Knights of Munkelstein sat silent on the hill overlooking Sylvania as the last rays of sunlight disappeared behind them. Sir Orgen studied King Dominic, who was lost in thought. The giant could feel his king's pain. "We can still head back, sire. I don't think we've been spotted yet," Brenden suggested.

The Black Knight's plea snapped Dominic out of his stupor. He turned to the knights, and one-by-one looked each man in the eye. To James Bastile, it felt more like their king was peering into their souls.

"The past five days have been emotionally draining, as I am sure you can all imagine," Dominic began. "For twelve long years, you have all trusted that I would return to Munkelstein; although, I am certain not one of you could have imagined my return would be so...strange. You have been a more loyal group of men than any king deserves and, for that, I will be forever in your debts. While I have no right to ask you to blindly trust me once more, that is exactly what I must do." He carefully studied each man. If there was anyone among them not willing to die for their king at that moment, he wasn't showing it.

"Sire, I must admit, before your return, I had lost hope you would ever return to Munkelstein," said Burton Redjon. "And until two days ago I was not certain you had indeed returned. However, I can no longer deny that it is my king I see sitting before me. I have always been your loyal subject and will do whatever you ask of me, my lord." The Red Knight paused, then smiled and added, "Plus, we rode all this way. It would be a shame to have to turn around now."

251

"Thank you, Burton. I do not feel worthy of such loyalty, but I promise you, if we survive this, I will spend the rest of my days earning it," the king replied. "If there is anyone who does not wish to proceed, now is the time to turn back. I promise, I will harbor no resentment," the boy offered.

"What are we waiting for? Let's go get your family," urged Sir Bastile. The rest of the knights shouted their agreement with James; with one exception.

King Dominic saw the reluctance and said to his friend, "Brenden, I understand your concern for my safety and I appreciate it very much. But I need you to trust me one last time. I realize the person you see sitting before you is a young, frail looking boy, and not the warrior you have loved and respected for most of your life. However, answer this question for me: If the man you knew twelve years ago were sitting in front of you now, and not a boy, would you trust him? Would you allow him to lead you on this quest?"

Without hesitation, Sir Orgen replied, "Aye, sire, I would. But that man was a fierce soldier who I have seen best men more than twice his size with little effort. I mean no offense, my lord, it's just…you are not that man, at least not yet. And should you go into Prince Mathias's fortress, I fear you will not return. I would not have that same fear with your previous self," the giant said assertively.

"Your point is well taken, Brenden. Make no mistake, I have no illusions of leaving Sylvania Manor alive. My sole mission tonight is to free an innocent family whose only crime was unknowingly harboring a coward. Were it not for my selfish plan to save myself, the Bennett family would be sitting in the safety of their home as we speak; instead of cowering in the dungeon of a lunatic." The resolve in the king's eyes as he spoke, was enough for Sir Orgen to see that the boy would not be swayed. "One last question, my friend: Would the Dominic Segarius you knew before, not be willing to make this same sacrifice?"

The giant nodded his affirmation to this. "Aye, he would indeed," the Black Knight said reluctantly. He had to hand it to Dominic, the boy was every bit as persuasive, as he ever was as a man.

The Knights of Munkelstein sat overlooking Sylvania as the last bit of sunlight disappeared behind them. Time had run out. It was time for King Dominic to surrender himself to his brother.

"For a boy so young, he should be much more nervous than he appears," Sir Krebow thought.

"Before I surrender myself, there is something you all should know," the king said. "Something that I hope will provide you with a little faith in me." Then King Dominic proceeded to explain to the knights how, for almost fifteen years, he had a man working inside Sylvania. A man so keen, he had positioned himself as one of the prince's most trusted advisors.

Just as Dominic finished explaining his rescue plan, the Sylvania Manor doors opened. Two groups of large men dressed in full battle armor, with large steel blades strapped to their hips, hurried out of the building. The twenty Sylvanian Royal Guardsmen began to weave their way towards the eight riders from Munkelstein.

Sir Orgen and Sir McConnell's hands instinctively went for their swords. "It's ok," Dominic reassured. "Relax they aren't here to fight." He then reached his hand into his satchel, ensuring everything was still there, and waited.

The Royal Guards of Sylvania marched, single file, through the town; navigating the maze of roads and alleys. When they had cleared the last ring of buildings, they assumed a two-abreast marching order. When they were within a few yards of King Dominic and the Knights of Munkelstein, the Royal Guard stopped.

A man from the front line took two steps forward and announced, "His eminence, the great Prince Reynaldus Wilhelm Mathias, has requested the presence of Dominic Philip Segarius to the prince's council room."

"Our KING, is not going anywhere with you, you dumb ox," Sir Krebow shouted. "Tell your mediocre prince, if he wishes to speak to the King of Munkelstein, he had better get off his arse and come out here himself. It's a nice evening. We don't mind waiting."

"We have our orders. Dominic Segarius is to come with us," the head of the Royal Guard shouted back. "Prince Mathias has requested only Dominic's presence, the rest of you can leave or stay here if it suits you. The prince does not care which you choose."

"Now listen to me, you ugly bastard, your prince has already displayed an immense amount of disrespect by not greeting the king himself. If you think for one moment we would...,"

Dominic raised his hand, and Sir Krebow stopped midsentence. The boy let the silence hang in the air for a moment, then said, "Tell Prince Mathias I need proof my family is alive first. Then, and only then, will I surrender to him."

Without hesitation the messenger replied, "Prince Mathias understands your concern and assures you that he is a man of his word; however, if you require proof that the Bennetts are indeed alive, you will have to come with me."

The situation was becoming tense and Dominic became concerned. If his men reacted, and a fight broke out, his family would be killed. "This was not supposed to happen," he thought.

Sir Orgen leaned over to the king and whispered, "Sire, this was not part of the plan. I will not let you go in there alone."

The king turned to his friend and smirked. The gesture was meant to be reassuring, but Sir Orgen felt no such assurance. The only assurance Brenden Orgen felt at that moment, was that his king would never leave Sylvania Manor alive.

"Very well," said the boy as he dismounted his horse. "Best not keep my brother waiting."

18

You Can Run...

As Dominic was following the head of the Sylvanian Royal Guard to meet his destiny, his family was enjoying their first taste of the air outside their prison cell.

Only moments ago, the stranger's voice told the Bennett family that the time for their escape was now. Without hesitation, they stood and readied themselves to move. They quickly made their way towards the rumbling sound coming from across the dungeon and found a newly created opening in the wall. The Bennetts hurried through the opening and found themselves standing in a dimly lit corridor, where they were greeted by a frail looking old man.

"I am Kelin Semtun. King Dominic has sent me to rescue you. Follow me and do not say a word," the stranger said.

"Oh my God! Thank you so much for helping us," Maggie Bennett cried as she wrapped her arms around their savior.

"Shhhhh! Ma'am if you wish to live through this you will keep your mouth shut and do exactly as I say. Do you all understand my words?" the man scowled. Maggie immediately melted away from Kelin. The stranger seemed old and frail, but his voice was strong and heartless. None of the Bennetts said a word, however, even in the poorly lit corridor, Kelin could see the slumped expressions and nodding heads of their acknowledgement. "Good. There will be ample time for hugs and 'thank-yous' once you are free of this place. Now, follow me. And stay close."

The four shadowy figures worked their way through a vast network of corridors. Randy tried to keep track of every turn, in case they were found out and had to run. But they had made too many quick turns, and he soon lost track. "For an old man, he is surprisingly agile," Randy thought. The man who called himself Kelin was surefooted and walked as quickly as any speed walker. Randy had to almost run to keep pace with the old man.

After a few minutes of meandering through the maze, the fugitives made one final sharp right turn; which brought them to a long narrow corridor. The escapees sprinted down the hallway for a few hundred feet, where they were finally greeted by a dead end.

Kelin and the Bennett family were standing in a narrow corridor, surrounded on three sides by walls made of large, oddly shaped stones. There were no doors or windows. No stairs or ladders. The only way forward was behind them.

"Dead end," Randy said. He was about to ask the old man if he knew where he was going when they heard voices coming from somewhere behind them. "Oh man, we're screwed. Now what?" Randy asked in a panicked voice.

The old man shot Randy a look which said both: 'Quiet you idiot' and 'Oh Ye of little faith'. Kelin surveyed the hallway behind them and, when he was certain they were not being followed, he stepped to the right side of the wall and ran his hands across the smooth stone surface until he found what he was looking for. He slipped his fingers into two shallow handholds and without hesitation, slid the wall open.

"That wall must weigh more than a ton," Randy thought. Before he could give it any other consideration, he was being shoved through the fresh opening in the wall.

"Move. Unless you'd rather stay here with them?" the old man offered, motioning to the sound of soldiers in the distance behind them.

They now found themselves in a dark vestibule, at the base of a steep, brick stairway.

"Hurry, up the stairs," the frail voice directed behind them.

As the Bennett family ascended the stairs, the old man slid the wall back into its original position, making certain it was closed securely. Attached to the inside of the wall, near its base, were three large metal bolts; which appeared to Rose to be locks. Kelin slid the large bolts into place in the floor then headed up the stairway after the Bennetts.

"We're safe. For now," the old man said.

They were about halfway up the stairway when Randy looked back and was shocked to see old Kelin Semtun sprinting up the steps behind them. The man moved with the grace of a mountain goat, leaping from crag-to-crag. Kelin quickly passed the Bennett family; arriving at the top first. It appeared to Randy that Kelin wasn't winded in the slightest.

The fugitives were perched on a small stoop, surrounded by three brick walls. "Dead end," Randy thought again, but dare not say.

"Is everyone alright?" the old man asked. "Let us a rest a moment so you may catch your breath."

He couldn't see Kelin, however, Randy couldn't help thinking the old man was directing this at him.

"No, I think we're good. How did you...I mean you move so fast," Randy stuttered.

Without acknowledging Randy, Kelin replied, "That was the easy part. Once we step through this wall there is no going back." Touching the false wall in front of them, he continued, "Beyond this lies the main hallway, which leads directly to the front foyer and, beyond it, your freedom. No matter what, or who, you see, do not stop and do not speak. Is that understood?" Kelin asked with an urgency which told the Bennett family the situation was dire.

"Yes, we understand," Randy replied. "Is Dominic here? Where are we meeting him?"

"Sir, as a favor to your son, I have agreed to risk my life to rescue your family from this place. If you do not want my help, you are certainly welcome to continue on without me. However, if you wish to live, do yourself a favor, heed my words: no matter what, or who, you see, do not stop and do not speak. Tell me you understand," Kelin chastised.

Randy could sense the old man's agitation, and while he appreciated the man's help, he needed to know that his son was safe.

"I understand Mr. Kelin," Randy whispered. "Believe me, I want my family out of this hell more than you can know. But

Dominic is part of our family as well. I will not leave my son behind. I have to know he's safe and that he is coming with us."

Kelin could see that the man he had just rescued from certain death, had no intention of leaving without his son. This left him with two options: tell the Bennetts the truth, Dominic was sacrificing himself for them, or, lie and tell them the boy they called 'son' would be meeting them outside. If it were up to Kelin, he would always prefer the truth. But Kelin Semtun wasn't a weak, frightened man; unlike the family he saw standing before him. As he contemplated this, the decision made itself.

"Prince Mathias, your brother has arrived!" shouted a voice from the other side of the wall.

"Where is my dear Dominic?" an eerily familiar voice replied.

Maggie felt Rose's fingers dig into her arm.

"Mom, that's the crazy old man," Rose whispered almost inaudibly.

Kelin shot her a quick, "Shhh," and the frightened girl buried her face in her mother's shoulder.

Randy pushed gently on the wall in front of them. "It must be another secret exit," he thought. Kelin quickly grabbed Randy by the wrist and wrenched sideways. When he was certain the man had gotten the message, the spy of Munkelstein released him. Embarrassed, Randy pulled his arm back and gently rubbed his wrist. Kelin then put his index finger to his lips; the universal sign for "Shhh", placed his ear to the wall, and listened.

"Ahhh, there he is, my baby brother. My, my time sure has been good to you, has it not?" cackled the voice beyond the wall. "Bring him to me. We have much to discuss."

19

Family Reunion

After navigating the maze of buildings, Dominic at last found himself standing in the large marble foyer of Sylvania Manor. He surveyed his new surroundings, looking for any strategic advantage he could find. The foyer itself was unimpressive. Other than a few candelabras placed haphazardly around the entrance and hallways, there was nothing of importance that he could see. In fact, it seemed to Dominic the entire building was desolate.

From where he stood, there were three hallways leading from the foyer and into the manor. Directly in front of the boy, was a long hallway which appeared to run the entire length of the building. The two other hallways, one immediately to his left and the other to his right, were much shorter. The hallway to his left was only a few steps long and turned sharply right. The hallway on his right was the same length but turned left. He couldn't tell where these two hallways lead so Dominic focused on the long hall directly in front of him.

The main hall had six doorways; three on each side. "Or are there seven," he thought. Just passed the first door to his left, Dominic spotted a slight recess in the wall. It was subtle, "Almost invisible," he thought. To Dominic the recess appeared to be the same shape and size as the rest of the doorways in this hallway. "Interesting," he thought.

"Prince Mathias, your brother has arrived!" shouted the man King Dominic had followed from the Sylvania main gates.

A moment later, a door opened at the far end of the hallway and a voice shouted, "Where is my dear Dominic?" An old man came shuffling through the doorway and into the hall. "Ahhh, there he is, my baby brother. My, my time sure has been good to you, has it not?" cackled Reynaldus. The prince motioned to his guard, "Bring him to me. We have much to discuss."

The guard proceeded down the hallway, "Follow me," he ordered Dominic. The boy followed reluctantly.

When they were a few steps past the recessed area in the wall, Dominic stopped. "This is it," he thought. He wasn't sure why, but he '*knew*' this was the spot. "I'm not going any further until I've seen my family," Dominic said defiantly. "We had a deal, my life for theirs."

"Oh, my dear boy, you are certainly in no position to make demands. Or do you forget where you are?" Reynaldus sneered.

"Let them go, NOW!" the boy screamed. "They're innocent. They haven't done anything to you. Let them go and I'll come quietly. Otherwise, I'm not taking another step." With this, Dominic sat down on the floor, crossed his legs and slung his bag across his lap. If he was going any further, "They'll have to drag me," he thought.

"Still the same stubborn boy I see. Very well," Reynaldus said, motioning to his guard. "Samuel, go and tell Gregor to fetch the Bennett family."

Samuel turned to leave and for the first time since he left for Sylvania, King Dominic was starting to doubt his plan; but before Samuel had taken his first step, a man came running down the hall behind them shouting, "My lord, they're gone! We've looked everywhere, but, they seem to have…vanished."

"What do you mean they've vanished, Gregor?" asked a visibly perturbed Reynaldus. "I sent you to retrieve the Bennett family an hour ago. Why is this the first I'm hearing of this? Where are they?!" he demanded. Dominic felt the tension in the hallway rise. "Gregor, unless you wish to have your worthless head removed, I suggest you start talking," the prince said, no longer smiling.

Then Dominic noticed something odd. Funny how he hadn't seen it until now. It was clearly there from the moment Reynaldus stepped into the hallway. Gripped in the prince's right hand was the staff of Dyog Ronndewo; and the familiar cerulean blue crystal, mounted atop it, was glowing. The boy sat, mesmerized by the light's beautiful blue glow; watching as it grew in intensity. The light quickly became so bright, the boy had to shield his eyes from it. "Whatever is about to happen, will not be good, for anyone," the boy thought.

"Sire, we've been scouring the catacombs for the past hour and can find no sign of the Bennett family," Gregor explained. "They appeared to have escap...."

BOOOOOM.

Before Gregor could finish his sentence, a thunderclap erupted and a bright blue bolt of energy shot from the staff. The bolt hit Gregor in the chest with such force, his body was thrown forty feet across the foyer and smashed the man into the Sylvania Manor's large wooden entry doors.

The blast was loud and bright, and disoriented Dominic. He could hear nothing but a loud ringing in his ears and his field of vision was filled with spots of light. The boy closed his eyes and rubbed them hard, trying to clear away the spots which had suddenly clouded his vision. When he opened his eyes again, Prince Mathias was standing only a few feet from him, smiling the most wicked smile.

"Do you see what happens to those who disappoint me, brother?" the prince asked calmly.

Reynaldus stepped forward and grabbed Dominic by the face, turning the boy's head to show him his handy work. Behind them, in a heap, lie Gregor. His shirt had been burned from his body and smoke rose from where Gregor's chest should have been. Dominic quickly realized he could see straight through the dead man's torso.

Fear set in and Dominic began to shake. "What have I done?" he thought.

"It appears we have a traitor in our midst," said Reynaldus. "Samuel, summon the council to the meeting room at once. If anyone refuses, or resists in any way, you have my authority to remove their livers and feed it to their children. Do I make myself clear?" the prince asked his guard, his eyes still locked on Dominic.

"Aye, sire," Samuel replied. He turned to leave then looked back at the prince and asked, "What about him? Shall I have Barnard come keep an eye on him until I return?"

Family Reunion

"No, I think we'll be ok here. Won't we brother?" Reynaldus said rhetorically. Dominic, who was still in a state of shock, did not seem to hear the prince. "See, I'll be fine." Samuel bowed to the prince and headed for the door. "One last thing, Samuel," the prince shouted, "dispatch the rest of the Royal Guard to search for the Bennett family immediately. They are not to step one foot off Sylvanian soil. Do you understand me?" As the prince spoke, the crystal began to glow once more.

20

You Can Run...
(Part 2)

Kelin strained to hear the commotion in the hallway beyond them. There had been an explosion and he was trying desperately to understand what had happened. "Aye sire," a voice said. "What about him? Shall I have Barnard come keep an eye on him until I return?"

The spy had been listening intently and heard what the prince had done. He turned to the Bennetts and for the first time since they met, Randy saw what looked to be fear in the man's eyes.

"Be ready," Kelin said. "We'll only have one opportunity."

Kelin looked to Rose, who was cowering behind her mother. The spy knew how hard this must be for her, but he needed the girl to be strong if they had any chance of making it out of Sylvania Manor alive. The old man stepped to Rose and put his hand on the girls' shoulder.

"I know this is hard for you and I know how scared you must be; but I need you to trust me. Can you do that for me?"

Rose gave a slight nod of her head. As frightened as she was, she wanted nothing more than to be gone from this evil place.

"When it's time to move you must do as I say. If we stay here, they will find us and I promise you, you don't want that." Kelin gave Rose a second to accept what he had told her then asked, "Can you run, or would you like me to carry you?"

Sniff, sniff. "I can run," Rose replied.

"Then, let us run," Kelin said with a smile.

21

The Battle on the Hill

The seven Knights of Munkelstein remained upon their horses, watching as their king started towards Sylvania Manor without them. Nineteen Sylvanian guardsman stayed behind to watch over the intruders from Munkelstein.

Years later, it would be argued who was the first to show steel; although Sir Bastile still swears it happened like this:

"So, tell me friend, are all the citizens of this town as ugly as you?" Sir McConnell politely asked the guard closest to him.

"Stephen, show some respect. These Men are our hosts and we should be polite," said Sir Jameson. "You would not be so rude if you saw their women. I've seen more attractive sows," the Gold Knight added.

The Battle on the Hill

"Thomas, do you suppose Prince Mathias sent these men here to babysit us, or to clean our boots?" asked Sir Krebow.

Sir Jameson asked the guard closest him, "Well boy, which is it? Are you here to babysit or clean our boots?"

The guard said nothing, but the knights could see their insults were having an effect on the Sylvanian Royal Guardsmen. Sir Moren climbed from his horse and started towards the guards in the front row, being sure to step directly into a fresh pile of equine dung. In unison, the nineteen guardsmen reached for their swords.

"Whoa, boys I do not want to start any trouble. After all, we're clearly outnumbered, more than two-to-one, if my math is correct," Elijah Moren said. When he was no more than a step or two from the Sylvanians, the Blue Knight stopped and addressed the green-eyed man closest him. "Here you are, boy," he said, lifting his manure covered boot, "get to it. These are my good boots and I want them spit shined before King Dominic returns."

The green-eyed Sylvanian had had enough of the insults and began to draw his sword. Before he had pulled the blade more than a few inches from its scabbard, the Elijah Moren withdrew a dagger from his belt, lunged forward and drove it into the man's throat. The movement was so fast and fluid, the knight had the blade tucked back into his belt before the other Sylvanian Royal Guardsmen could comprehend what they had just witnessed. It wasn't until the perforated Sylvanian was lying on the ground, clutching his neck, that any of his countrymen reacted; and by the time they did, the Knights of Munkelstein were already upon them.

Sir Orgen, who was in a full sprint towards the Sylvanians, pulled his dagger and hurled it at his nearest enemy, striking the man between the eyes. Without breaking stride, the Black Knight pulled his blade from the man's face, and with dagger once again in hand, he pirouetted, slicing the throat of the guardsman unlucky enough to be closest to him. While the giant was dicing his way through the enemy, Sir James Bastile found himself surrounded by three Sylvanians.

It was well known, in many of the kingdoms, that James Bastile was one of the deadliest men alive with a blade. Had the three Sylvanian guardsmen who chose to surround him that night, realized who they were up against, they may have reconsidered their attack; however, in battle there is rarely time for second guessing. The man closest to the green knight, a strong baby-faced man, attempted to overpower James with a violent chop of his sword. Sir Bastile easily blocked the initial attack and, as the Sylvanian was drawing his sword back for second attempt, James Bastile quickly brought his sword up through the man's lower jaw and skewered his brain stem. Baby-face was dead before his body hit the Sylvanian soil.

Sir Bastile immediately turned his focus towards his next two foes, a short-pig faced man and a dark complexioned bald man. The soldiers were still in awe of how fast Sir Bastile moved and quickly regretted their decision to challenge this man; but their regret would be short lived. As if shackled together, the two men attempted to fight Sir Bastile side-by-side. Had they flanked the Munkelstein knight, they may have lived a few moments longer. The Green Knight feigned a forward thrust to his left, which caused both opponents to react. The pig-faced man, to Sir Bastile's right, reacted to the knight's bluff and inadvertently drove his sword into his bald partner's wrist; slicing through its tendons and causing the man to drop his blade. Realizing what he had just done, pig-face reacted to his brother's howl of pain, rather than to Sir Bastile's blade, and was quickly stabbed through the heart. The bald soldier desperately grasped for his sword with his good hand and never saw the knight's blade as it came down and punctured the Sylvanian's lungs.

As James Bastile was finishing off the three Sylvanians, Sir Michael Krebow spotted two Royal Guardsmen running from the battle, towards the outer most ring of buildings. He quickly mounted his steed, Sapphire, and, as if reading the White Knight's mind, the horse bolted after the men. The Sylvanians had a significant head start on the horse, but Sapphire was fast and determined. When the stallion had drawn to within a few yards of the fleeing soldiers, Sir Krebow pulled his dagger and threw it at the man to his right. The blade struck the Sylvanian between his shoulder blades, burying itself to the hilt. The man fell forward, dead.

The second Sylvanian suddenly broke hard to his left, attempting to outmaneuver his pursuers, but Sapphire seemed to want this man even more than Sir Krebow. At full gallop, the horse instinctively turned to follow the fleeing guardsman; it took Sapphire only a few seconds to catch up to the man. When the horse sprinted past him, the Sylvanian thought he had actually made it to safety. Then, just as he had this thought, the Sylvanian's world began to spin, as if he were rolling down a hill, and then, everything went black. Michael Krebow's blade was so sharp, it was said the knight often shaved with it. The sharpness of his blade, coupled with the speed at which Sapphire was galloping as they passed the Royal Guardsman, meant the Sylvanian never felt the blade strike his neck and sever his head.

The Battle on the Hill

Without breaking stride, Sapphire turned back to the battleground. By the time Sir Krebow had regrouped with his countrymen, the battle was nearly over. Only two of the Sylvanian Royal Guard remained, and they had been disarmed.

"Please, sir, I have a family. Spare me, please. I will do whatever you ask," begged the smaller of the two men. He looked to be no more than twenty-years old and certainly had not seen battle before.

"And you?" Sir Elijah Moren asked the other prisoner. "Will you do anything for us as well, or do you wish to die here tonight?" Sir Elijah, as he preferred to be called, wore the scowl of a man not to be trifled with.

"I am no coward," the larger, red haired soldier replied. "I have more respect for myself and my country than this coward. Do what you will with me." Sir Elijah could see in this man's eyes that he was not afraid to die. "This is quite the dilemma," the Blue Knight said. "After all, we don't need them both, do we Sir McConnell?"

"We most certainly do not," Stephen replied. "Sir Orgen, which man do you feel has earned the right to die by Sir Elijah's blade?" the Grey Knight asked the giant.

Brenden Orgen stepped in front of the two kneeling prisoners and drew his sword. The smaller prisoner's eyes grew wide at the sight of the giant standing before him, yielding the razor-sharp piece of steel.

"Please, please, please. Oh god please, please, please," the boy whimpered.

"Your god is not here with you tonight, my boy. Only the Knights of Munkelstein and we are not so merciful," Sir Orgen said coldly. "You, brave soldier of Sylvania," the Black Knight said as he raised his sword to the throat of the defiant prisoner. "I respect your courage. To kneel in the face of death and smile, is most noble. Therefore, I will give you the first opportunity to answer our questions. But know this, I never ask twice so answer me truthful and you may very well sleep in your own bed tonight."

"Go to hell you bastard. I will tell you nothing," the red-headed Sylvanian spat. Brenden had to admit, this man was very brave. Or very, very stupid.

The giant kept his sword to the soldier's throat, but turned his gaze to the man's frightened friend. The smaller man was now visibly shaking. He met the giant's gaze and saw that his captor was smiling at him. Without breaking eye contact, Sir Orgen thrust his sword through the throat of the red-headed prisoner. He withdrew his blade from the guardsman's neck and the man fell dead. The Black Knight sheathed his sword

and knelt in front of the last of the nineteen Sylvanian
Guardsmen sent to watch over the Knights of Munkelstein
that night.

"Son, I do not wish to kill you and I have a feeling you do
not wish to die," Sir Orgen said, with what sounded to Sir
Redjon to be compassion. "I will offer you the same deal I
offered your dead friend here," the giant said, motioning to the
dead man. "Answer our questions and I swear on my life, and
the lives of my brothers, you will leave here unharmed."

"Yes, please, anything. I will tell you anything," the
frightened man begged.

"First, tell me your name," Brenden asked.

"My, n-n-n-name is Franklin Gregory sir," the soldier
stuttered.

"Pleasure to meet you Franklin Gregory. I am Sir Brenden
Orgen and these, as I am sure you undoubtedly have guessed,
are the brave knights of Munkelstein." The tone and tempo of
Sir Orgen's voice had a calming effect on Franklin and the boy
gave a weak grin. "There, that's better," he continued.
"Franklin, I assure you, we have no desire to stay here any
longer than we have to. The faster you help us, the quicker we
can leave this wretched place. Will you help us Franklin?" the
giant asked.

"Yes, Sir Brenden. I will do whatever you ask."

Burton Redjon was watching the boy closely to see if this was a game, or if he was being sincere. The prisoner had just watched eighteen of his brothers slaughtered in front of him, so fearing for his life was a natural response. But, in Sir Redjon's opinion, there was something off with this boy.

"Good, that's good Franklin. So, here's the deal: if I think you are lying to me, or playing tricks, or if you are anything other than truthful with me, I will not show you the same mercy as we showed your friends here," Sir Orgen said. "Do we have a deal?"

"Yes, yes. Deal. Whatever you want. Just, please, spare me. For my son's sake," Franklin begged.

"Ok then, Franklin, first question: is the Bennett family still alive?" Sir Orgen asked.

"Sir? The Bennett family? I don't know anyone named Bennett," Franklin replied.

"Come now Franklin. What did I just tell you? Honesty is your only path to tomorrow," the giant said coldly as he reached for his sword.

"NO! I swear I don't know who that is. I've never heard of the Bennett family. PLEASE! I'm telling you true, I swear," Franklin said, on the verge of tears.

The Black Knight gave a look to Sir Jameson which said, "What do you think? Is he telling the truth?" Sir Jameson replied with a look which said, "I have no idea."

"Calm down Franklin, calm down. I believe you. Here's a question I am certain you know the answer to: How many more men does the prince have in that main building there?" Sir Orgen asked, pointing to Sylvania Manor.

"In Sylvania Manor? Ummm, I believe there are a total of fifty men in the Royal Guard and well, not including us," Franklin said motioning his eyes around the field of carnage, "that would leave about thirty-two. But I don't know if they are all in the manor. Some may be in the armory or supply buildings. There is no way for me to know for sure."

Sir Orgen kept his eyes locked on Franklin, looking for any sign the boy was lying. "The men within Sylvania Manor, where would they be stationed?" he asked.

"I can't say for sure," the boy replied. "There are two hallways off the main foyer which lead to the barracks and other living areas for the men. But there are also prison cells below ground so some of them could be down there. I've never seen the cells myself but I have heard that the prince almost always has prisoners down there. Apparently, the key to his defeating King Dominic is being kept in one of the cells," Franklin explained.

Sir Orgen and Sir Jameson exchanged a glance which said, "That's where the Bennetts will be."

"Last question Franklin: are there any traps between here and Sylvania Manor? That's quite the maze of roads and buildings you have there. Wouldn't want to come across any more of the ferocious Royal Guard, now would we?" Sir Orgen asked.

All eyes were now on the boy. If Franklin showed any sign he was not being fully truthful, it wouldn't be a matter of if he would die, it would only be a matter of which knight killed him first.

"I didn't know you were here until we marched out to meet you a short while ago," pleaded Franklin. "And as far as traps being set for you in the city, I do not know what Prince Mathias has planned, I swear," the boy insisted.

Brenden studied Franklin for a moment. He believed the boy had been honest with him but his instincts told the giant that this boy knew more than he was saying. "I wish I could believe you Franklin, but you haven't given me anything of substance." The Black Knight stood and drew his sword. "Goodbye, Franklin," he said.

"Wait…. wait!" Franklin shouted. "There's more, the prince, he lied about…*ugh*"

The giant heard the soft, 'whoosh', sound of something

whizzing past his head. An instant later a trademark eight-inch silver dagger, carried by all Munkelstein Knights, was protruding from the boy's chest. Franklin clutched at the knife, eyes pleading to Sir Orgen for help, and collapsed to the ground. The last of the nineteen.

A furious Sir Orgen spun around to see which of his brothers had wielded the death blow on the boy. "Whoever did this is going to pay," he shouted. "He was just about to give us something we could actually use."

"The boy was playing you for a fool, Brenden" said Burton Redjon casually, as he turned from the giant and started back to his horse, Titian.

"He was about to tell us something about Prince Mathias's plan you fool! He could have helped us maneuver our way through the town! I assured him he would leave here unharmed!" the giant shouted. Sir Orgen did not much care for Burton Redjon, or his cavalier attitude towards his king and kingdom. They had come to blows on a few occasions but Sir Orgen never doubted the Red Knight's loyalty to Munkelstein or his brother's. "This is unacceptable Burton," he shouted. "You will pay for this, you traitorous bastard."

The Red Knight stopped abruptly and turned to face his brother. He had had enough of the giant and his condescension towards him and the rest of the Knights of Munkelstein. "Traitor?" Burton asked. "Are you so blind and arrogant that you do not see what is plainly in front of you? The boy was playing you," the Red Knight said as he placed his hand on his sword. After a moment's reflection, Burton turned and resumed his march towards Titian, but was halted by the unmistakable sound of a sword being drawn. He quickly unsheathed his own blade and spun on his heels, and growled, "I have waited a long time for this." When the Red Knight turned back, he expected to see the giant standing at the ready, sword in hand, but what he saw surprised him.

"Brenden, do not even think about it," yelled Thomas Jameson, sword in hand. "Now is not the time. Our king needs us and yet you two bicker like school children."

The Black Knight had closed half the distance to, a completely unaware, Sir Redjon when Thomas Jameson intervened. For such a large man, the giant moved with the quiet stealth of a large predator.

"There was something off about this boy, Brenden. I saw it as well," continued the Gold Knight. "While I do not condone Burton's methods, I will defend his actions with my life. To do otherwise, would not be in the best interests of King Dominic, or Munkelstein." The Gold Knight paused to allow both men to calm down and reevaluate their next decision.

Brenden stood stoic for a moment, chest heaving with anger, glowering at Burton Redjon. The giant looked down at Thomas Jameson, who had unflinchingly pulled his sword in defense of Sir Redjon, and then surveyed the battlefield. The other knights looked concerned, but seemed willing to let the two adversaries hash things out themselves.

After another few moments, Sir Orgen's posture relaxed. "You're not worth it," he said to Burton.

"Alright then. If you ladies are finished, we have work to do," joked James Bastile.

"Let's get moving. Our king needs us," ordered Sir Jameson.

As the knights of Munkelstein hurried toward Sylvania Manor, Thomas could see the anger still residing in Brenden's eyes. Perhaps Franklin reminded him of the young King Dominic, or maybe the giant didn't like to be made a fool. Whichever it was, it would have to wait until the king was safe.

"Come, brother. You'll feel better when that bastard Reynaldus is dead once and for all," Sir Jameson said, but the giant did not seem to hear.

22

...But You Can't Hide

What's the matter Dominic? You're awfully quiet. Rat got your tongue?" Prince Mathias asked, grinning ear-to-ear.

He had been waiting for this moment for most of his life and it was finally here. Reynaldus wanted nothing more than to kill this pest who shared the same womb as he; but not before he made his brother suffer.

"Please, don't be frightened brother, my men will find your 'family'. And when they do, I have a treat in store for you all. First, I am going to peel the skin from dear old Randy's bones and wear him like a cloak. Mother Maggie will suffer a much less painful fate when she is fed to my dogs. Don't worry, they haven't eaten in days so it should be fairly quick. And finally," the prince paused, savoring the moment, "the brilliant little

Rose, her I will save for last. I have a special surprise for your big sister. Should I tell you? No, I can't. After all it is a surprise, wouldn't want to ruin it. Oh, but I'm just bursting to tell you. What do you think, do you want to know? Of course, you don't. Everyone loves a good surprise."

Dominic was just coming out of his fog; his hearing had returned, although there was still a slight ringing. The boy heard Reynaldus saying something about dogs, which he didn't quite understand. But then the old man, his brother, started to talk about hurting his sister, Rose. A moment earlier, King Dominic was frightened and disoriented, now, at the sound of his sister's name, his nerves steeled and fright was replaced with anger.

"Do not touch them. Don't you lay a hand on my family or you will never live to regret it," King Dominic demanded.

For the first time in more than a decade, Prince Reynaldus saw the brother he once knew. Until now, he had seen only a frail looking boy, but the power and resolve Dominic now displayed, was that of a King.

"Or what, brother? How will you kill me? You are alone here and your friends, rescuers, whatever you choose to call them, are most certainly dead by now. It's just you and I, and if I wanted, I could end your life in an instant. Just ask poor

Gregor there. Now, where was I? Oh yes, Rose. I have something special planned for Rose."

*   *

"He's sent his guards out to look for you," Kelin whispered, his ear still placed firmly on the false wall. The spy listened as the prince toyed with Dominic. Boasting about how he was going to torture the Bennett family.

Randy had been straining to listen to what was being said, but, as the stairway was narrow, there was room for only one to listen at the wall. However, when he saw Kelin's expression suddenly change from deep thought to repulsion, Randy asked, "What are they saying Kelin?" The old man said nothing as he continued to listen to the commotion beyond the wall. "Tell me," Randy demanded. He knew whatever Kelin had just heard, it was not good. Kelin did not acknowledge him.

In the past five days, Randy Bennett had been through hell and was done waiting for answers. He shoved his way next to Kelin and pressed his ear against the cold wall.

"I have something special planned for Rose Bennett, the voice bragged. "Rosey, as her daddy calls her, will be suspended from the ceiling by her feet. Her arms will be tied to ropes and shackled to the floor. Then, at my command, my men will slowly hoist young Rose up, stretching her arms. They will continue to pull as the girl's tendons tear and her bones are pulled from their sockets. They will continue until her flesh tears and her little arms are ripped from her body," Reynaldus said coldly. "Do you know what the best part is, brother? The best part is that you will have a front row seat. You will beg me to show her mercy and you will beg me for my forgiveness and you will beg me to kill her and end her suffering. And only when I am certain you have suffered as I have suffered, your majesty, will I show you how merciful I can be. Do you understand me, BROTHER?!"

He could not believe what he was hearing. The man who had been holding him captive was threatening to do despicable things to his little girl.

"And while you watch your family die before you, remember it was you who killed them. Do you hear me, boy? It is you who has brought this on poor Rose, not me!"

Randy had heard enough. No one was going to threaten the lives of his family as long as he still had breath in his lungs. Without realizing what he was doing, Randy reacted.

"AHHHHH!" There was a sudden explosion of dust and debris in the hallway as Randy Bennett came bursting through the wall behind Dominic.

The elder Bennett was now standing in a well-lit hallway. In front of him were his son and the oldest man Randy had ever seen.

"Dominic, are you ok buddy?" he asked. Randy had no idea what was happening in the hallway in front of him, but there was no time to try and figure it out. The madman was threatening to savagely torture his little girl and he knew this would be his only chance to get his family out of this place. "Come with me D, we're going home. Hurry Kelin, get the girls out of here. NOW!" Randy ordered.

Kelin stepped through the wall first, pulling the girls behind him. He turned right and sprinted for the exit. Prince Mathias would have dispatched them all in an instance had he not been taken aback by what he was seeing.

"Seamus? Is that you? After all I have done for you," the prince said as the crystal started to glow a brilliant blue, something Randy had seen once before.

"Girls, RUN!" Randy screamed.

The happiness Reynaldus felt only a moment earlier, had vanished. "How dare they," he thought as he raised his staff above his head then drove it into the floor. He was going to kill the traitor calling himself 'Seamus Breitling'. But Prince Mathias underestimated a father's love and watched as Randy stepped in front of the blast. The bolt of blue light hit Randy in the shoulder, knocking him off his feet and slammed him into a nearby wall.

Maggie had just reached the Sylvania Manor exit when she heard the explosion. She turned to see her beloved lying in the hallway, blood rushing from his head. In a panic, Maggie broke free of Kelin's grip and ran to Randy's side.

Rose turned and sprinted to her father, crying, "Nooooo. Daddy, please noooooo!"

Randy lie on the floor, motionless, smoke rising from his shirt. Maggie pulled her husband to her and screamed, "NOOOOOOOO! God, no, please. Randy, you're ok baby, you're ok. Please, Randy, wake up honey. We need to go now, Randy. Wake up!" But deep down, Maggie knew her husband was gone.

The blast from the crystal had struck Randy in his shoulder, shattering bone and burning through his flesh. The bolt of electricity did not hit Randy's vital organs. However, unfortunately, for the Bennett family, the impact from the shot of light, threw Randy into the wall headfirst, breaking his neck.

"Daddy. Wake up daddy, please, wake up," Rose begged, sobbing uncontrollably. Just minutes ago, her dad was holding her tight, telling her everything would be alright. Now, he lay lifeless in front of her. Rose let out a howl of pain and anger, "NOOOOOOOOOOO!"

It was all unraveling. When he left Munkelstein to rescue his family, Dominic was convinced his plan would work. Now, as he sat there in the hallway, he realized he had been naïve. The boy didn't know how his former self would have handled this rescue mission, only that he had felt confident his plan was the best course of action to save his family. Now, as he sat there, the boy knew his actions had killed them all.

The king remained seated in the center of the hallway, face-to-face with evil. Every piece of the boy wanted to lunge at the crazy man and avenge his father's death. But Dominic was no longer the strong, fearless warrior he had been twelve years ago. Besides, how could he have known how truly powerful Reynaldus had become? That certainly wasn't part of the plan.

His father was lying dead behind him, yet Dominic remained seated. He desperately wanted to run to his dad's side and hug him. He wanted to comfort Rose and tell her it would be alright. To kiss his mother and say, "I'm sorry". But the boy knew there was nothing he could do to bring back the man who raised and protected him for the past twelve years, and it broke his heart. Dominic would have given anything at that moment to hear his father's voice again. To tell his dad how much he loved him and that he was sorry; so, so sorry.

A Dish Best Served Cold

Because Dominic Segarius wasn't strong enough to take care of Reynaldus years ago, Dominic Bennett's father was now dead. It was all his fault and all the King of Munkelstein could do was sit.

"Maggie, Rose, come with me, please, I beg you," Kelin urged the Bennett girls. He knew his attempts were futile, but he had to try.

"Look what you made me do, Seamus," Reynaldus said disgustedly. "If that is your name. You made me kill poor Randy. It should have been you, you, you snake. Now, it appears you are going to make me kill poor Maggie as well. Such a shame too, my dogs are so hungry. Oh well, I guess they'll just have to settle for a cold meal," the prince said as he raised the staff above his head.

"Wait!" King Dominic yelled. He plunged his hand into his bag and pulled out the vial. "If you harm one more fiber of my family, I swear, I will drink this," he said, holding the small bottle to his mouth.

"So? Drink up," the prince replied. He paused for a moment then looked at the boy and said, "Looks like it's last call for your dear mother as well." The crystal began to glow its brilliant cerulean hue.

"Don't you recognize its beautiful golden color brother?"

King Dominic urged, as he held up the vial. "It's the nectar of the Celavian Root." Reynaldus stopped at this, and lowered the staff. "You know the Celavian Root, don't you brother? After all, you used it to kill our father, King Roland. Did you not?"

23

A Dish Best Served Cold

The Knights of Munkelstein had just cleared the last alleyway, and were approaching the steps to Sylvania Manor, when they heard the screaming.

"James, Michael, Elijah and Thomas, stay here and keep watch. Cry out if you need help," Sir McConnell directed, giving orders like a seasoned general. "Burton and Brenden, follow me."

Sir Redjon had been wrong about Franklin. There had been no traps set for the Knights of Munkelstein in the Sylvanian alleyways. A fact which was not lost on the Black Knight. "What is Burton hiding?" he thought as he sprinted up the marble steps towards the screaming voices.

The Red Knight threw his shoulder into the manor doors, but they wouldn't budge. "There's something in the way," he said.

Sir Orgen took three huge steps backward, then ran full

speed into the heavy doors; the impact from his large frame threw the doors open with a crash.

On the floor in front of them, lie the corpse of a man whose chest cavity appeared to have been burned out. The body was lying on its back, staring up at the ceiling, a hole in his chest large enough to fit a small pumpkin. Further down the main hall was an even stranger scene.

Standing nearest the foyer entrance was a man who only Sir Orgen had ever met. A man named Seamus. "This was the man King Dominic had told the knights was his 'man on the inside'," the giant thought. Huddled in the hall, just beyond Seamus, was the source of the screaming. Lying over a second lifeless body were two women dressed in the strangest outfits Brenden had ever seen. "That must be the king's family," the Black Knight muttered. The women were sobbing and clutching the dead man tightly.

A few feet passed the women, sat King Dominic. He was seated in the middle of the hallway, holding something in his hand and yelling at the old man standing in front of him.

"REYNALDUS! Back away from our king at once," shouted Sir McConnell.

Prince Reynaldus looked up to see three large men standing in his home. They were not from his Royal Guard.

"Sire, are you hurt?" Sir Orgen asked.

"I'm fine, Brenden. My brother and I are just working out the details of my surrender," the king replied to his friend. "Reynaldus, I will make you one final offer: let my family, and my men, go at once and I will surrender myself to you, without a fight," King Dominic offered.

"So, now my baby brother thinks *he's* the one making the demands? Do you really think this is a negotiation boy?" the prince asked. "What are you going to do, kill yourself? Go ahead, drink it. You're dead already."

"It occurred to me that if you simply wanted me dead, you would have killed me when you first found me in Clarkston," the king replied. "I saw you, standing there at the edge of Eden, watching me like some creepy pedophile. No, you want me to suffer first, and you want the satisfaction of taking my life yourself." King Dominic could see that he had struck a nerve with his brother. It was time to turn things to his advantage. "Imagine what people will think of you when they discover you became king only after I killed myself. Some may think you were too afraid to do your own dirty work," the king said mockingly. "How would that look? The great Prince Mathias, afraid of his little twelve-year old brother. Couple that with the fact you also killed your own father, a man loved by his people, well, they might just think you've become a mad-dog," King Dominic said, a slight smile on his face. "You know what they do to mad-dogs? Don't you Reynaldus?"

Anger was boiling within Prince Mathias. He had planned every detail of his revenge and now it was unfolding rapidly. His mind was swirling, scheming of a way to get things back on track. Reynaldus was so lost in thought, he almost didn't notice the three new intruders advancing on him; almost.

The Knights of Munkelstein had stealthily advanced down the hall to within only a few yards from where their king was seated, when Prince Reynaldus shouted, "Take one more step and I will fry you all!" The knights froze. "Regardless of how your king dies tonight, and die he shall, his death will assure my place as King of Munkelstein once and for all. You would all be wise to remember that fact!" The knights stood motionless, each apprising the situation; strategizing their next move.

With nothing between him and the prince, Stephen McConnell had the best chance to get to Reynaldus. He was standing less than ten feet from the prince, which for Sir McConnell was just two long strides. But the risk far outweighed the reward. If he was too slow, they would all die.

King Dominic was directly in the path between the prince

and Sir Redjon, so the Red Knight did the next best thing: he slyly took one long stride to his right. This subtle step put the knight directly between Prince Mathias and the Bennett girls. Shielding them from another potential attack.

Sir Orgen was standing between his brothers, and directly behind his king. The best he could hope to do was to shield King Dominic, should Reynaldus try to make good on his threat to kill the boy.

"So, what do you say, brother, do we have a deal?" King Dominic asked, directing the prince's attention back to himself.

The door behind Reynaldus, at the far end of the hallway, suddenly opened and ten large men hurried out. A small group of the Prince's Royal Guard had been searching the catacombs below Sylvania Manor for the Bennett family. Having heard the loud explosion earlier, they abandoned their post and hurried to see what was happening. The Sylvanian guardsmen filed in behind Prince Reynaldus, swords drawn. Reynaldus raised his hand, signaling the men to stop.

"No, we most certainly do not have a deal. Why don't I just go ahead and destroy your family and your friends right now? Sure, once they are all dead, you will drink your poison and die, but you will die knowing total, all-consuming sorrow

299

for what your actions have caused. It may not be the way I planned it, but the end result will be the same, brother," Prince Mathias said, smiling again. It was only a matter of moments before the crown would finally be his. "Yes, I think I like my plan better."

The cerulean crystal started to glow again. King Dominic could see in Reynaldus's eyes that he meant what he said. The boy had one last move.

"Stop or I will smash it!" the king yelled.

Reynaldus looked down to see King Dominic holding a rock over an odd-looking piece of metal, preparing to crush it. "And why would I care if you destroy that trinket?" Reynaldus asked.

"Do you not know what this is? Clearly you don't. This was given to me decades ago by a very powerful man. You remember Dyog Ronndewo, don't you brother? Come to think of it, he had a staff much like the one you now hold," King Dominic said.

"The very same," Reynaldus bragged. "So, what? Why do I care about a gift from a ghost?"

"Dyog called this 'trinket', as you call it, a Piece of Time," King Dominic replied. "And with it…"

"One can turn back time," Reynaldus interrupted. "Yes, he

told me about it before he turned me into this grotesque old pile of skin you see me before you now."

"Then if he told you about the Piece of Time, he must have also told you that it can turn back time for the person possessing it. Did he also tell you it was this Piece of Time which allowed me to become the boy you see before you now? I'm certain he must have," the king said, condescendingly.

"Your stall tactics will not work brother. It's time to say goodbye now. It really has been a wonderful evening," the Prince replied. "Say hello to father for me, won't you?"

Dominic let out thunderous laughter, "HAHAHA! You still don't see it, do you? And here I thought you were supposed to be the smart one. I can either pulverize this Piece of Time, rendering it completely useless, or I can give it to you. It would then be yours to use as you wish," the boy asserted. "I'll bet it has to suck having to get up to pee five times a night."

"Of course!" Reynaldus thought. He was so consumed with revenge he had totally missed the obvious. He felt like a fool for not having seen it sooner. Perhaps his new found old age was effecting his mind.

Prince Mathias lowered the staff. "That is a tempting offer indeed. I let your family, and your goons, go and in exchange I get the Piece of Time *and* I get to kill you myself? You have turned in to quite the negotiator, baby brother." Just as Reynaldus was about to agree to Dominic's terms, a thought occurred to him, "How do I know the Piece of Time will work? That crazy old wizard called his magic *Disposable*. Disposable means 'to be discarded after use.' You have clearly already used it and therefore it is ready to be discarded, is it not?"

"Do you remember the old woman who slept in the gutter around the corner from where father bought his tobacco?" King Dominic asked.

Reynaldus nodded, "Yes I do. She was a vial smelling woman who rooted through other's trash bins. What of her? Is this another stalling tactic? I warn you I have run out of patience."

"One day I caught her pulling an old, broken, mirror out of the trash and I asked her, 'Why do you take what other people have thrown away? After all, it is useless garbage.' She said something to me which I have never forgotten. The old woman looked at me and said, 'Just because something has been discarded, does not make it garbage. Its true value lies with the person who possesses it'." It suddenly occurred to Dominic that perhaps his encounter with the old woman, all those years ago, was not a coincidence. "So, you see brother, the Piece of Time is only useless to me, but that does not make it garbage."

A Dish Best Served Cold

Reynaldus pondered this thought for a moment. He was growing weary and wanted this to be over, once and for all. "Alright, I will let your family go; however, your men will remain here until I am assured the Piece of Time has worked. If it does not, then, well, you know what will happen," said the prince casually. "Ladies, you are free to leave. And Rose honey, no hard feelings, ok."

With the prince's words, the sadness which had been consuming Rose Bennett turned to rage. The madman had just mercilessly killed her father, and was now was gloating. As Rose turned to Reynaldus, with hate in her eyes, she spotted a small metal blade tucked into the belt of the giant man standing behind her little brother. Before she could think about what she was doing, Rose Bennett bolted around the man in the red armor and pulled the dagger from the giant man's belt. She slipped between the giant and the man in the grey armor, and ran for Prince Mathias. The Stephen McConnell was too busy watching Reynaldus and never saw Rose duck past him. Thankfully for Rose, someone had been keeping a close eye on her.

Sir Orgen had seen the pain in Rose's face from the moment he entered Sylvania Manor and was concerned for the girl. When Rose made her move, it was so quick that the girl had almost slipped by Sir Orgen, en route to Prince Mathias. As she ran past him, the giant reached for the girl, narrowly grabbing the slightest bit of her collar with his thumb and index finger. He yanked Rose back with all his strength, wrapped his arms around her and pivoted her away from Prince Mathias. Had he reacted a fraction of a second slower, it would have been Rose lying dead on the floor.

The bolt of brilliant blue light shot from the crystal, struck Sir Orgen in the left side of his back and exited through the right side of his chest, before blowing a small chunk out of the wall behind him.

For a few moments, Rose was trapped under the giant. She was flailing for air and thought she would most certainly die there. Just as the girl was drawing her last breath, Sir McConnell pulled his friend and brother off her. Rose gulped in precious oxygen and, when her lungs were full once more, she began to sob uncontrollably.

"Look what you made me do Rosey. Here I give you your life back and you try to kill me. Tell me why I shouldn't return the favor Rose. TELL ME!" Prince Mathias bellowed. "How dare she!" he thought.

"Because if you do, I will destroy it, along with any chance you have of regaining your youthful self," King Dominic proclaimed. The look on his brother's face told Reynaldus his brother was serious.

A Dish Best Served Cold

The prince considered his options for a moment, then replied, "Very well. Rose, you and your mommy have exactly ten seconds to leave my home. In eleven seconds, you'll watch your mommy die and in twelve seconds...well, let's not count to twelve."

Kelin quickly grabbed Rose, threw her over his shoulder and ran for the front doors. "Come Maggie. NOW!" he yelled. With this, Maggie snapped out of her malaise and ran after Rose and Kelin.

"Seamus my friend," shouted Reynaldus, "you and I have some unfinished business to discuss. I'll be seeing you very soon, you traitorous pig. On that you can be certain." But Kelin was out the door with the Bennett girls before the prince could finish his threat.

With Maggie and Rose safely outside, King Dominic slid the watch to Prince Mathias. "A deal is a deal," he said, keeping the vial at the ready.

Reynaldus turned and motioned to the guard nearest him, to retrieve the Piece of Time. The guardsman rushed forward, scooped up the watch and handed it to Prince Mathias.

The prince studied the piece of magic. "How does it work?" he asked.

Dominic hesitated, contemplating what he should tell

305

brother. The king had just lost both his fathers, as well as a very dear friend, at the hands of this monster. Giving him the key to his youth was unpalatable to the boy.

Sensing Dominic's hesitation, Prince Mathias ordered, "Men, if he does not answer I want you to hunt his family down and kill them, slowly."

Reluctantly, the king said, "At the top of the watch is what's called a crown." The irony of this was not lost on Reynaldus. "Use the crown to adjust the dials the number of years you want to go." Dominic waited while the Prince adjusted the watch.

"Now what?" Reynaldus asked.

"You see the two buttons on the side of the watch?" King Dominic asked. The prince nodded. "Press the top button to go back in time, or the bottom button if you choose to go forward. That's it," the king explained. "Remember, it doesn't change time for everyone, just for you," the boy reminded. "Now, let's hope he falls for it," he thought.

Reynaldus stared at the watch for a few moments. This was it. All he had to do next was press the button, and then kill his brother. It was almost over. "Men," he said to his guardsmen, "If this doesn't work, kill the two ogres, but leave the boy for me." He gave his brother a smile and pressed the button.

24

5:1

T he four Knights of Munkelstein standing guard outside Sylvania Manor, watched as their brothers rushed to rescue King Dominic. Moments later, they were surrounded by twenty armed Sylvanian Royal Guardsmen. The prince's guards had apparently seen the massacre on the hill and decided caution was their best approach. They split off into two groups of ten, surrounding the severely outnumbered knights.

The Knights of Munkelstein instinctively maneuvered themselves into a defensive position. Sir Bastile and Sir Elijah turned to protect their left flank and Sir Krebow and Sir Jameson protected their right.

Not many people would think that twenty against four

would result in a stalemate; however, for a few minutes neither side made a move.

The Sylvanian Guardsmen had no idea it was actually seven men who slaughtered their brothers earlier that evening, and not just the four standing before them, so their reluctance to attack was understandable. It wasn't until Sir Bastile spoke, that the stalemate ended.

"Allow me to introduce myself: I am Sir James Tobias Bastile, perhaps you've heard of me," the Green Knight began. "This handsome young man in blue, to my right, is Sir Elijah Moren. The old, ugly man behind me is Sir Thomas Albert Jameson which makes the man to his left Sir Michael Robert Krebow. We are Knights of Munkelstein, and as your friends up on the hill can attest, we are very skilled at our job. I cannot promise you that your deaths tonight will be painless, or quick; however, I can promise, that if you stay and fight, you will indeed die." Bastile waited a moment, to let his threat sink into his enemies brains, then stepped forward and asked, "So, who's first?" And drew his blade.

With sword in hand, Sir Bastile approached the three guardsmen nearest him. Almost in unison they each took a hesitant step back. The man in the middle naively asked, "Are you really Sir James Bastile?"

"Only one way to find out, my boy," the Green Knight quipped as he unleashed his steel upon them.

The battle lasted only a few minutes. Most of the Royal Guardsmen had seen the carnage on the hill and had lost their resolve for this war. There were very few among the remaining Sylvanian Royal Guard who believed in Prince Mathias and fewer still willing to die for him. So, when Sir Bastile stepped forward and killed three of their brothers, with little effort, nearly half of those remaining fled.

With the Sylvanian Guard at a much more manageable number, the knights went to work. Sir Jameson ducked the attack of a young ambitious guardsmen, stepped behind the boy and stabbed him through his heart. In his youth, Thomas Jameson was much faster and would have turned back quicker, but those days were long behind him. Before he could turn to face the four men behind him, the guardsman closest to him drove his blade into Sir Jameson's left shoulder. The knight heard his skin split and felt searing pain, followed by the warmth of blood running down his arm. A lesser man would have flinched at the intense pain, but a lesser man could never be a Munkelstein Knight. With adrenaline pumping, Thomas rushed the man, locking their blades together. While the Sylvanian stood his ground, contemplating his next move, the

Gold Knight pulled the dagger from his belt, jammed it into his foe's stomach and twisted the blade. The guardsman let out a howl of pain and fell to the ground, clutching his stomach; only moments away from death. Without hesitation, Sir Jameson turned in search of his next victim, but in the time it took him to dispatch the two Sylvanian's, Sir Krebow had finished off the three remaining soldiers on their flank.

Behind them, on the left flank, Sir Bastile, sword in hand, was standing over the last remaining soldier. The Sylvanian was lying face down in the dirt, trying to crawl away to safety. The Green Knight was about to let the man go; after all, the Sylvanian had just had twelve inches of steel run through his right lung and did not have long to live. But when the doors to Sylvania Manor burst open, and two screaming women and one old man came running out, Sir Bastile no longer felt merciful. With one fluid motion, the knight swung around, pierced the Royal Guardsman's neck, swung back to face his brothers and sheathed his sword.

"Fun's over boys. Our brothers need us," shouted Sir Krebow as he hurried up the steps.

25

The Best Laid Plans

The old man standing in the hallway of Sylvania Manor that night, holding the antique watch, appeared to be about 200 years old. In reality, the elder Segarius brother was only fifty-five that day; however, the transformation Reynaldus had undergone when he accepted Dyog Ronndewo's proposition made him appear, and feel, much older. But, as he would soon discover, exchanging years of your life for power, only ages one's body; it does not change the number of years you have been alive. Perhaps, Prince Mathias was right, maybe his new-found age was effecting his mind.

Assuming he was now 150 years older, Reynaldus Wilhelm Mathias adjusted the Piece of Time to 1 8 0. "Did he really think I'd fall for his pathetic attempt to kill me?" the prince thought before pressing the bottom button. Immediately, a violent storm broke out above Prince Mathias. The storm was so intense, and unexpected, it completely disoriented all who were in the Sylvanian Manor main hallway that evening. An instant later, the storm was gone.

When the shock of the storm began to wear off, Dominic readied himself. He'd know soon enough if his plan had worked.

"Prince Mathias," one of the guardsmen called. "Prince Mathias sir, where are you?"

Lying on the floor, in the exact spot the prince had been standing, was the brown tattered robe of Prince Mathias.

The guardsmen stepped forward to claim the robe and was startled by what he found. There, lying inside the tattered cloth, was a baby. The guardsmen jumped back, startled by what he had seen. "What have you done?" he shouted at King Dominic.

The king stood slowly, faced the Sylvanians and said, "Sir McConnell, Sir Redjon seize my brother please. Kill anyone who tries to stop you." He had hoped his brother would fall for his plan to kill him. "If he had just pressed the top button, this would all be over," he thought. King Dominic's new plan would be to bring Reynaldus back to Munkelstein. Maybe under better conditions the boy would grow to be less hateful. The chances of this being the case were small, but he had to try. After all, he wasn't about to kill a baby. No matter how evil he may be. Then the boy felt it: the unmistakable point of a blade poking his ribs.

"Change of plans, my lord," the familiar voice said behind him. Slowly Dominic turned his head to see Stephen McConnell standing behind him, blade pressed to the boy's back. "I can't let you take him," he said.

"Stephen, what are you doing?" Sir Redjon asked, dumbstruck.

"Daniel, grab the prince and go. You, you, you, and you go with Daniel and protect Prince Reynaldus with your lives," Stephen McConnell ordered the Sylvanian Royal Guardsmen. "The rest of you get rid of him," he said motioning to Sir Redjon.

"You son-of-a-bitch. We were your brothers," yelled Sir Redjon, as he drew his sword.

The five remaining Royal Guardsmen began their advance on Sir Redjon just as the rest of the Knights of Munkelstein burst into the foyer. Stephen McConnell grabbed Dominic around the neck and turned him towards the knights.

"Stay where you are or I will kill him where he stands," yelled Stephen.

Disposable Magic

It was the first time the king saw the entirety of the carnage
which had occurred in the hallway that night. Lying directly
behind Sir Redjon was Dominic's father. A man willing to give
his life to save those he loved. The boy's heart broke. "Mom,"
he thought. How could he ever look his mother in the face
again without feeling shame for what had happened? Tears
began to trickle down the king's face. He closed his eyes for a
second and when he opened them again, he saw his friend,
lying dead at his feet.

If it weren't for Sir Brenden Orgen, things would have
turned out much different. The one thing King Dominic
knew above all else, was there was no one in Munkelstein who
loved and believed in the king more than Sir Orgen.
Complete and total sadness now consumed the boy as he
remembered his old friend. Dominic tried to fight back the
tears which were streaming down his face. As he raised his
hand to wipe his cheeks, he realized he was still holding the
vial of Celavian Root.

"Take another step and see how serious I am," Stephen
McConnell yelled at the knights as he squeezed Dominic's
neck tighter.

Randy Bennett, an innocent man who raised and protected
Dominic, was dead because the king hadn't taken care of

Reynaldus decades ago; as was his friend and most loyal subject, Sir Brenden Fredrick Orgen. Anger suddenly filled the boy. He squeezed the vial tight and jerked his hand back. The gold liquid flew from the vial, striking Stephen McConnell in the face.

Instinctively, the traitor released the king from his grip and began to frantically wipe the poison from his eyes and mouth. Once freed from Stephen's grip, King Dominic fell to the floor, in anticipation for what was about to come. An instant later, four silver daggers struck Stephen McConnell in the chest. The traitor of Munkelstein, grasped at the blades protruding from him as he fell to his knees, blood spewing from his mouth. He tried to speak but could only mutter, "P...P...P."

Stephen McConnell, former Knight of Munkelstein, died saving King Dominic Segarius's family, exactly as Dyog Ronndewo had foretold.

When the five Sylvanian Guardsman saw Stephen McConnell lying on floor, blood pouring from his chest and mouth, they dropped their swords. It was now five-against-five and they were at a distinct disadvantage. A wise man had once said, "Stepping back will not be easy, but staying will mean your certain doom." The Sylvanians seemed to understand this as well.

When James Bastile saw his friend, Brenden lying dead on the floor, he drew his blade and charged the unarmed guardsmen. "I'll kill you all, you bastards!" he shouted.

King Dominic rose from the floor and cried out, "James no! They will have their day, but it will not be this day."

The Green Knight halted his assault, before it began, turned to the king and asked, "You would let them live? He was our brother. These cowards do not deserve our mercy," Sir Bastile argued.

"James, I understand your pain. He was my friend as well. Sir Brenden Orgen has saved my life more times than I can count and, when I was at my weakest, he came to my defense. If not for him, not one of you would have believed I returned. It is because of Sir Orgen that Prince Mathias is no longer a threat."

"At least not for now," Sir Krebow thought to himself.

James Bastile stood for a moment and considered his kings words. He could gut the five cowards before the other knights could react. "And really," he thought, "would any of them even try to stop me?"

But Sir Bastile did not charge the unarmed Sylvanian guards. As a loyal Knight of Munkelstein, he did what he swore to do years ago: he obeyed his king.

316

"Sire, the prince," Sir Redjon cried out, "they've taken him. We must hurry before they are gone for good."

Elijah replied, "They've taken a baby. I'm certain we don't have anything to worry about, Burton."

"If they make it into the Sylvasatanian mountains we'll never find him. What happens as Reynaldus grows and starts to remember who he is? It took King Dominic only five days to regain his memories once he returned," Sir Redjon explained. "And he lived in a different world for twelve years," he added.

Dominic thought about this for a moment. Burton was right, they needed to find Reynaldus, and fast. "Michael, Elijah, search Sylvania Manor for any stragglers and do what you must to ensure we suffer no further casualties. When you're finished, search the place for any information which may help locate where they may have taken the prince," the King instructed. "Burton, James, take these men down to the dungeons and see what they know. Surely one of them has something useful he'd be willing to exchange for his life." The Knights of Munkelstein reacted to their king's orders without hesitation. "We don't have a lot of time, so act quickly and thoroughly."

"As you wish sire," Burton replied. Sir Redjon turned to

the five Sylvanian soldiers standing before him and shot them a devilish look which told them he was going to enjoy what was about to happen. "You heard the king, get your asses moving," he ordered. He then turned to the Green Knight and asked, "Coming?"

"I wouldn't miss it," James replied with a smile, as he hustled after.

A moment later, Sirs Krebow and Moren were sprinting down the hall to Prince Mathias's chamber.

"What will you have me do, sire?" asked Sir Jameson.

"How's your arm, Thomas?" the king asked with concern in his voice.

"My arm, sire?" the knight replied, puzzled by the question.

"I noticed you favoring your left arm. Were you injured? Can you still fight?" asked a concerned King Dominic.

It took a moment for Thomas Jameson to understand what his king was asking, then he suddenly remembered he'd been stabbed. "Oh, that. Forgot all about it. Just a scratch, my lord. It would take more than a tiny poke from this worthless lot to keep me out of the fight," he replied.

"That's good, Thomas. I need your help," the king replied.

Sir Jameson knelt before his king and asked, "What would you have me do, my lord?"

The Best Laid Plans

King Dominic watched the loyal, fearless man kneeling before him and felt ill. He did not deserve to be treated with such respect after the pain he had brought to those he loved.

"Please, Thomas, rise," the king commanded. "I need you to find a cart. I won't leave them here," the king said with pain in his voice.

An instant later, Thomas Jameson was sprinting out into the night.

26

Until We Meet Again

For the first time since waking up in the cold, dank dungeon, Dominic Bennett-Segarius was alone. Only five days earlier, he was a twelve-year old boy playing in his yard; filled with excitement at the thought of having a chance to face the Black Knight in battle. Now he stood in a foreign place, surrounded by carnage, as the King of Munkelstein. Had he only known then that the Black Knight was not his enemy, but a close friend. Actually, he was much more than a friend. The Black Knight, Sir Brenden Fredrick Orgen, was his brother. Certainly, he was more of a brother than Reynaldus had ever been.

King Dominic Segarius knelt beside his friend and brother, and placed his hand on the giant's chest. Tears filled his eyes as he spoke, "I'm sorry my friend, please, forgive me. You have always believed in me, even when I did not believe in myself. Were it not for you, I would certainly be dead, as would my family. It is not fair that you lie here while I live. I can only promise that your death will not be in vain," the king said as he sobbed over his fallen friend. "I will live the rest of my life in honor of you, this I swear."

After a few minutes of quietly reflecting on the life of the Black Knight, and the exploits the two men shared, King Dominic gently kissed his friend on the forehead and whispered, "Goodbye brother. I will never forget all that you have done for me." Wiping the tears from his face, Dominic rose to his feet and turned to face his father.

Randy Bennett was lying only a few steps away from where the boy was standing, but the walk over to his father was the longest of his life. With every step, dread and sadness filled the boy's soul. "Sir Orgen died a warrior," King Dominic thought, "and would be happy knowing he died in service to his king." But his dad was different. Randy wasn't a warrior and he certainly did not sign up for this.

Dominic stood over his father for a moment, unable to move any further. He looked down and said, "You were an innocent man who unknowingly aided in the escape of a coward in hiding from a lunatic. You were a great man and an even better father. You did not deserve to die like this,"

Dominic struggled to say. The king felt his knees buckle and he fell to the floor. He grabbed his father's lifeless body, held him in his arms, and wept.

He remembered the day his dad bought him his favorite gift: a plastic sword. Dominic carried the sword everywhere. He loved the gift so much, he even brought it to school one day. When his dad showed up to Clarkston Elementary one day, at the request of the principle, instead of getting angry with son for bringing the 'weapon' to school, Randy hugged his boy and said, "Next time, let's leave this at home, ok buddy?"

He remembered the best birthday ever, and how his dad dressed as a king's servant. The man looked ridiculous, and Dominic knew his dad only did it to make his son happy. When he asked his dad if he we would dress up for the party, without hesitation Randy said, "Absolutely I will!" And when Dominic told his father that the costume would make him look silly, his dad replied, in his best crotchety old man's voice, "If that is what's required then, dang nabbit, that's what I'll do."

Every memory brought a deeper sadness to Dominic's heart. He sat there holding his father as memories of their good times together flooded his mind. The boy wasn't aware he was smiling as he wept. They had certainly had a lot of fun in their brief time together.

Gazing down at Randy's lifeless body he thought of all the things he was going to miss about his dad: the way he smelled, the sound of his laughter, his smile, how much the man loved his wife, his selflessness towards his family, how when he talked to you, he made you feel like you were the only person who mattered, his silly voices and his stupid dad jokes. But mostly, Dominic was going to miss being Randy's little boy. His dad was gone and the King of Munkelstein felt completely alone.

"Sire, I've found a cart."

The sound of Sir Krebow's voice snapped Dominic out of his deep thoughts. "Give me a minute please, Thomas," King Dominic said through tears and sniffles. He gave Randy another tight squeeze and kissed his cheek. "Thank you for everything, dad. I will never forget all you have done for me," he said through his tears. "I promise, I will watch over your girls for you."

King Dominic gently laid Randy's head down, brushed the hair from his dad's face and stood. "I'm sorry daddy," he said one last time as he wiped his face in his shirt.

The king rose, turned to Sir Jameson and said, "Come Thomas, let's get them home."

27

Lest We Forget

W e've had our men out searching for him for weeks but still no sign, my lord," said Sir Redjon.

"Thank you, Burton," replied King Dominic. "Thomas, where are we with deciphering the information recovered from Sylvania Manor?"

The Gold Knight stood to address his king. Every night since their return from Sylvania, the knights had been pouring through the stacks of papers and drawings they confiscated from prince's chambers. They had discovered little information as to the whereabouts of Prince Mathias. Sir Jameson was about to tell the king that they had found nothing of consequence, when he spied the empty chair across from his. The chair of Sir

Brenden Orgen sat empty in the War Room and it gave Sir Jameson pause.

"Thomas? Is everything alright?" the king asked.

"Hmmm."

"Are you ok?" King Dominic asked again.

"Aye, I'm fine," Sir Jameson said solemnly. "We've read through more than half of the papers we took from Sylvania but so far we have found nothing which might help us locate Prince Mathias," the Gold Knight said.

"Thank you, Thomas. Stay on it and let me know if you need assistance," the king replied. "We have many wise men in Munkelstein whom I am certain would be happy to help you. Perhaps fresh eyes...," the king was cut-off before he could finish.

"That won't be necessary, sire," Sir Jameson said confidently. "If there is something to find, we'll find it." The truth was, before they left for Sylvania, he would never have believed that one of his brothers could have betrayed them. Sir Jameson was not ready to trust anyone outside the War Room anytime soon.

"Very well. Let me know if you find anything," King Dominic replied. He understood why Thomas did not want *outsiders* helping him, and he didn't blame the man. He wasn't sure who he could trust anymore either.

325

"Does anyone have anything they wish to discuss before we end for the day?" King Dominic asked.

"Aye," said Sir Elijah. King Dominic gave the young knight a nod which said, 'Go ahead.' "Thank you, sire. I was wondering, what will you do now?" the Blue Knight asked.

"What do you mean, Elijah?" the king replied, although he was certain what Elijah meant.

"Well, my lord, it seems to me you have two families which need you: the Bennett family and your Munkelstein family. You cannot be in two places at the same time," Sir Elijah said. "Will you stay with us, or go back to Clarkston?"

Dominic knew this question was coming, and to him, the answer to this question was easy. It was the answer to the other question which was going to be far more difficult.

"Ahhh, that, 'what will you do now'. The answer is very simple Elijah, I will be staying in Munkelstein. Actually, the decision was made for me twelve-years ago," the king replied.

"Sire?" asked Michael Krebow.

"The magic I used to travel to Clarkston could only be used once, by me at least. So, even if I wanted to return to Clarkston, I would have no way to get there."

"For what it's worth, I am very happy you are staying, sire" replied Elijah.

King Dominic gave the young knight a smile and then said, "Any other questions?"

"Just one, my lord," said Sir Krebow. "We have been told by Burton and Kelin Semtun that, before he, umm, transformed, Prince Mathias possessed a weapon of unimaginable power."

"You have heard correctly, Michael," replied the king.

"Sire, where is this weapon now? If it were to fall in the wrong hands, well, I don't have to tell you what could happen," Sir Krebow urged.

King Dominic surveyed the knights, who were all watching him intently. He wasn't sure how they would react to his response, but what was done, was done. "I had the staff of Dyog Ronndewo destroyed," the king said bluntly. "It is no longer a threat for us to concern ourselves with."

"But, sire," continued Michael, "if you had kept the staff of Dyog Ronndewo perhaps you could have used it for good."

Dominic could see in their faces that the other knights had the same concern as their brother. He contemplated Sir Jameson's observation a moment and replied confidently, "Brothers, I do not believe any good could ever come from such dark magic. After witnessing the devastation and pain a weapon of that magnitude could cause, I had the staff destroyed," the king explained. "I for one will sleep better knowing the world has been rid of that abomination."

Michael nodded his agreement as he sat; although the king could sense the knight's disapproval of his decision.

"Alright then, if there's nothing else, that concludes our business for today," the king said, changing the subject. "But before we adjourn, I'd like to say something. A few weeks ago, I stood in this room frightened and confused. At the time, there was only one person who believed in me. I have no idea why Sir Orgen had such faith in the scrawny kid who magically appeared in Munkelstein. But had he not believed, wholeheartedly, in who I was, there would have been many more deaths that night. Sir Orgen is a hero and I will be forever in his debt." King Dominic paused, his head bowed, hand resting on the giant's chair.

The five remaining Knights of Munkelstein, bowed their heads in remembrance of their fallen brother. After a few moments of silence, the king continued, "So long as I am king, the chair of Sir Brenden Fredrick Orgen will remain empty, lest we forget."

"Sir Orgen, you were my brother and my friend and you will be forever missed," said Sir James Tobias Bastile.

"You were a loyal friend to those lucky enough to know

you, and merciless to those who opposed you. You will be missed my friend," said Sir Thomas Albert Jameson.

"You were the biggest man I ever met. I'm just glad you were on our side. I shall miss you every day my brother," said Sir Elijah Phillip Moren.

"You were the bravest man I have ever met. You always spoke your mind and your loyalty was never in doubt. You are, and shall forever be, missed," said Sir Michael Thomas Krebow, somberly.

The room fell silent. All eyes were on Sir Redjon whose head was still bowed in quiet reflection. The Red Knight suddenly realized his brothers were all watching him; waiting for him to share his thoughts on Sir Orgen.

The tension between the two men had come to a boiling point in Sylvania and they were all there to witness it. Disagreement aside, they were still brothers and brothers should be able to forgive each other their differences. If only Sir Redjon's brother were alive to forgive him.

"The last thing you said to me was 'You're not worth it, Burton,'" Sir Redjon started. "Your words are something which I will carry with me like an anvil for the rest of my days. You were abrasive and dismissive and felt you always knew what was best for Munkelstein, and I resented you for it. My jealousy and immaturity did not allow me to see how truly loyal and generous you were. I am sorry that it took your death for me to see what a great man and friend you were. I will miss you, brother." When he was finished, Sir Burton William Redjon lowered his head and began to weep.

28

Home

I love you baby," Randy said as he gently stroked his wife's face. They were lying in their warm king-sized bed; snuggled together under the down comforter and Egyptian cotton sheets. It was one of Maggie's favorite places to be and her favorite person to be with. Randy's arms wrapped around her tightly as he kissed her. A tear began to stream down Maggie's face as she dreamed of him. It was the happiest thought she could remember. But that's all it would ever be, a memory.

She hadn't slept for more than a few hours since awaking in their prison, and in those rare times when she did sleep, Maggie dreamt only of the old man and his cackling laughter.

As she sat in the sun, exhausted and wishing she were in bed with her Randy, Maggie imagined the softness of her husband's lips, the way his hands felt on her skin and how he smelled. It was perfect. "I love you too, my handsome man," Maggie replied.

"Have you decided what you're going to do mom?"

Startled from her sweet moment with Randy, Maggie sprung up to see her son standing next to her, blotting out the sun. "But he isn't really your son, is he?" she thought, and then immediately scolded herself. "He will always be your little boy, regardless of everything else." She couldn't bear the thought of losing both of her 'guys'.

Everything still seemed so unreal to Maggie. A few days after they arrived to Munkelstein, Dominic sat down with Maggie and Rose to tell them the truth about everything that had happened. What he told them, was just too unbelievable for Maggie to accept.

The Bennetts had raised their children to be good, honest people, and Maggie had never known her son to lie. However, what she had experienced was too, "Maybe *surreal* is more appropriate," she thought. As far as Maggie was concerned, magic and wizards did not exist; they were science fiction. This couldn't be real. However, she could not deny that what she saw in that dark cold place, was real. Randy lying dead, killed by a madman, was all too real. She only wished it weren't.

"Mom? Are you ok?" her little boy asked.

"Hmmm? Did you say something honey?" Maggie replied, half asleep and lost in thought.

"Will you stay?" he asked. "There's plenty of room and you'd never have to worry about money, or anything, as long as you live." Dominic had already lost his dad. He couldn't imagine losing his mother and sister as well.

"I'm sorry honey, we can't stay here. I just want to go home and make this place nothing more than a sad memory."

In the days since Randy's death, her son had somehow, changed. Yes, he looked like Dominic Bennett: same haircut, same smile; but somehow different. The boy she knew, couldn't even remember to brush his teeth; but he was no longer that boy. Standing before Maggie now, was a man living in the body of her little boy, asking her to give up her life in Michigan to stay with him. He was asking her to give up her friends, her family and everything and everyone Maggie knew, to stay in this place. A place full of nothing but painful memories. As much as she loved her son, she couldn't stand the thought of staying there a second longer.

"You can always come with us," she offered. "I mean, Clarkston is no Munkelstein, but at least we don't have dungeons," Maggie joked.

He knew his mom was only trying to lighten the mood, but Dominic wasn't in the mood for jokes. He had been dreading this conversation since they returned. Hadn't he broken her heart enough for one lifetime?

Dominic mustered up the courage and said, "I can't come with you." A tear formed in his eye, and ran down his cheek.

Maggie rose from her chair, wrapped her arms around her little boy and hugged him tightly. "It's ok buddy," she told him.

"Mom, I am so sorry. I never meant for any of this to happen. I miss him so much," the boy said as he broke into tears.

"I know honey, I miss him too," Maggie said struggling to contain her own tears. "Your dad loved you so much. You were the son he always wanted and he could not have been prouder of you."

Maggie held Dominic for a long while. She wasn't sure if she would ever see him again and Maggie wanted to remember exactly how it felt to hold her little boy.

"Are you sure you can't stay mom?" he asked once more.

"I wish I could honey, but I can't. It's too painful," she said. "I think Rose would like it here though. She seems to enjoy riding horses and there are plenty of cute boys," Maggie said with a smile. "But your sister has friends, and a family, who will miss her in Clarkston. I couldn't ask her to trade her family for a place with so many painful memories."

And there it was. While Dominic was Maggie's son, and Rose's brother, he wasn't really part of their family. He was just a stranger who barged into their home and destroyed their lives.

Realizing what she had said, Maggie quickly added, "You can always change your mind and come home with us, buddy."

"I can't," he replied. He then explained to his mother the magic he used to travel to Clarkston and how he was unable to return there. When he was finished, he told his mother, "We recovered the Gazing Glass from Prince Mathias's chambers. Whenever you and Rose are ready, you can use it to return home." Dominic paused, a sad expression on his face. "There's one more thing," he said, "once you leave Munkelstein, you will not be able to return."

"Let's worry about that later honey," Maggie said as she kissed her son's cheek. The past few weeks had brought enough tears to last a thousand lifetimes. The last thing Maggie wanted was to remember her final moments with Dominic through a vail of tears. She took her little boy by the hand and said, "Now, why don't you act like a proper king and show me around this place."

*   *

"So, how does this work?" Maggie asked. They had just returned from walking the Munkelstein grounds, for the final time, and now here she was, sitting at the desk in Dominic's room, holding a green jagged piece of glass in her hands.

"Just relax and focus yourself *through* the glass," Dominic told his mother. "As you do, you'll begin to see yourself standing in the middle of Eden."

They watched as their mom gazed intently through the Gazing Glass; unsure of what was going to happen next.

"I'll be right behind you mom," Rose said, trying to assure her mom that everything would be fine. Although, Rose had no idea if that was true or not. If she was being honest, she was scared to death.

"You'd better be," Maggie replied.

As she gazed through the glass, Maggie could suddenly smell the fresh sweet aroma of her rose garden and the faint scent of pine needles. A moment later, she could clearly see the three large oak trees standing guard over their yard. And then, before she realized what was happening, Maggie Bennett was home.

"Alright Rose, your turn," Dominic said, ignoring what they had just witnessed.

Home

"How...where...I don't understand," Rose muttered, trying to make sense of what she had just seen. Her brother had told her this would work, but to see it happen was another thing entirely.

"I know what you're thinking. I promise it's safe," Dominic said, trying to assure his big sister. He could see in her face that his words were not very comforting. "Don't worry, it doesn't hurt at all," he added.

Rose walked over to the chair her mother had occupied only moments earlier, and sat down. The seat was still warm. She ran her fingers across the map of the world lying on the desk in front of her. "Or at least, *my* world," she thought. She studied the map and wondered how her mother could have simply disappeared into thin air. One moment Maggie Bennett was clearly sitting at the desk, and the next, she was gone.

"It's ok, Rose. I promise, it's safe," Dominic ensured again.

"Please, come with us," Rose begged her brother. The thought of never seeing D again was awful. She still had not fully accepted that her father was gone. Leaving her little brother behind, in such a violent place, went against every instinct Rose had.

"I would if I could," he replied. "The glass won't work for me a second time."

"How do you know? Have you tried?" she asked. "I mean, just because some crazy old wizard said you could only use it once, doesn't make it true," Rose replied. "Promise me that, after I go through, you'll try."

She had a point. He hadn't tried to use the glass a second time; however, he had tried for years to use the Piece of Time. From the day he found the watch, Dominic had tried to make it work. No matter what he did, the watch wouldn't do anything. It wasn't until he found out about Disposable Magic that he understood why.

"I will. I promise," he lied.

As if sensing her brother's thoughts, Rose sprang from her chair and ran to him. She squeezed him tightly and buried her face in his chest. He squeezed Rose back and kissed the top of her head. His sister was the best friend he had in Clarkston. She had always stood up for him when the other kids picked on him for being different. He loved her more than he could ever tell her and wasn't sure what he was going to do without her in his life.

"I love you sis," he said, fighting back the tears. "I'll be right behind you."

"I love you too," she whispered.

They hugged a moment longer and then Rose returned to

the desk. She picked up the Gazing Glass and peered through it to the small spot burned into the little mitten.

"See you in a few," were the last words Dominic heard before Rose Bennett's body flickered twice and then, vanished.

EPILOGUE

I

Three Years Later

Maggie Bennett sat alone in her living room, watching television. Rose had moved to college only a few days ago, and this was the first time Maggie had the house to herself in, well, she couldn't remember. It had been three long years since she lost her husband, and her son. While losing her guys, was the saddest thing she could imagine, what made it worse was she couldn't tell anyone about it.

How do you explain to people that your twelve-year old boy was actually the king of a kingdom no one had ever heard of? In fact, after she returned to Clarkston and was able to wrap her mind around what had happened, Maggie searched for information on her son's kingdom. She scoured the internet in search of the smallest mention of Munkelstein, but her queries all had the same response: 'Did you mean: *mukaltin*'.

When the internet proved to be a dead-end, Maggie spent weeks in the library, pouring through books on kings, kingdoms and medieval times. Still, she found nothing. Exhausted, but undeterred, she then sought out history professors and scholars who all told her the same thing: 'There has never been a kingdom named Munkelstein, nor a royal family named Segarius.'

Had her Randy been alive, she may have been able to convince herself that Dominic never existed and the whole thing was just a bad dream. But her husband was gone and all that remained were pictures of her fellas.

A few months ago, Rose urged her mom to get back into the dating pool. She was worried about her mother and thought a distraction was just what Maggie needed. At first, Maggie was firmly against dating; Randy was the love of her life and she simply couldn't imagine being with anyone else. However, she had to admit it, she was lonely.

"Maybe next year," she said to herself as she munched her popcorn.

It was Friday night and Maggie Bennett sat alone, eating popcorn and watching one of her son's favorite movies: *Camelot*.

"Now him I'd date," she said as a young Richard Harris appeared on screen. The actor held a striking resemblance to Randy and it saddened her. "But you sir, are no Randy Bennett," Maggie said to the television and laughed. Then she felt it again, the feeling of being watched. It was happening more frequently lately and she tried to convince herself it was just some sort of PTSD.

Maggie paused the movie and looked out the window. The living room was at the front of the house and overlooked the spot where, fifteen years ago, their world changed forever. No one there. From her spot on the couch, however, Maggie could also see through the kitchen and into the backyard. She peered out the back window, searching for the root of her uneasiness. For just the briefest of moments, she could have sworn she saw a familiar blue flash of light. But quickly convinced herself she was only being paranoid.

Her uneasiness quelled, Maggie un-paused the movie and went back to ogling King Arthur. "You're a lucky woman, Guinevere," she laughed.

*   *

Knock, knock.

"Come."

Epilogue I

"Do you need anything before I turn in?" the girl asked.

"No thank you, Isabella. Sleep well."

"You as well, sire," she said closing the door behind her.

"Oh, Isabella, before you go. How are the nightmares?"

"He's not having nearly as many lately, my lord. But the one's he has now are much worse. Two nights ago, he awoke from a sound sleep screaming at the top of his lungs. It took us hours to calm him down. Maybe when he starts to talk he'll be able to tell us what he's dreaming about," Isabella mused. "Goodnight, sire," she said as she closed the door.

"Goodnight, Isabella," he said.

"That was close." he thought.

King Dominic lay in his bed, thinking about her. She looked just as beautiful as he'd remembered. He thought of her sitting there laughing and it made him smile. "Camelot?" he said, as he blew out the candle. "I love that movie."

The thought of his mom sitting alone on the couch saddened the boy. He wished he could knock on the door and say, "Hi mom". "Maybe next time," he said as he patted his covers.

Dominic closed his eyes and slowly drifted off to sleep with thoughts of family running through his head, and a familiar faint, blue glow, emanating from under his blanket.

II

Twenty-Five Years Later

"T"ell me why you have come, boy," a voice said in the darkness.

"I have been told a great and powerful man lives here and that he can foresee men's futures," the young man said, his voice quivering.

"Is that so? And just who might that be?"

The boy hesitated. If this was a trick, he was going to murder his brother. "A wizard by the name of Altrux Lival," the boy replied. "He is said to be more powerful than Dahagen and Dyog Ronndewo combined."

"I see. That does not answer my question though, does it? Why have you come here?" the voice asked again.

"I have come to hear my future. You see, my father's life is in danger and I would like to know how he will be killed, so that I may try to prevent it."

Epilogue II

"Unfortunately, for your father, I cannot disclose this information. It goes against wizarding protocol to divulge information which does not pertain to you. I will, however, tell you your future should you choose to hear it," the voice offered. "But, I warn you my boy, your excitement in discovering your fate will pale in comparison to the regret you will have for hearing it."

The boy watched as the cerulean blue light began to dance before him. As the light moved towards him, the boy could see that it was attached to an amulet worn around the neck of a man old enough to be his grandfather.

"Now let's talk about your future, Randal Bennett-Segarius."

ABOUT THE AUTHOR

Phil Maniscalchi is an automotive program manager and sales account manager in the Detroit area. He's a fan of Stephen King, Jonathan Maberry, Lee Child and countless other authors of fiction. Phil was born and raised in Detroit, Michigan along with his brother and four sisters. He currently lives in Clarkston, Michigan with his son King Dominic, his Daughter Rosey and their beautiful lab Coda. In his spare time, he teaches home improvements at the community center and lies on his couch eating Cheetos and watching Archer. *Disposable Magic* is the first novel by Phil, but not the last.